W9-CKM-433

BIGFOOT Boy 3

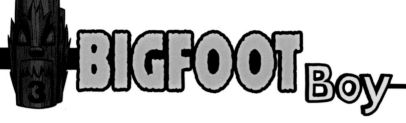

THE SOUND OF THUNDER

Kids Can Press acknowledges the financial support of the Government of Ontario,
through the Ontario Media Development Corporation's Ontario Book Initiative;
the Ontario Arts Council; the Canada Council for the Arts; and the Government
of Canada, through the CBF, for our publishing activity.

Published in Canada by
Kids Can Press Ltd.
25 Dockside Drive
Toronto, ON M5A 0B5

Published in the U.S. by
Kids Can Press Ltd.
2250 Military Road
Tonawanda, NY 14150

www.kidscanpress.com

Edited by Stacey Roderick
Designed by Rachel Di Salle and Marie Bartholomew

The hardcover edition of this book is smyth sewn casebound.
The paperback edition of this book is limp sewn with a drawn-on cover.
Manufactured in Shen Zhen, Guang Dong, P.R. China, in 4/2014 by Printplus Limited.

CM 14   0 9 8 7 6 5 4 3 2 1
CM PA 14   0 9 8 7 6 5 4 3 2 1

Library and Archives Canada Cataloguing in Publication

Torres, J., 1969–, author
      The sound of thunder / written by J. Torres ; illustrated
by Faith Erin Hicks.

(Bigfoot Boy)
ISBN 978-1-894786-58-4 (bound)   ISBN 978-1-894786-59-1 (pbk.)

      1. Graphic novels. I. Hicks, Faith Erin, illustrator II. Title.
III. Series: Torres, J., 1969– Bigfoot Boy.

PN6733.T67S69 2014   j741.5'971   C2013-908245-X

Kids Can Press is a Corus™ Entertainment company

BIGFOOT Boy

THE SOUND OF THUNDER

J. Torres and Faith Erin Hicks

Kids Can Press

For Titus, my little bigfoot.

Love, Da

For my brothers, who are now Bigfoot Men — F.E.H.

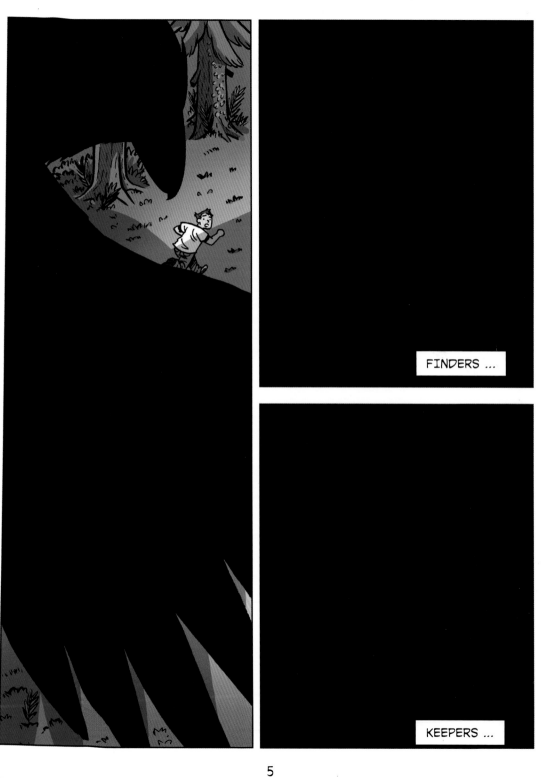

FINDERS ...

KEEPERS ...

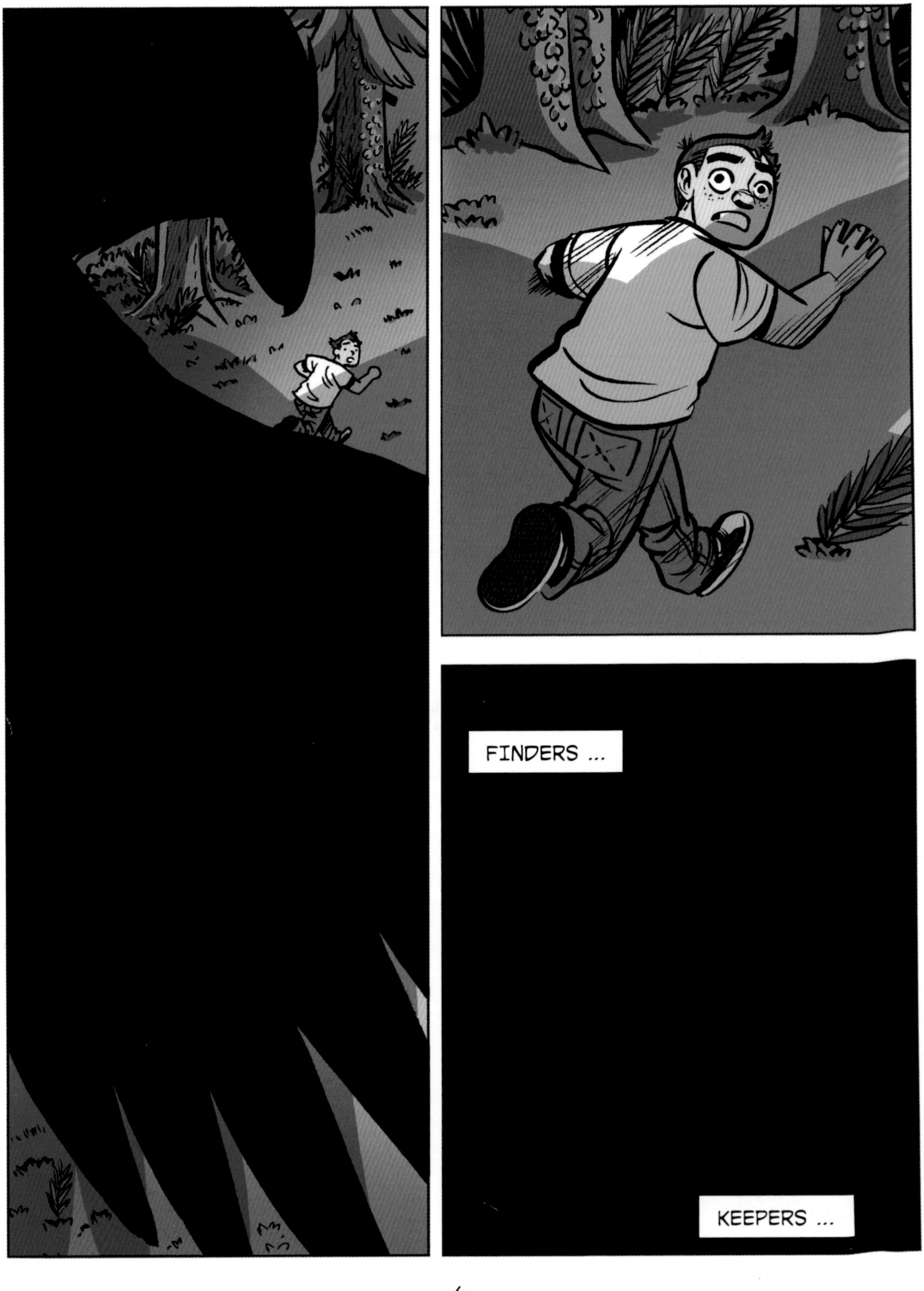
FINDERS ...
KEEPERS ...

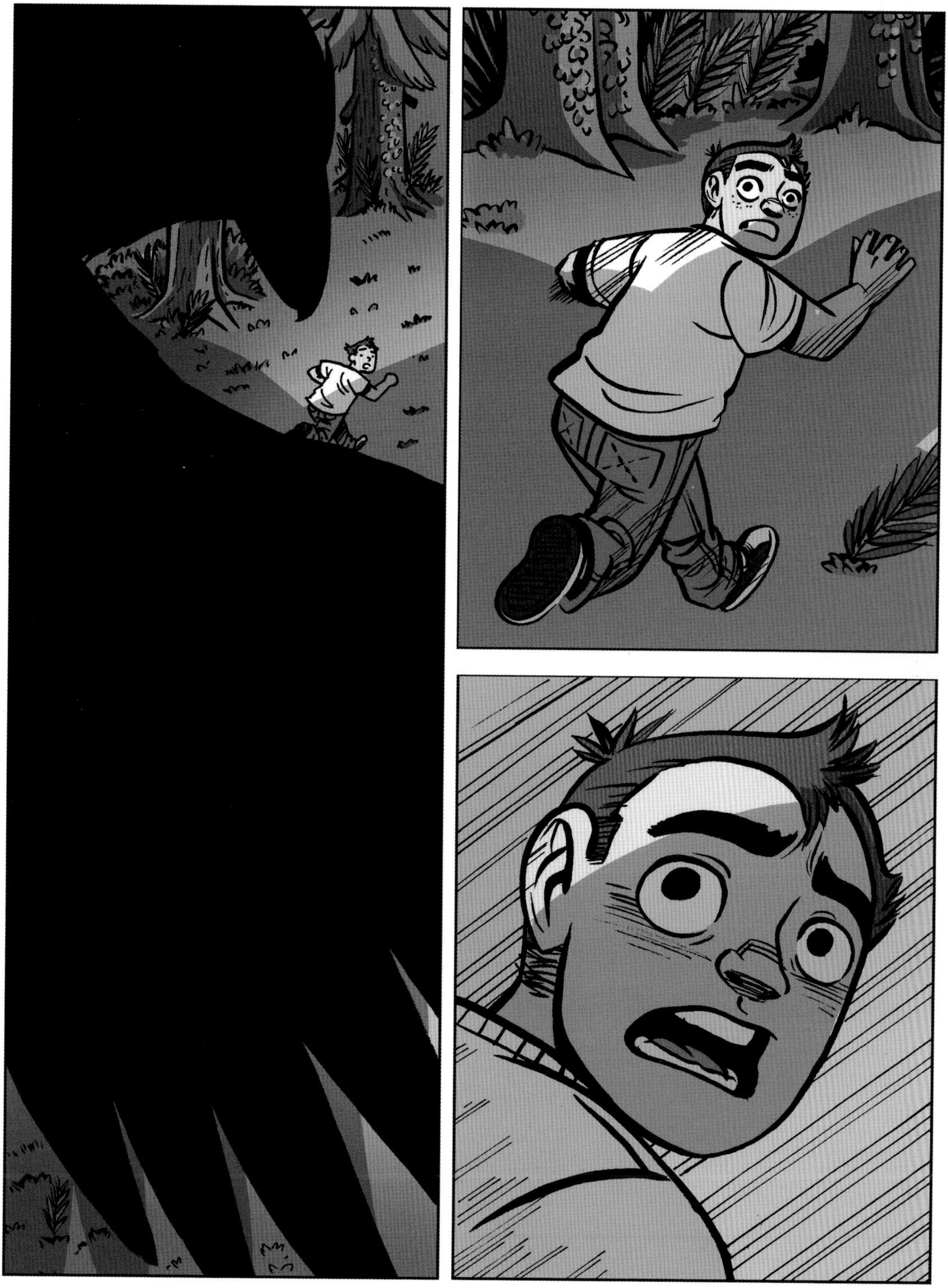

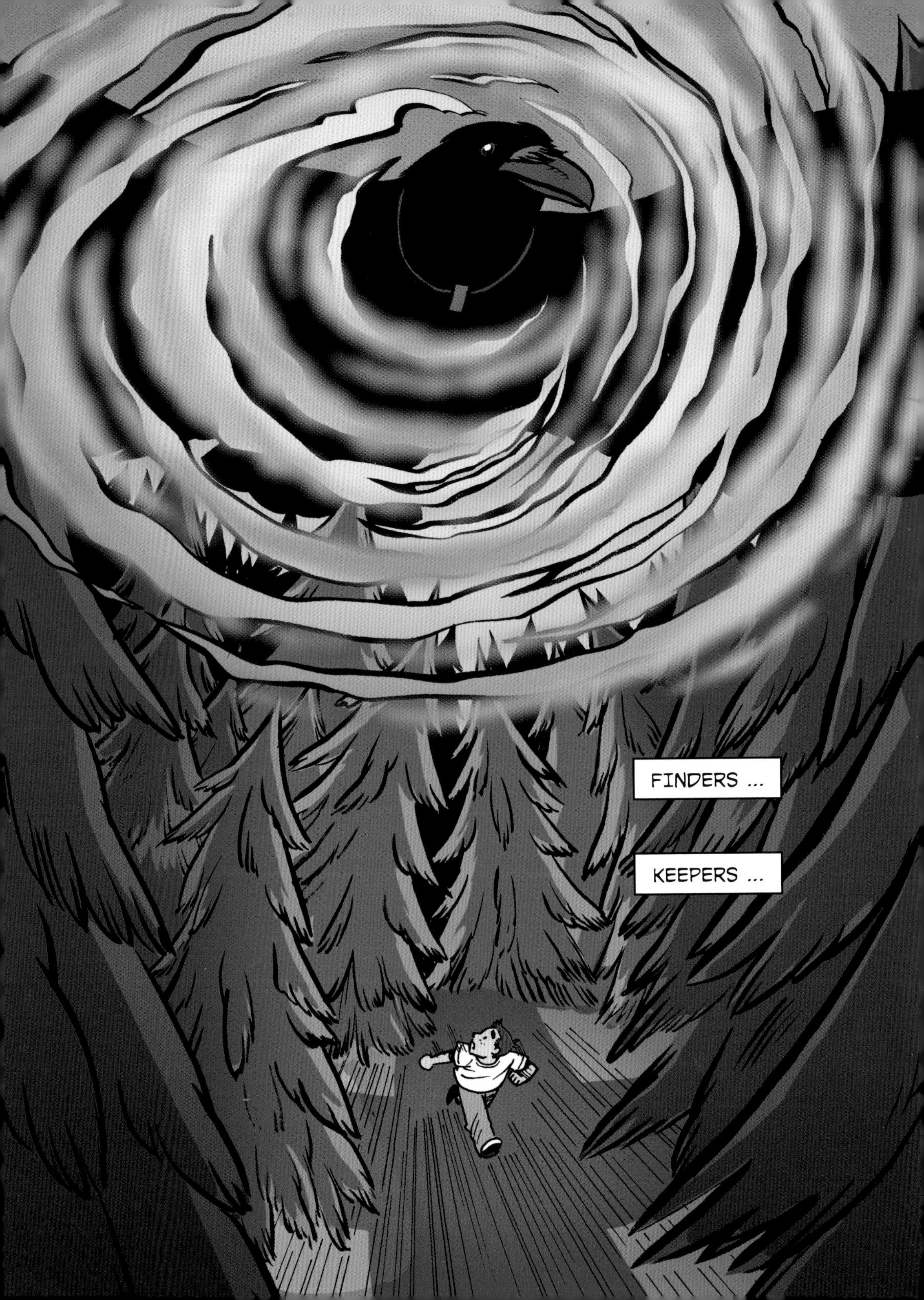
FINDERS ...
KEEPERS ...

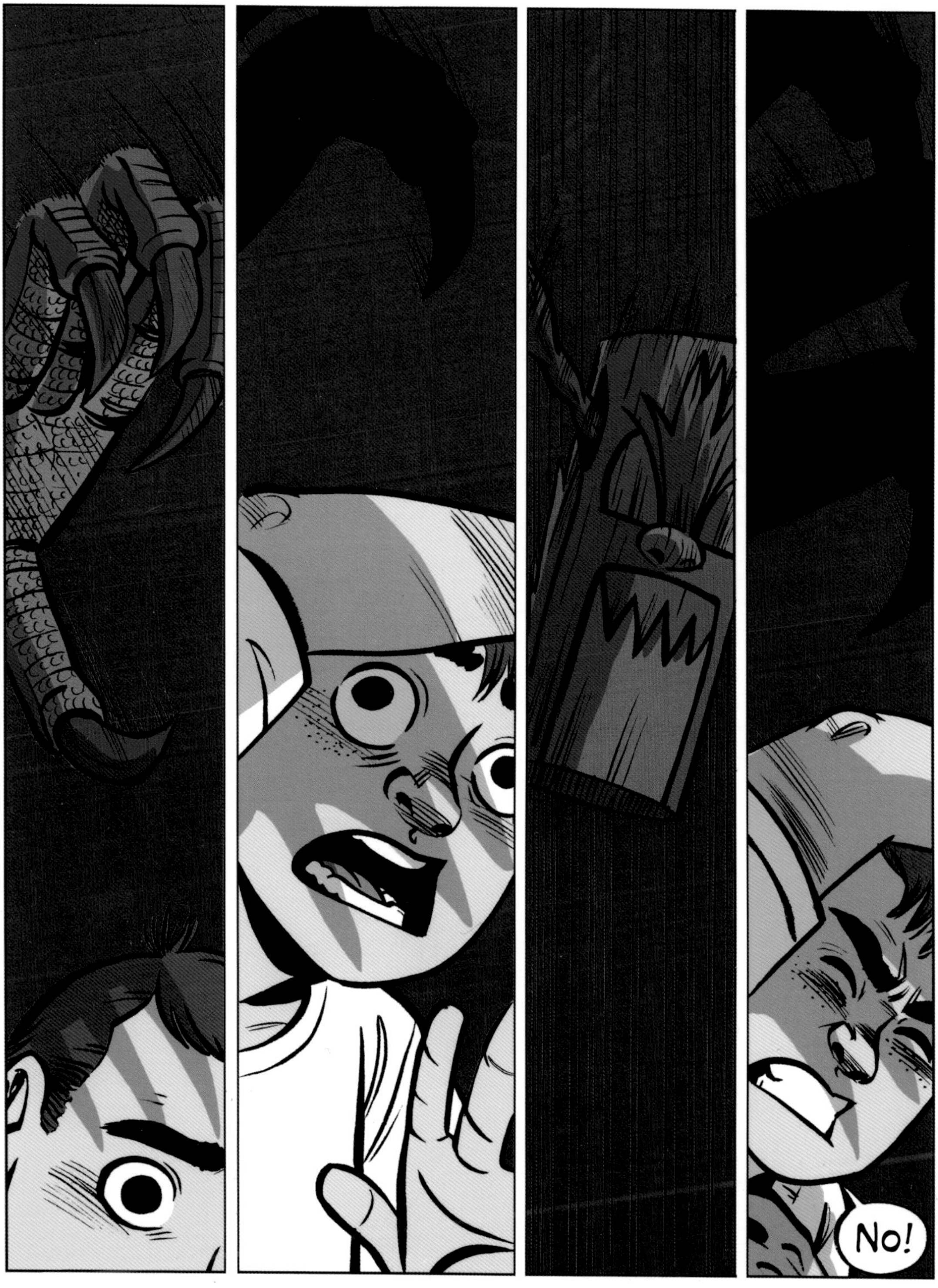
No!

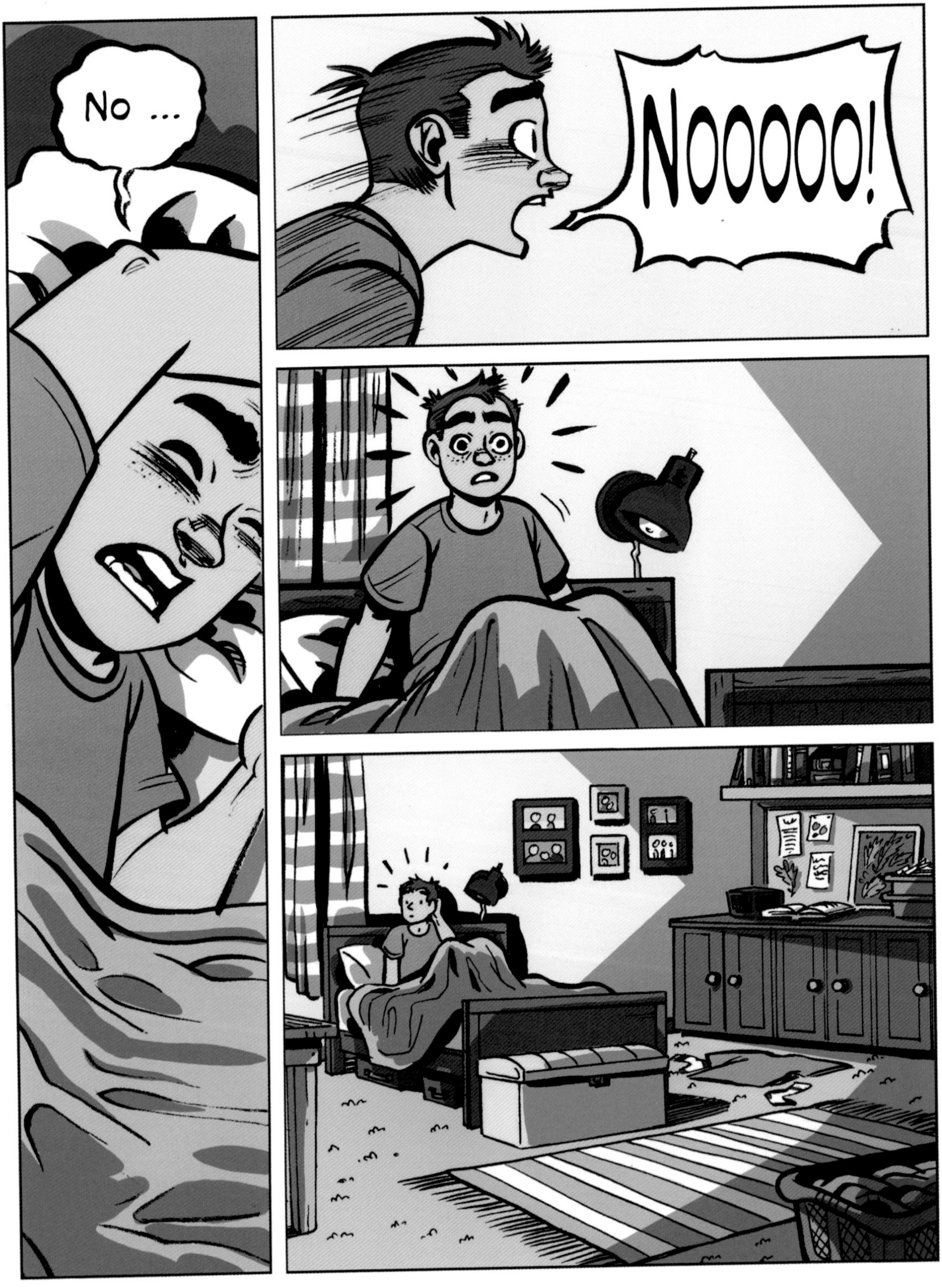
No ...
NOOOOO!

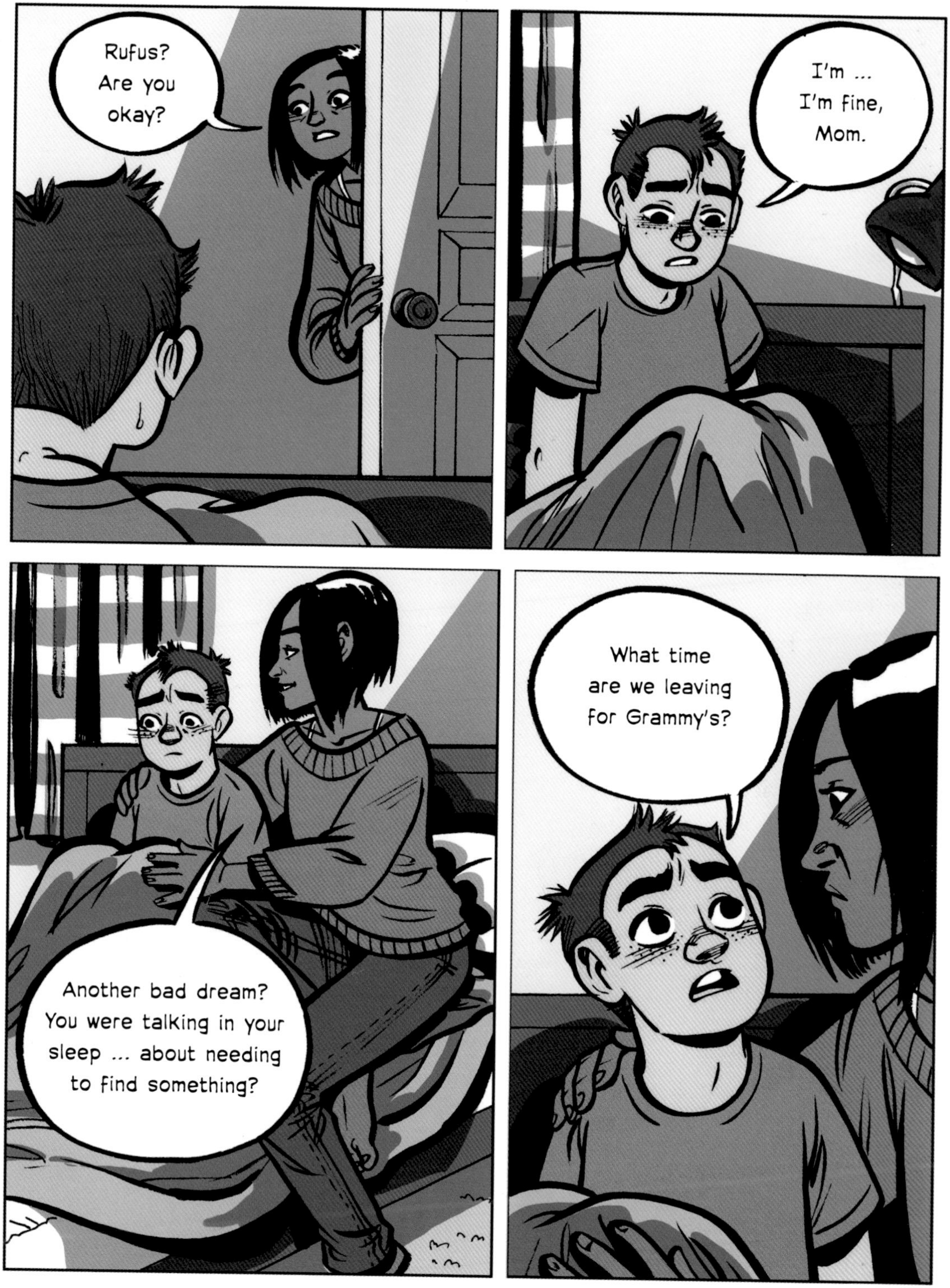

Rufus? Are you okay?
I'm ... I'm fine, Mom.
Another bad dream? You were talking in your sleep ... about needing to find something?
What time are we leaving for Grammy's?

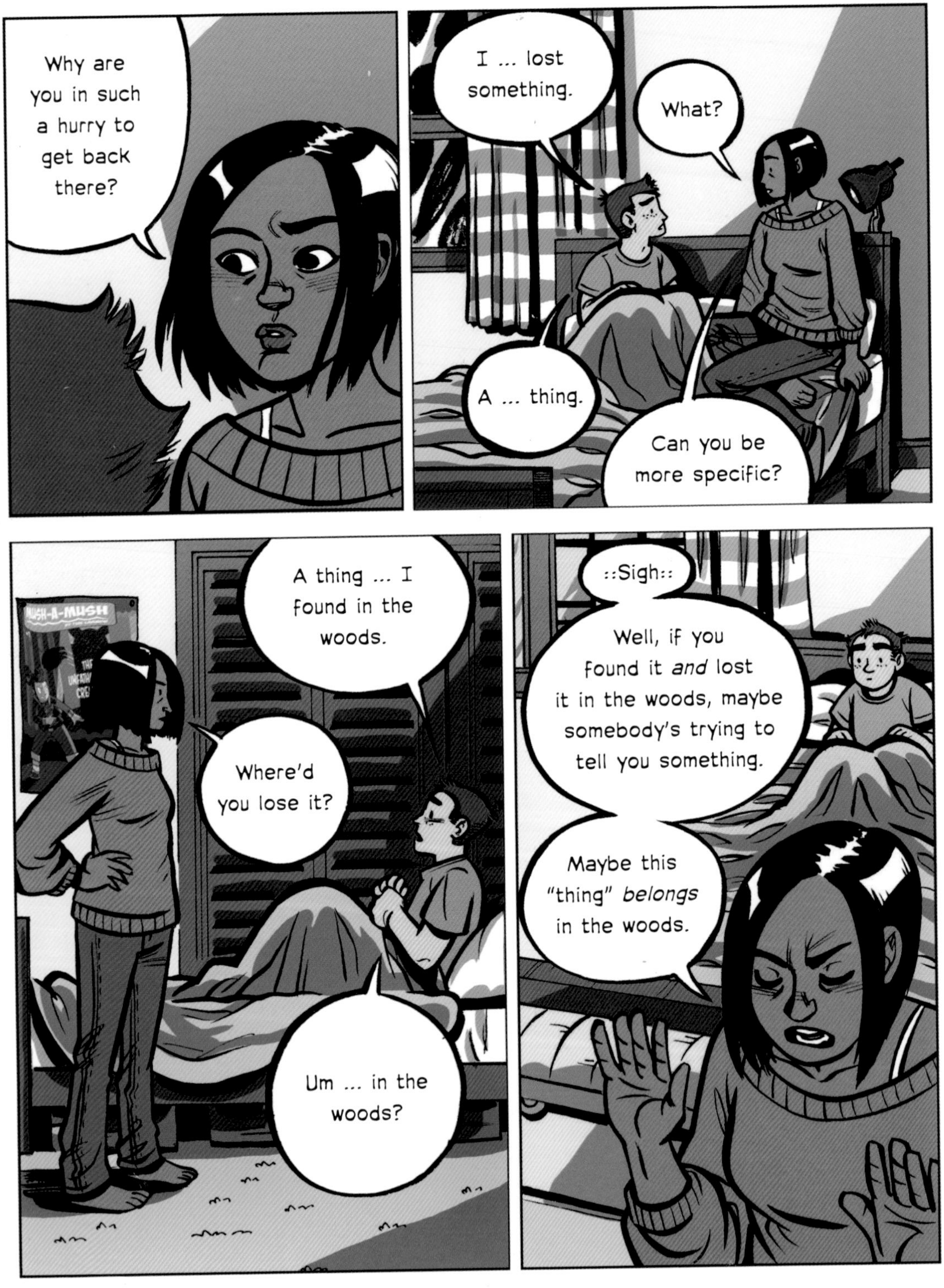
Why are you in such a hurry to get back there?
I ... lost something.
What?
A ... thing.
Can you be more specific?
A thing ... I found in the woods.
Where'd you lose it?
Um ... in the woods?
::Sigh::
Well, if you found it *and* lost it in the woods, maybe somebody's trying to tell you something.
Maybe this "thing" *belongs* in the woods.

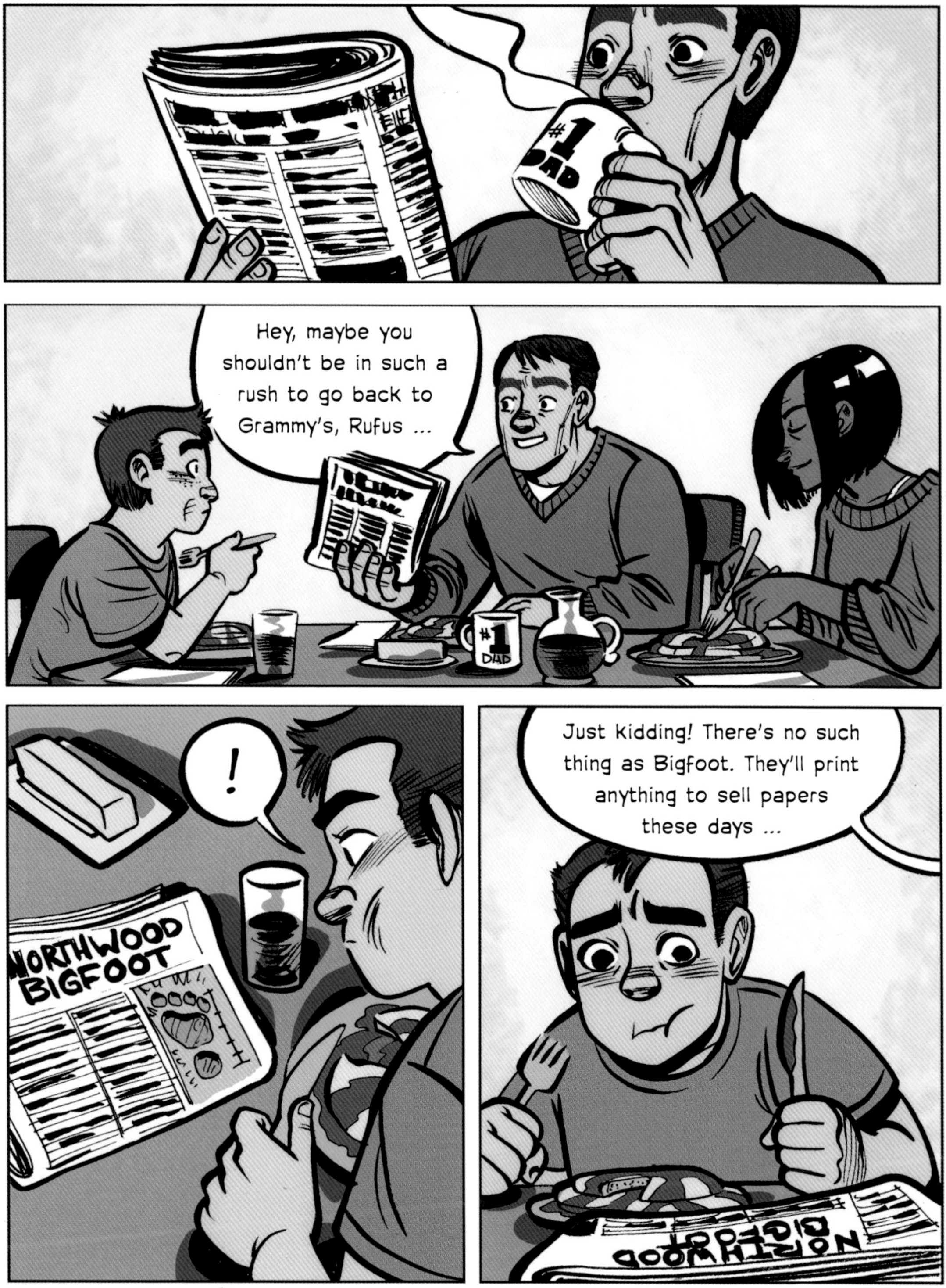
#1 DAD
Hey, maybe you shouldn't be in such a rush to go back to Grammy's, Rufus ...
#1 DAD
!
NORTHWOOD BIGFOOT
Just kidding! There's no such thing as Bigfoot. They'll print anything to sell papers these days ...
NORTHWOOD BIGFOOT

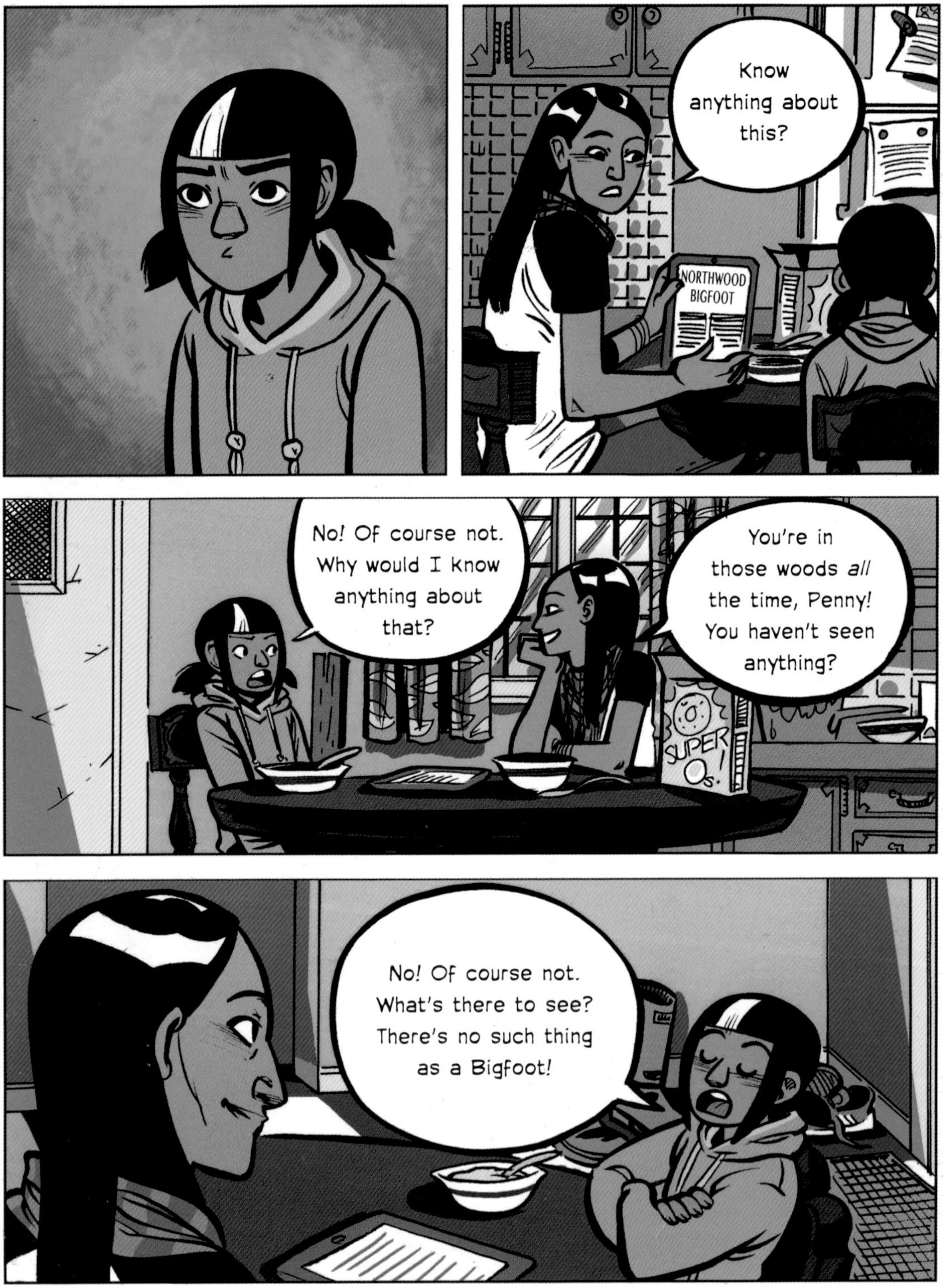
Know anything about this?
NORTHWOOD BIGFOOT
No! Of course not. Why would I know anything about that?
You're in those woods *all* the time, Penny! You haven't seen anything?
SUPER Os.
No! Of course not. What's there to see? There's no such thing as a Bigfoot!

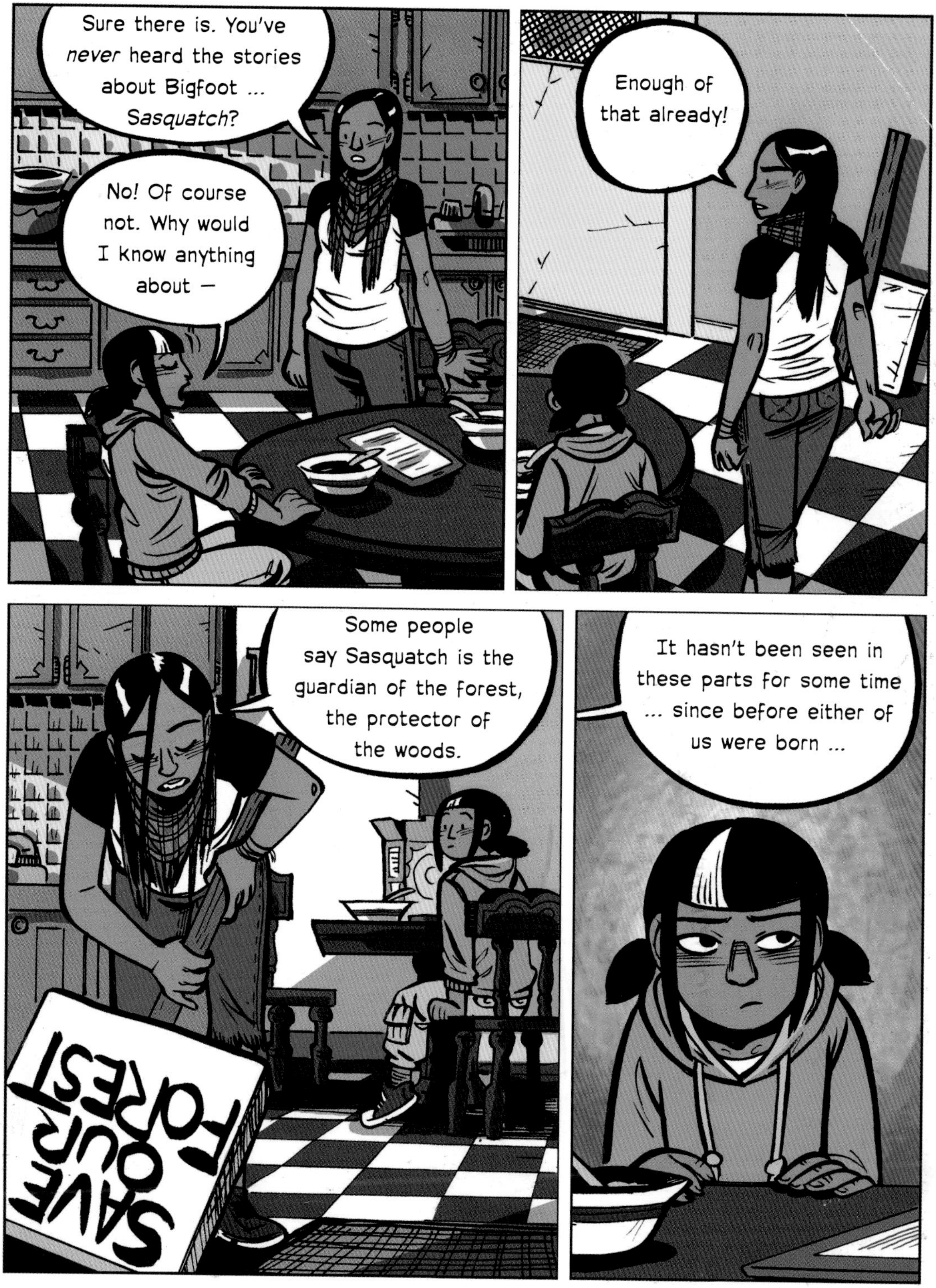

Sure there is. You've *never* heard the stories about Bigfoot ... *Sasquatch*?
No! Of course not. Why would I know anything about —
Enough of that already!
Some people say Sasquatch is the guardian of the forest, the protector of the woods.
SAVE OUR FOREST
It hasn't been seen in these parts for some time ... since before either of us were born ...

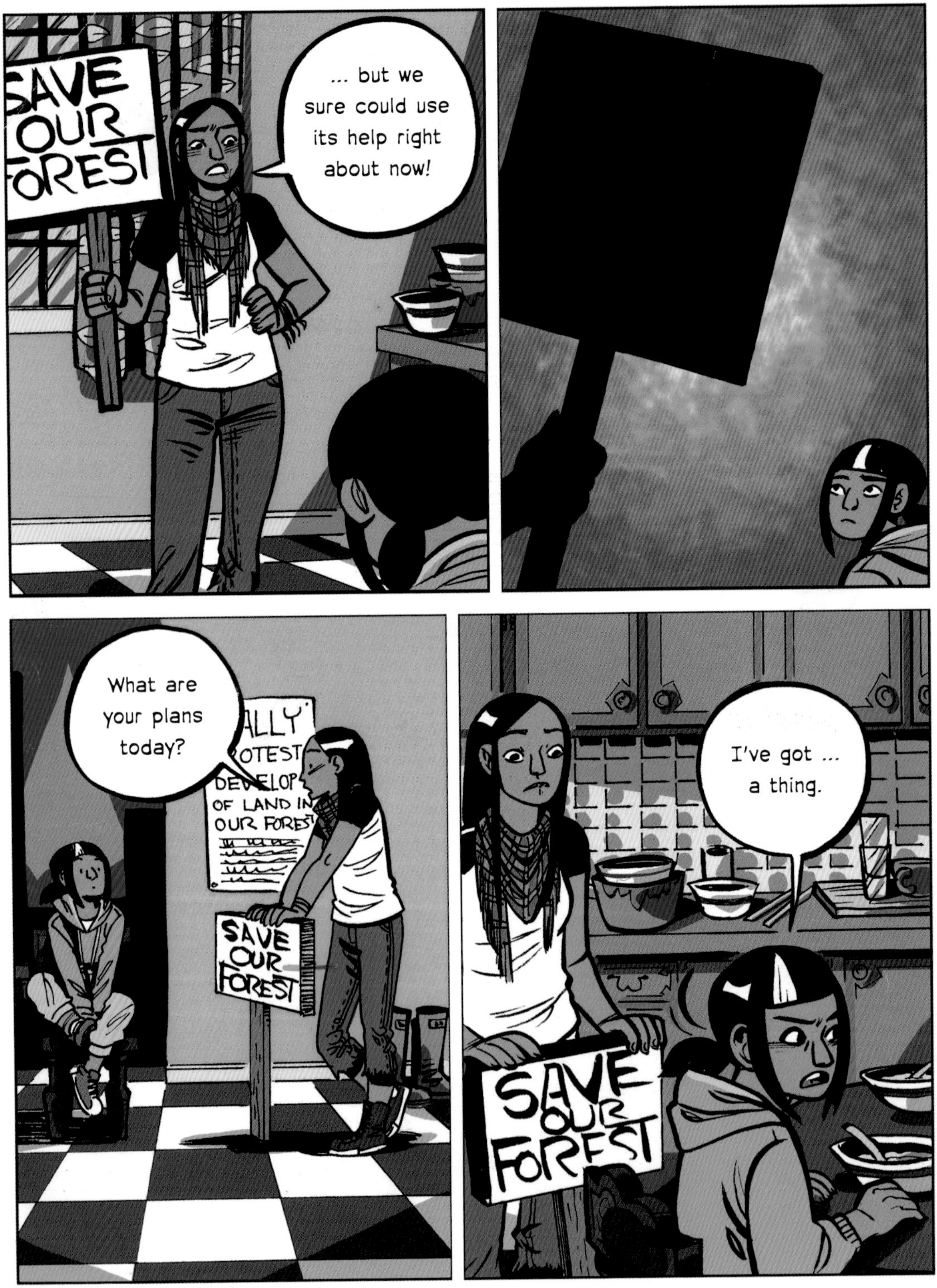
SAVE OUR FOREST
... but we sure could use its help right about now!
What are your plans today?
OF LAND IN
SAVE OUR FOREST
SAVE OUR FOREST
I've got ... a thing.

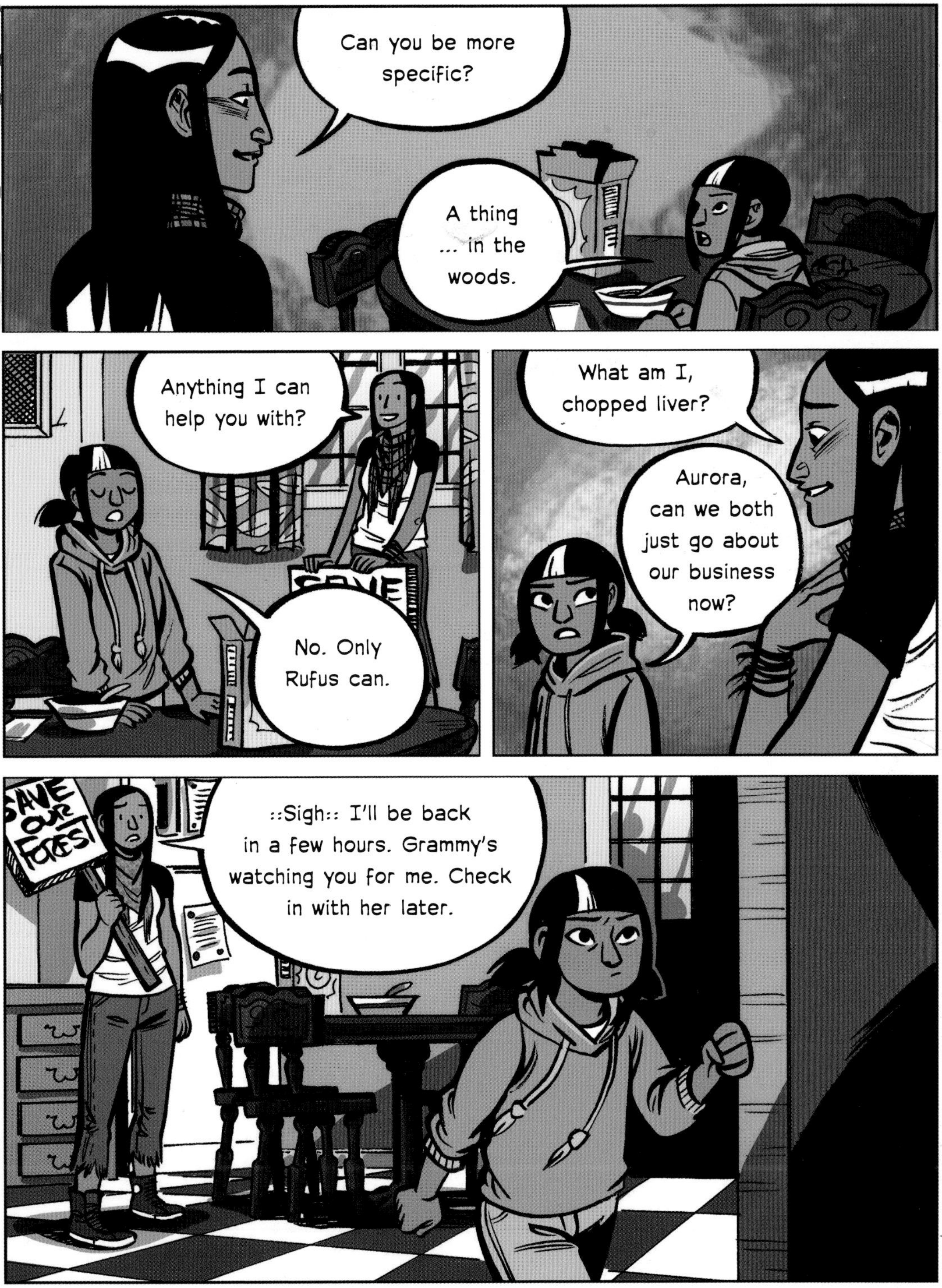
Can you be more specific?
A thing ... in the woods.
Anything I can help you with?
No. Only Rufus can.
What am I, chopped liver?
Aurora, can we both just go about our business now?
SAVE OUR FOREST
::Sigh:: I'll be back in a few hours. Grammy's watching you for me. Check in with her later.

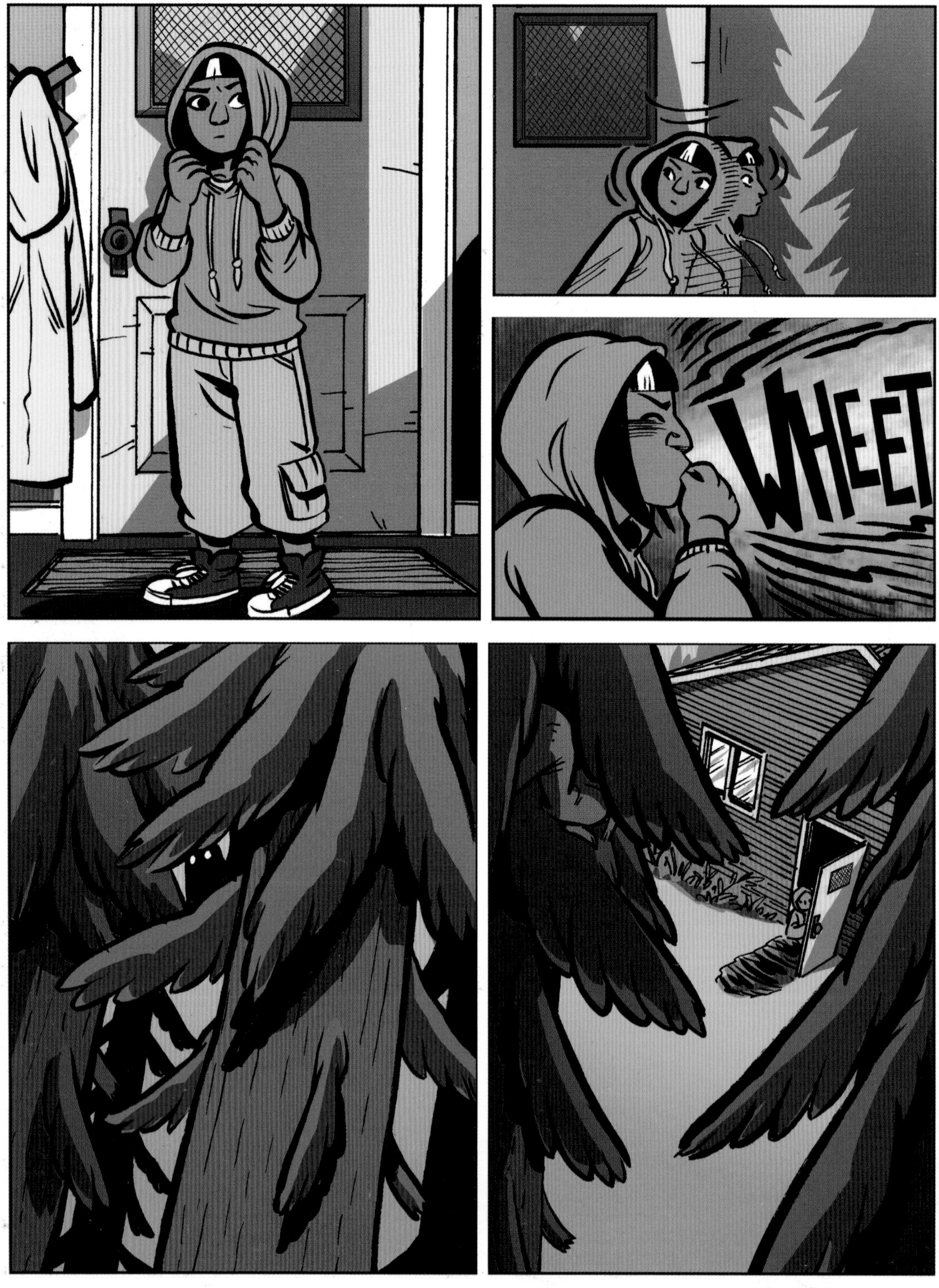
WHEET

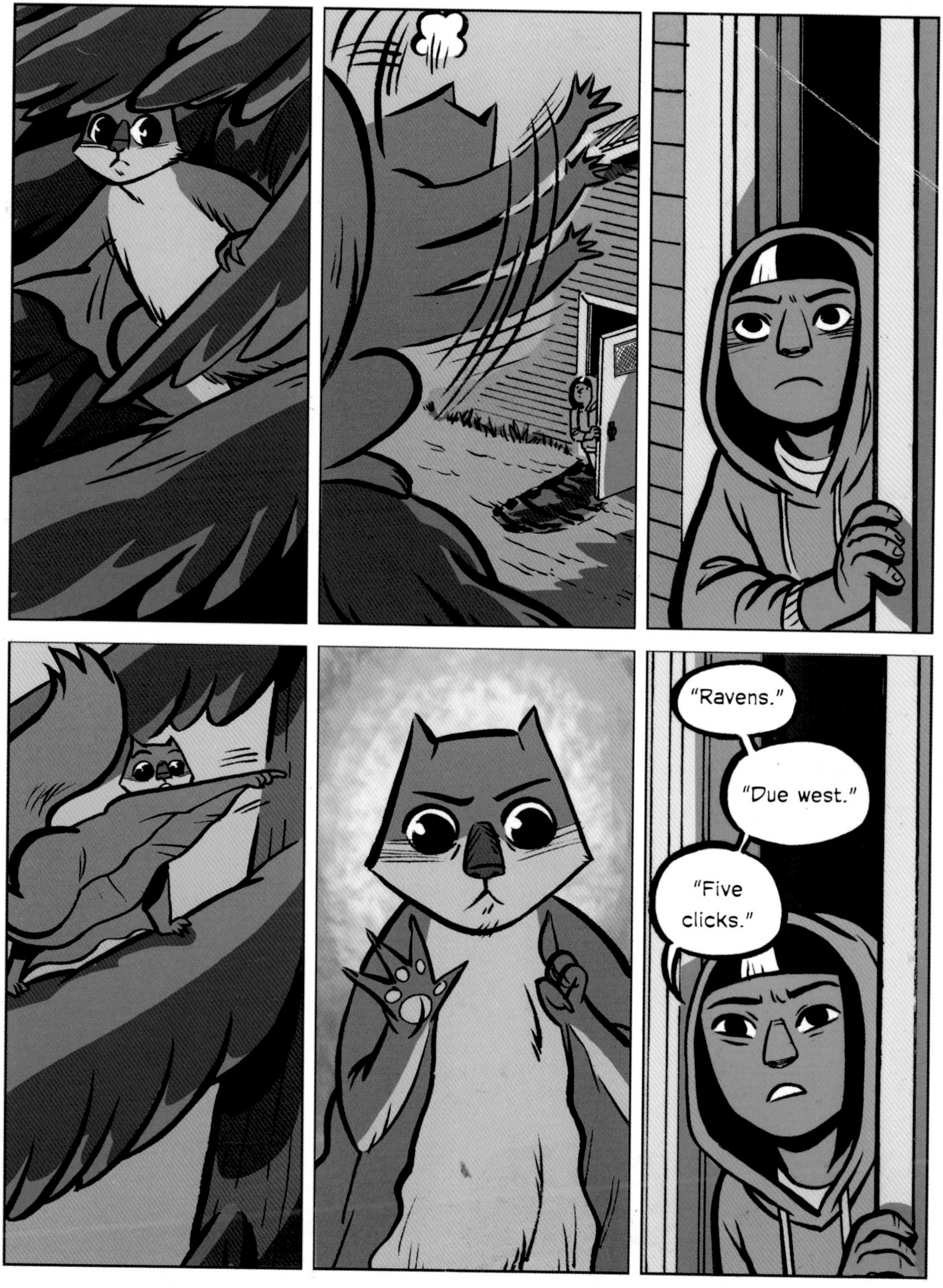
"Ravens."
"Due west."
"Five clicks."

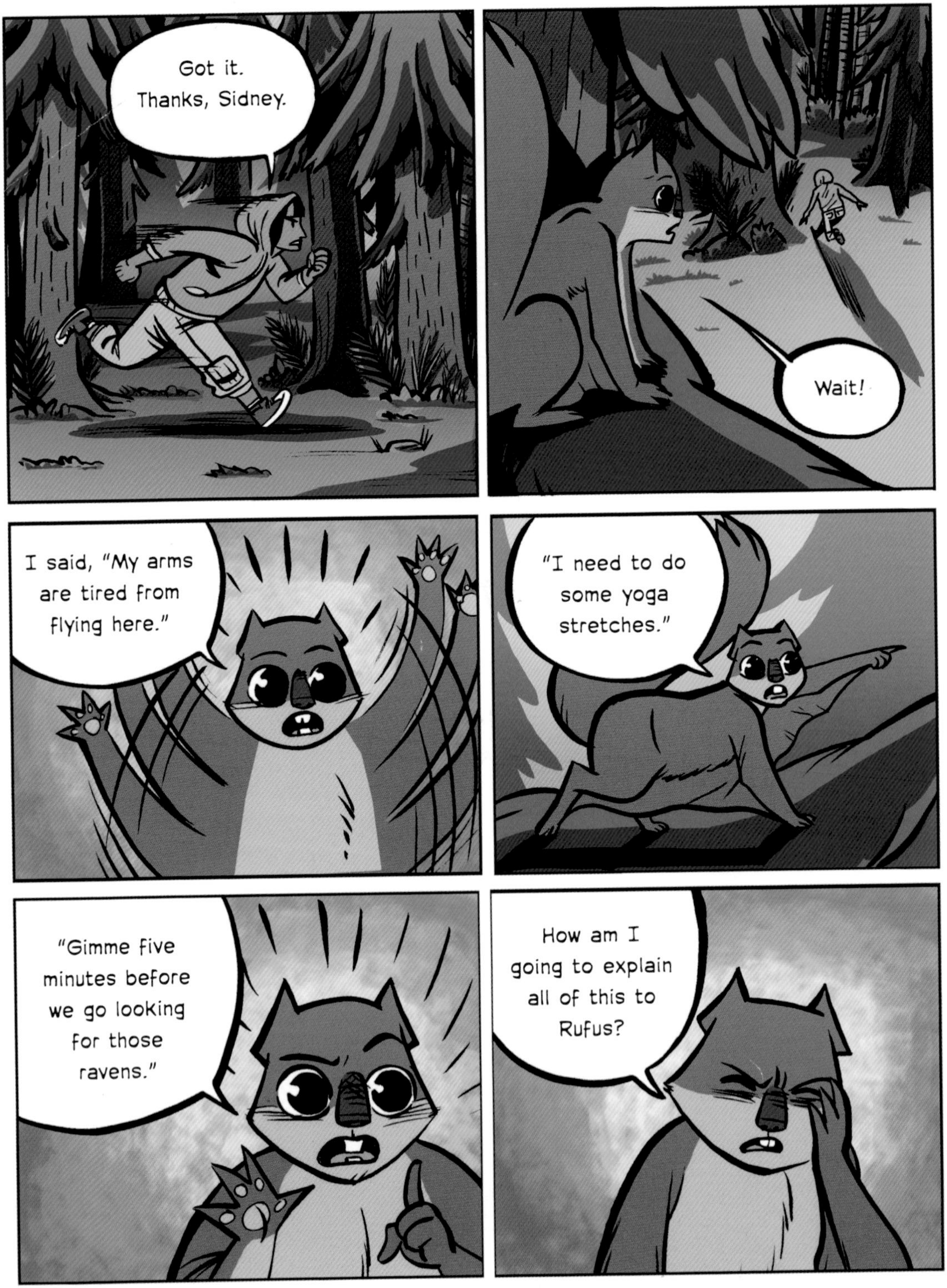
Got it. Thanks, Sidney.
Wait!
I said, "My arms are tired from flying here."
"I need to do some yoga stretches."
"Gimme five minutes before we go looking for those ravens."
How am I going to explain all of this to Rufus?

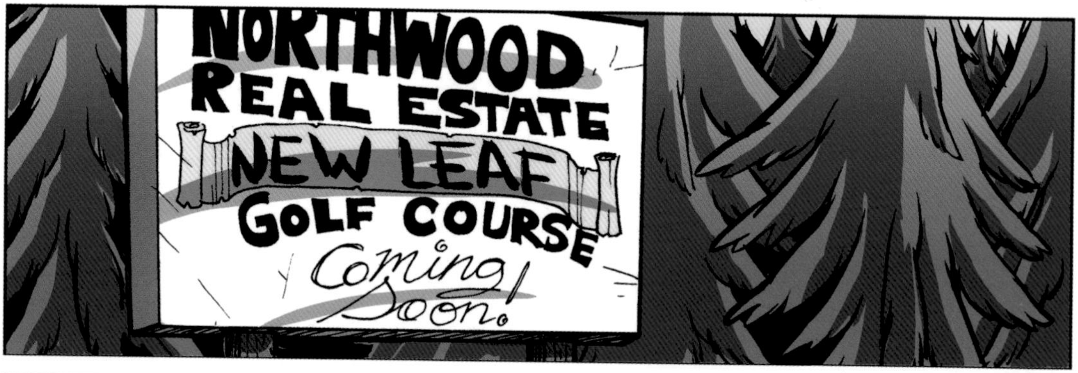
NORTHWOOD
REAL ESTATE
NEW LEAF
GOLF COURSE
Coming Soon!

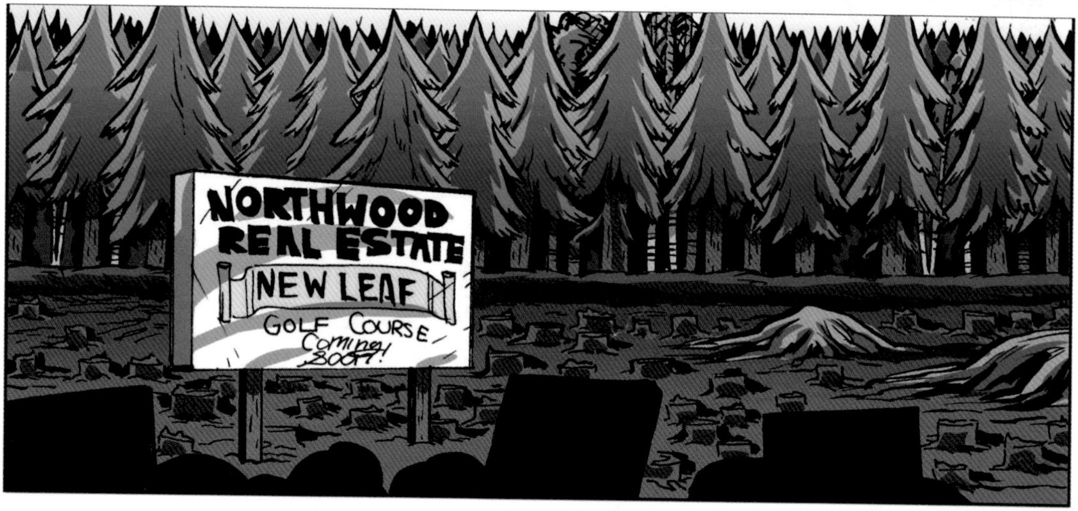
NORTHWOOD
REAL ESTATE
NEW LEAF
GOLF COURSE
Coming Soon!

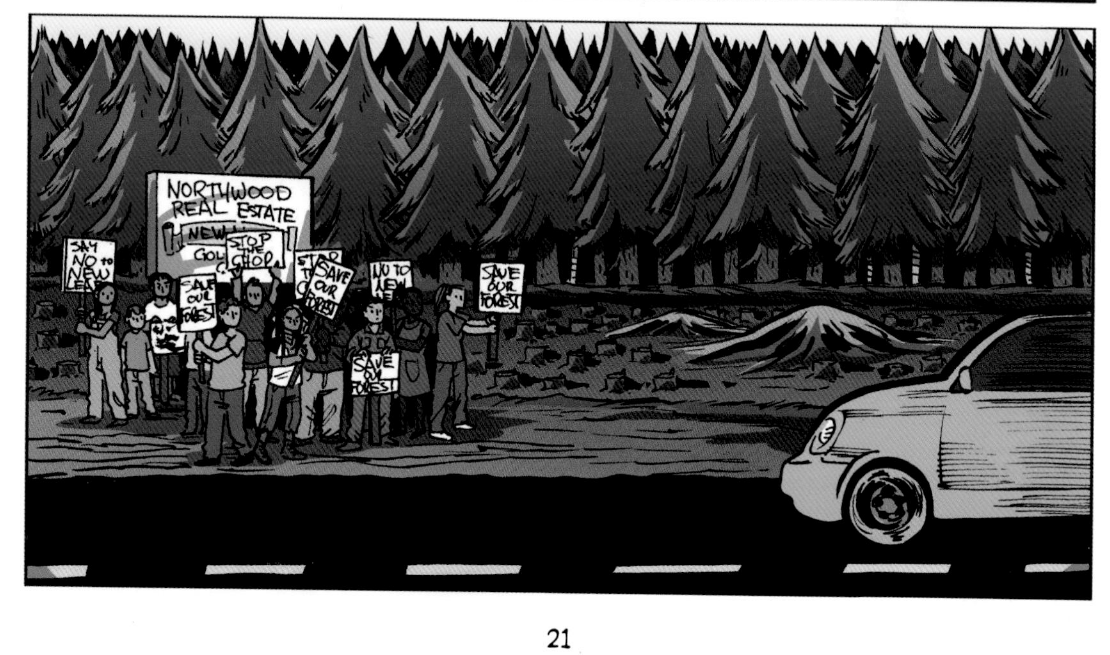
NORTHWOOD
REAL ESTATE
STOP THE CHOP
SAVE OUR FOREST
SAVE OUR FOREST
SAVE OUR FOREST
SAVE OUR FOREST

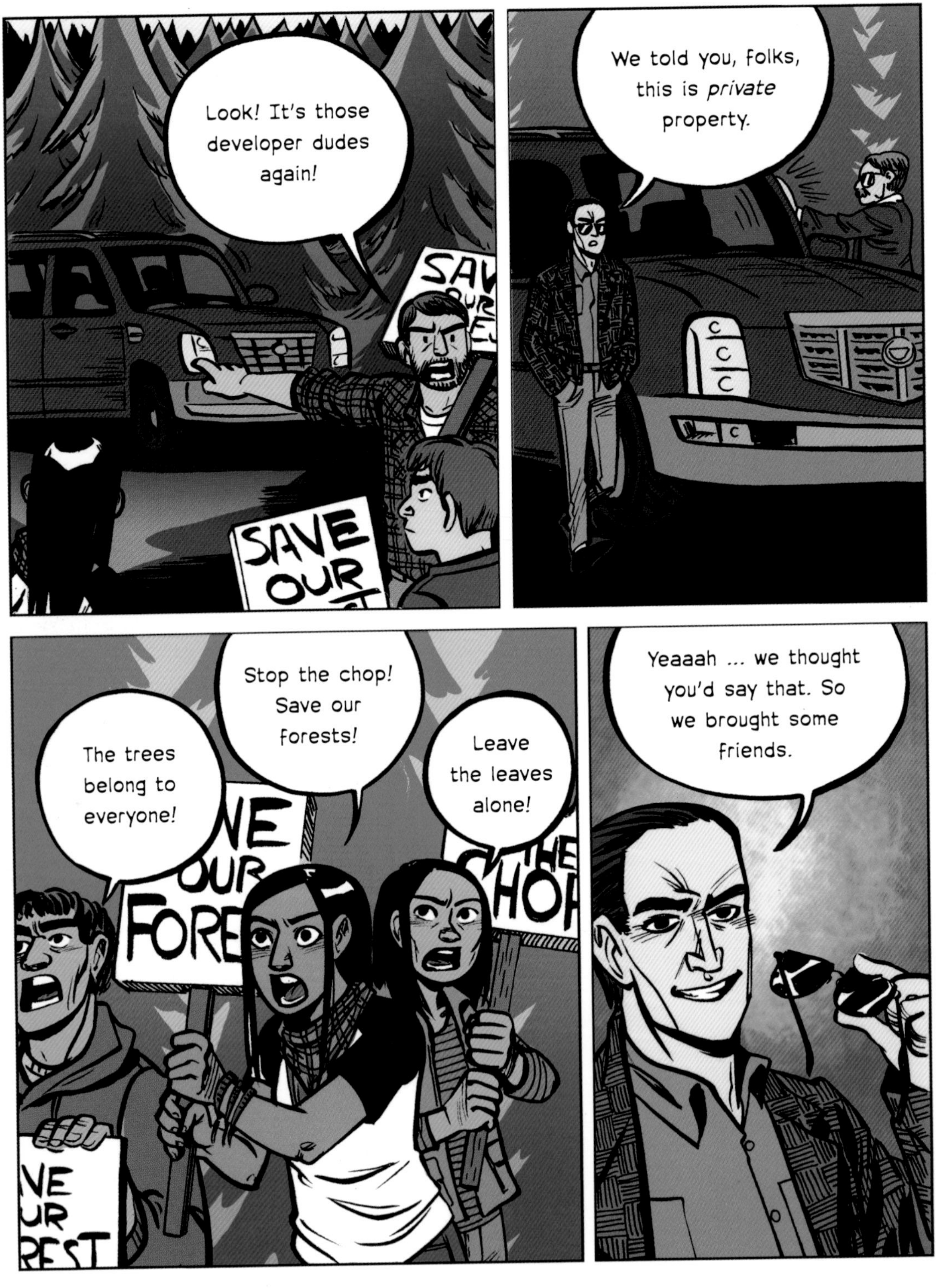
Look! It's those developer dudes again!
SAVE OUR
SAVE OUR
We told you, folks, this is *private* property.
The trees belong to everyone!
Stop the chop! Save our forests!
Leave the leaves alone!
OUR FORE
CHOP
VE UR REST
Yeaaah ... we thought you'd say that. So we brought some friends.

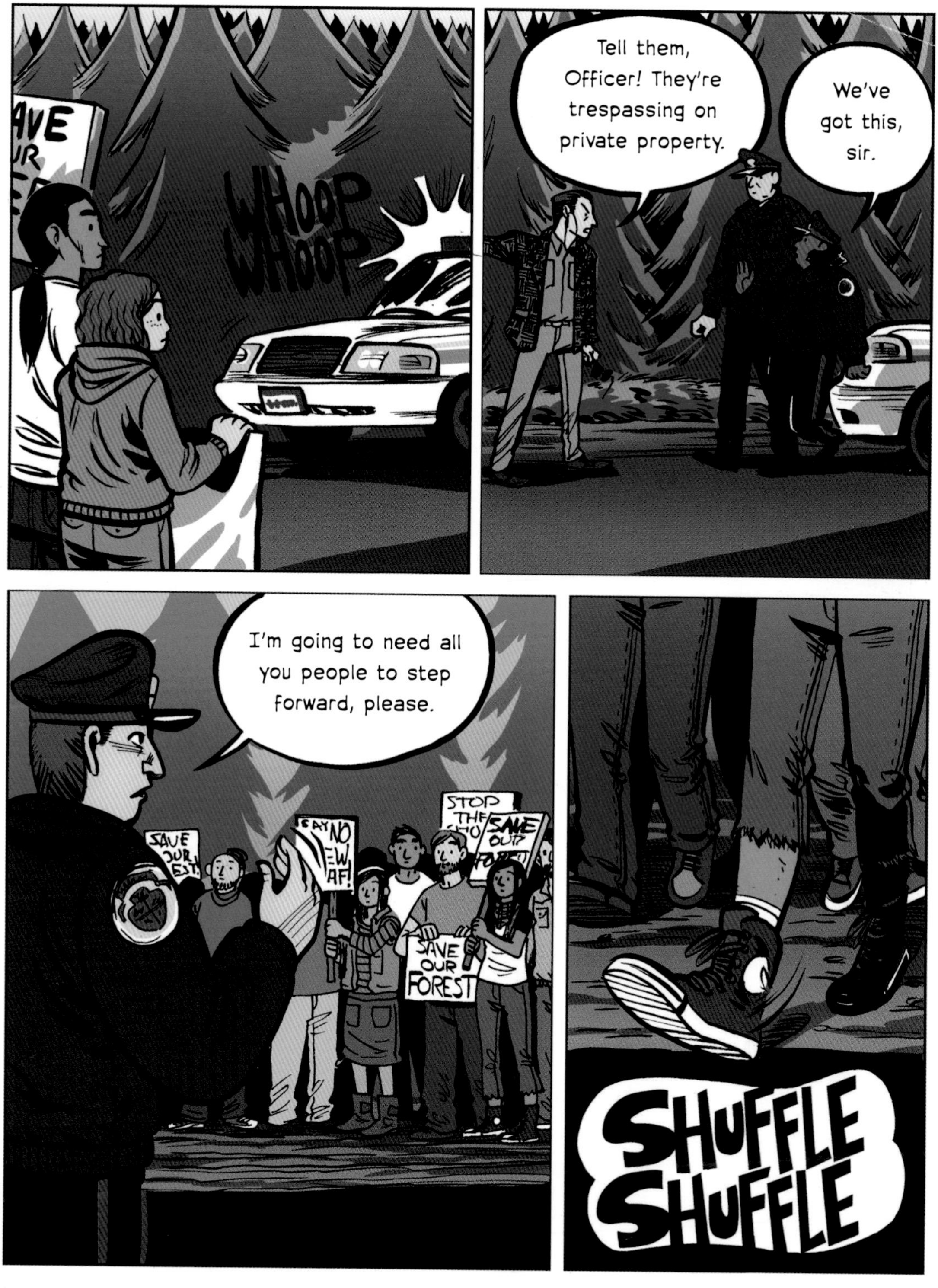
WHOOP WHOOP
Tell them, Officer! They're trespassing on private property.
We've got this, sir.
I'm going to need all you people to step forward, please.
STOP THE
SAVE OUR FOREST
SHUFFLE SHUFFLE

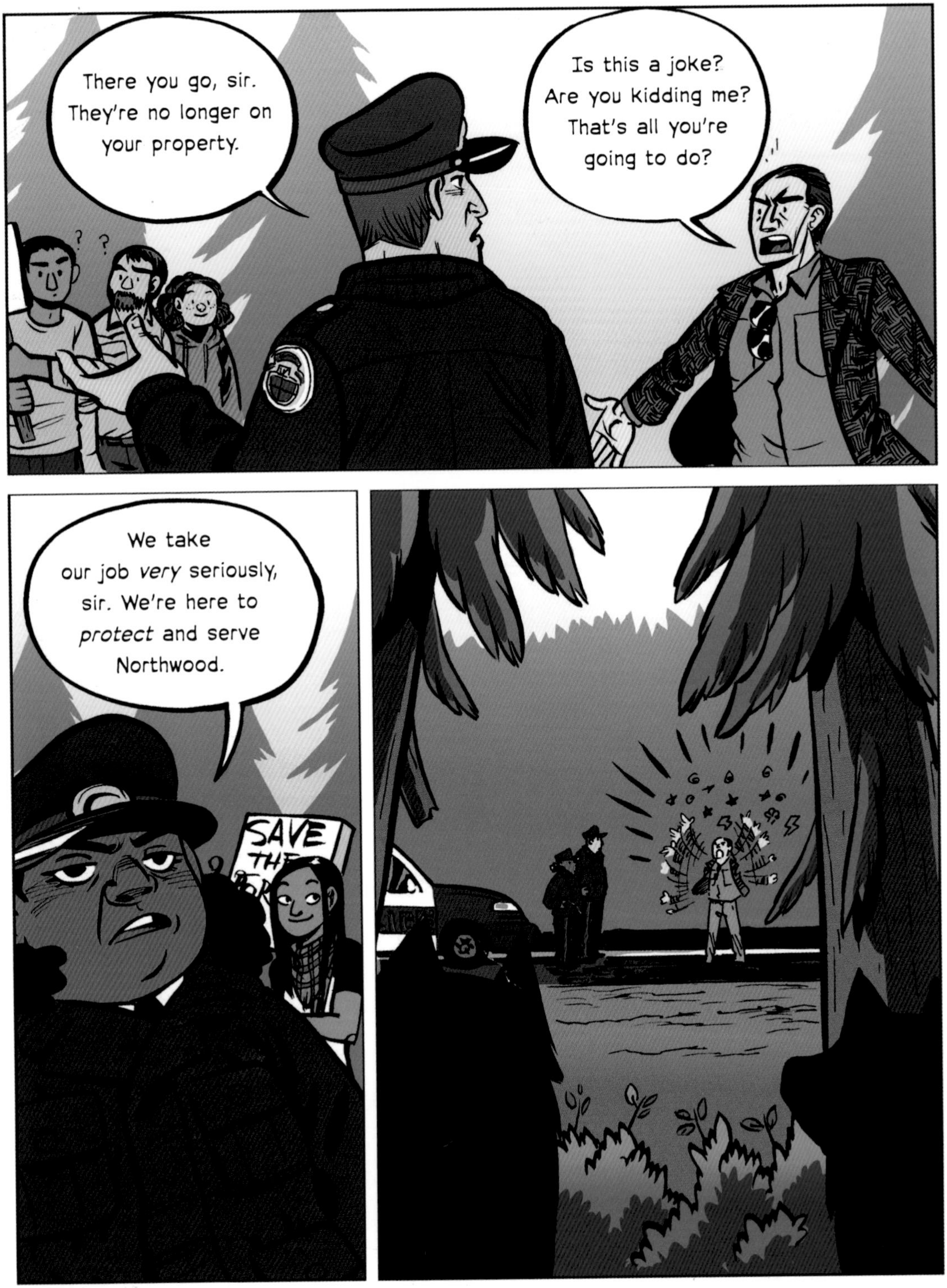
There you go, sir. They're no longer on your property.
Is this a joke? Are you kidding me? That's all you're going to do?
We take our job *very* seriously, sir. We're here to *protect* and serve Northwood.
SAVE

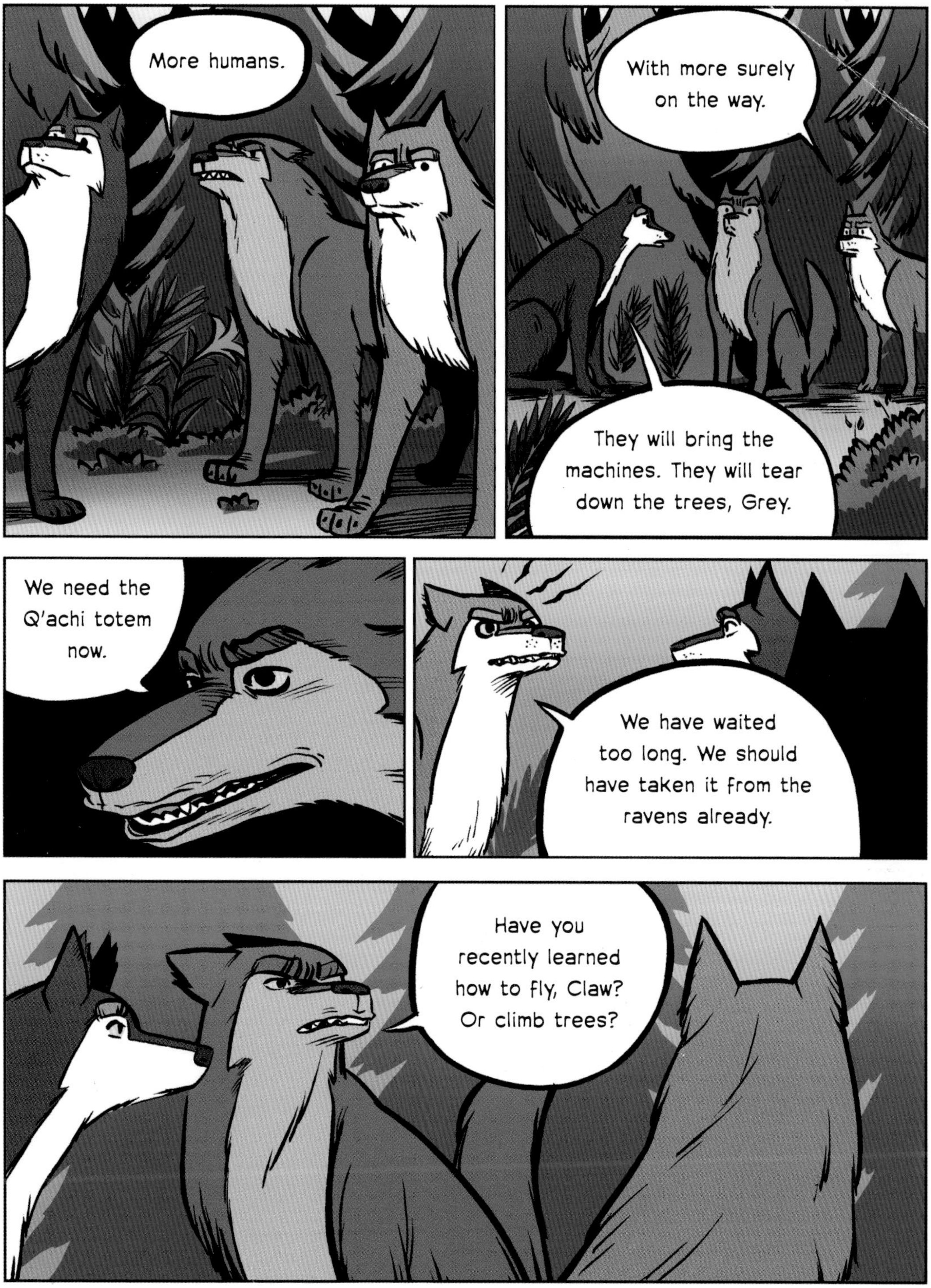
More humans.
With more surely on the way.
They will bring the machines. They will tear down the trees, Grey.
We need the Q'achi totem now.
We have waited too long. We should have taken it from the ravens already.
Have you recently learned how to fly, Claw? Or climb trees?

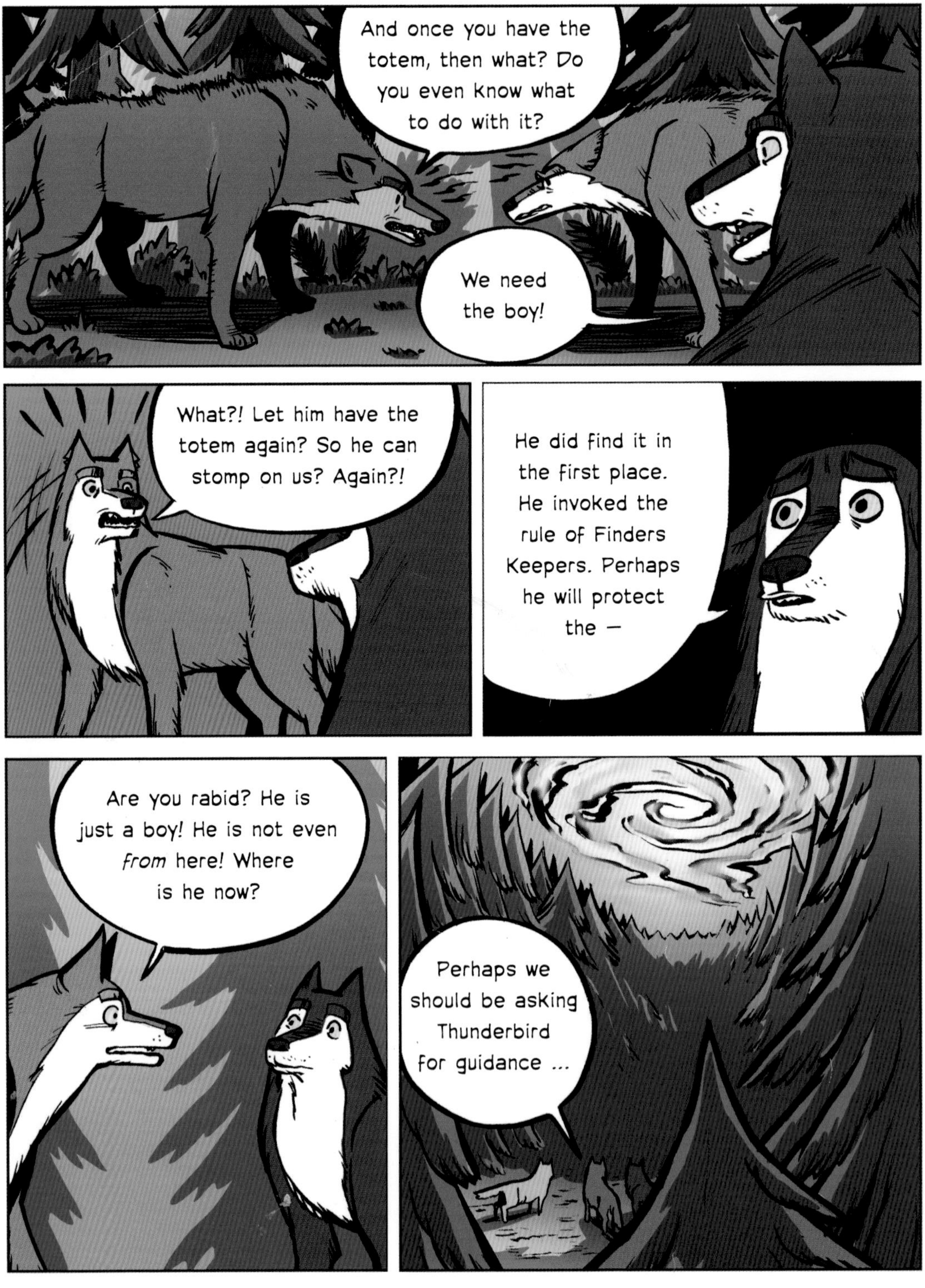

And once you have the totem, then what? Do you even know what to do with it?
We need the boy!
What?! Let him have the totem again? So he can stomp on us? Again?!
He did find it in the first place. He invoked the rule of Finders Keepers. Perhaps he will protect the —
Are you rabid? He is just a boy! He is not even *from* here! Where is he now?
Perhaps we should be asking Thunderbird for guidance ...

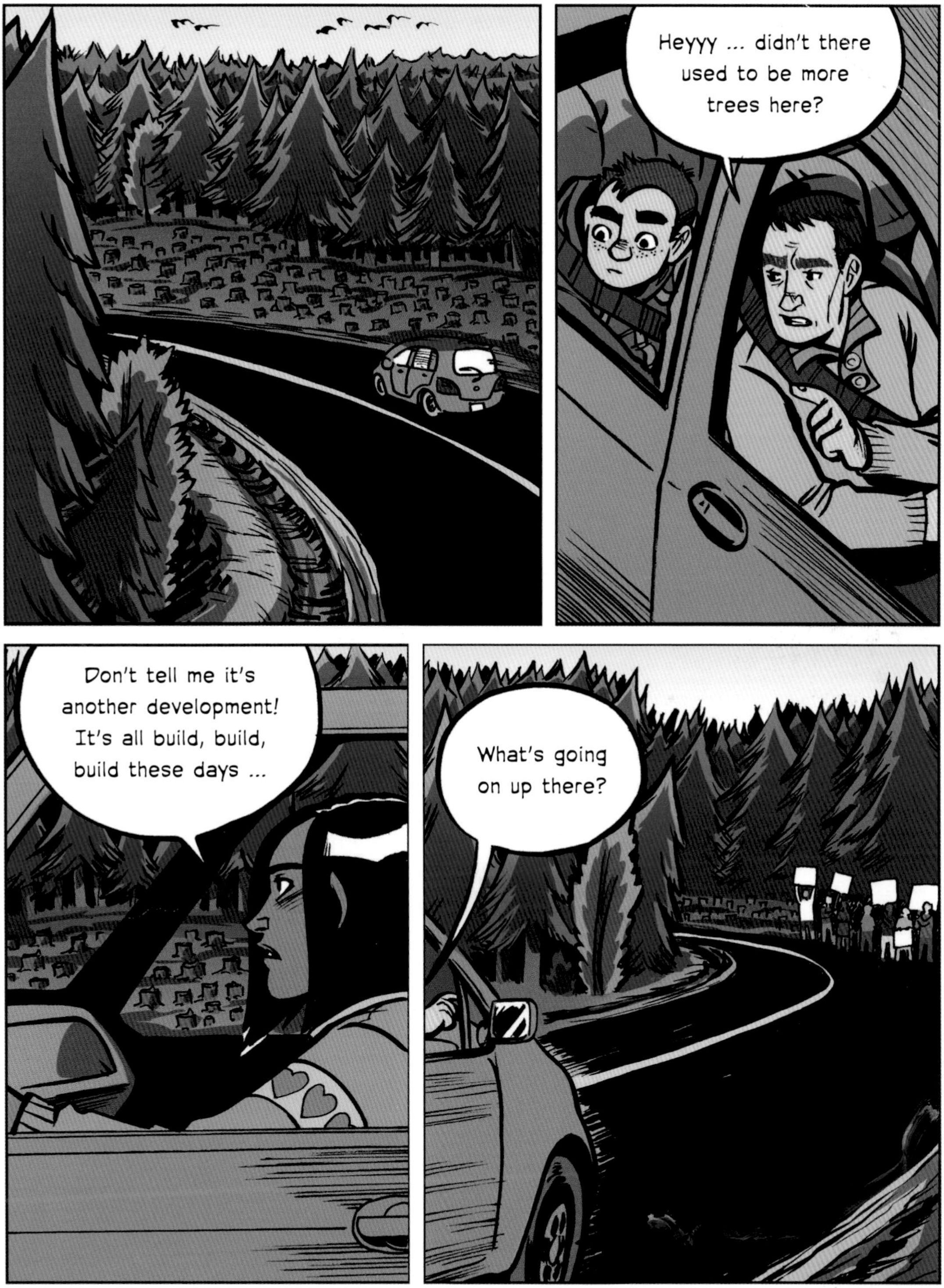
Heyyy ... didn't there used to be more trees here?
Don't tell me it's another development! It's all build, build, build these days ...
What's going on up there?

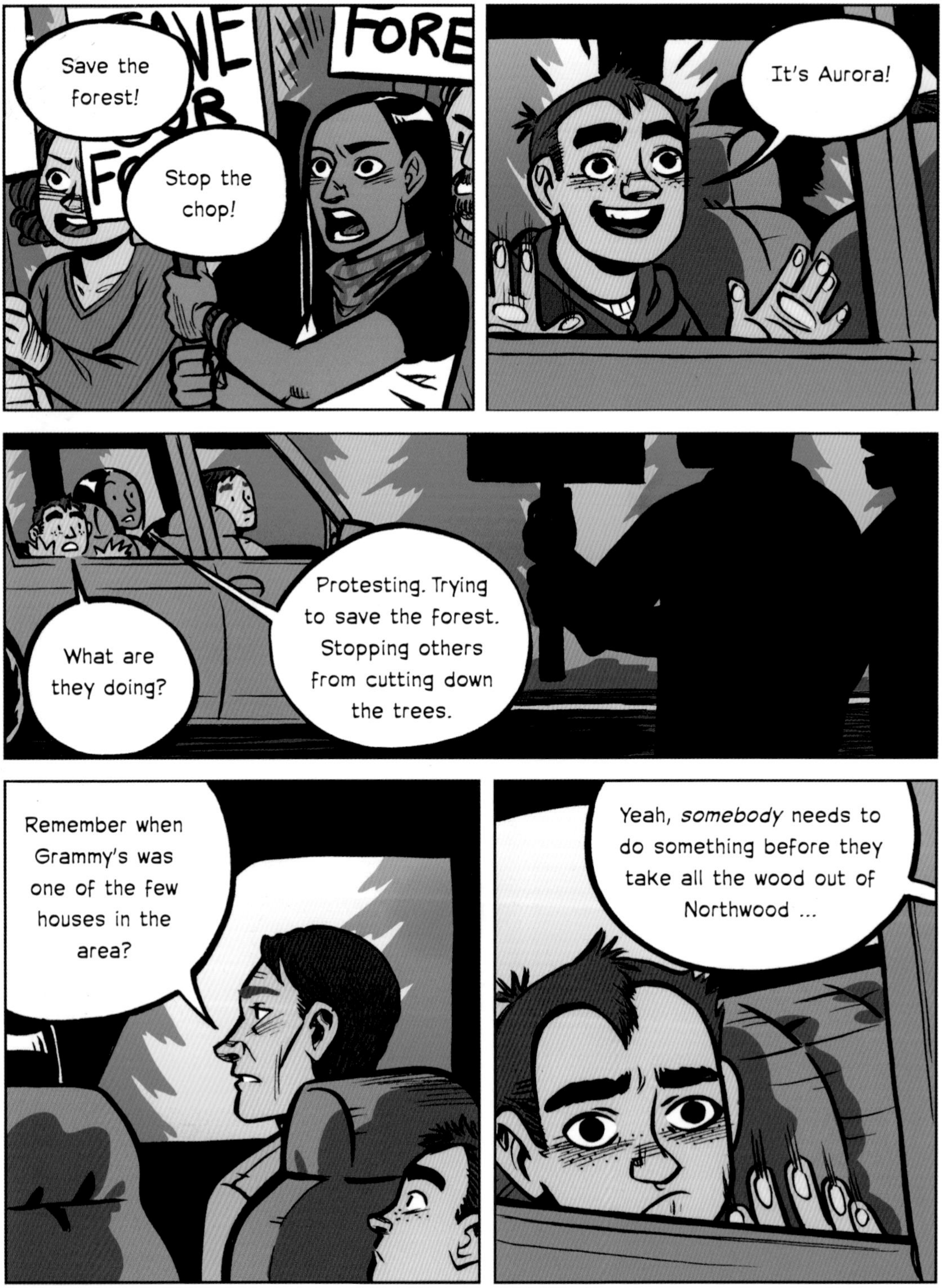
Save the forest!
Stop the chop!
It's Aurora!
What are they doing?
Protesting. Trying to save the forest. Stopping others from cutting down the trees.
Remember when Grammy's was one of the few houses in the area?
Yeah, *somebody* needs to do something before they take all the wood out of Northwood ...

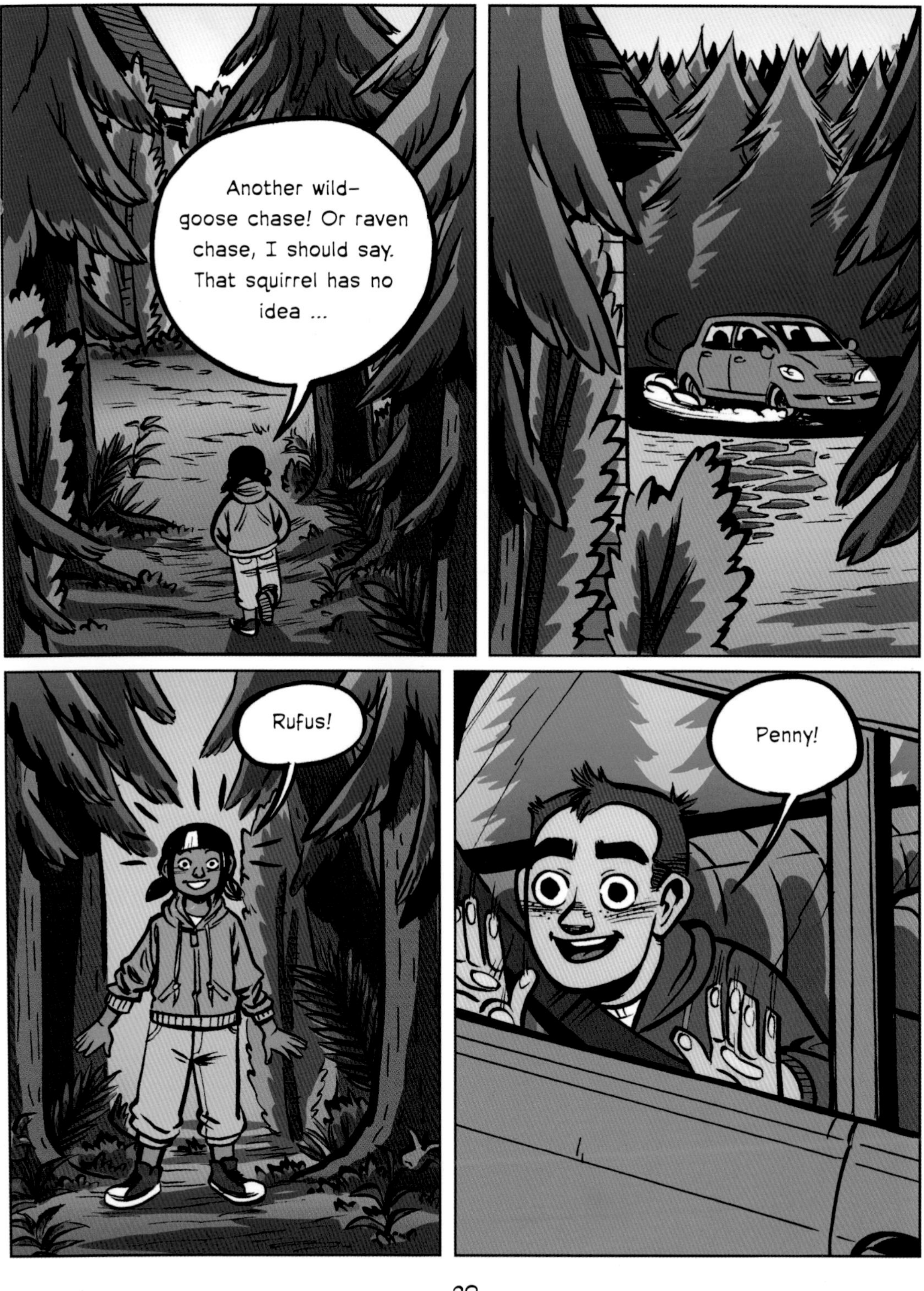
Another wild-goose chase! Or raven chase, I should say. That squirrel has no idea ...
Rufus!
Penny!

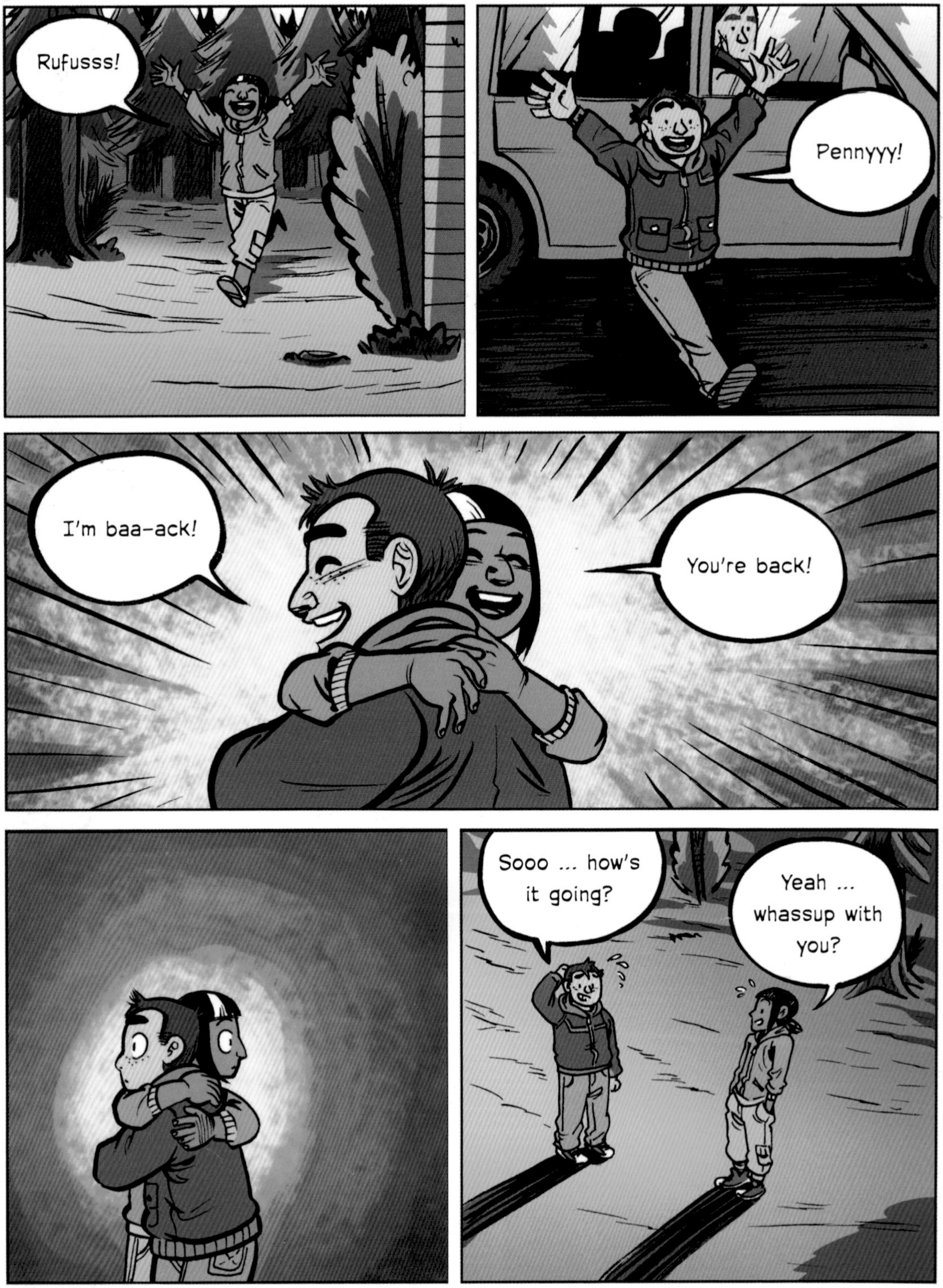
Rufusss!
Pennyyy!
I'm baa-ack!
You're back!
Sooo ... how's it going?
Yeah ... whassup with you?

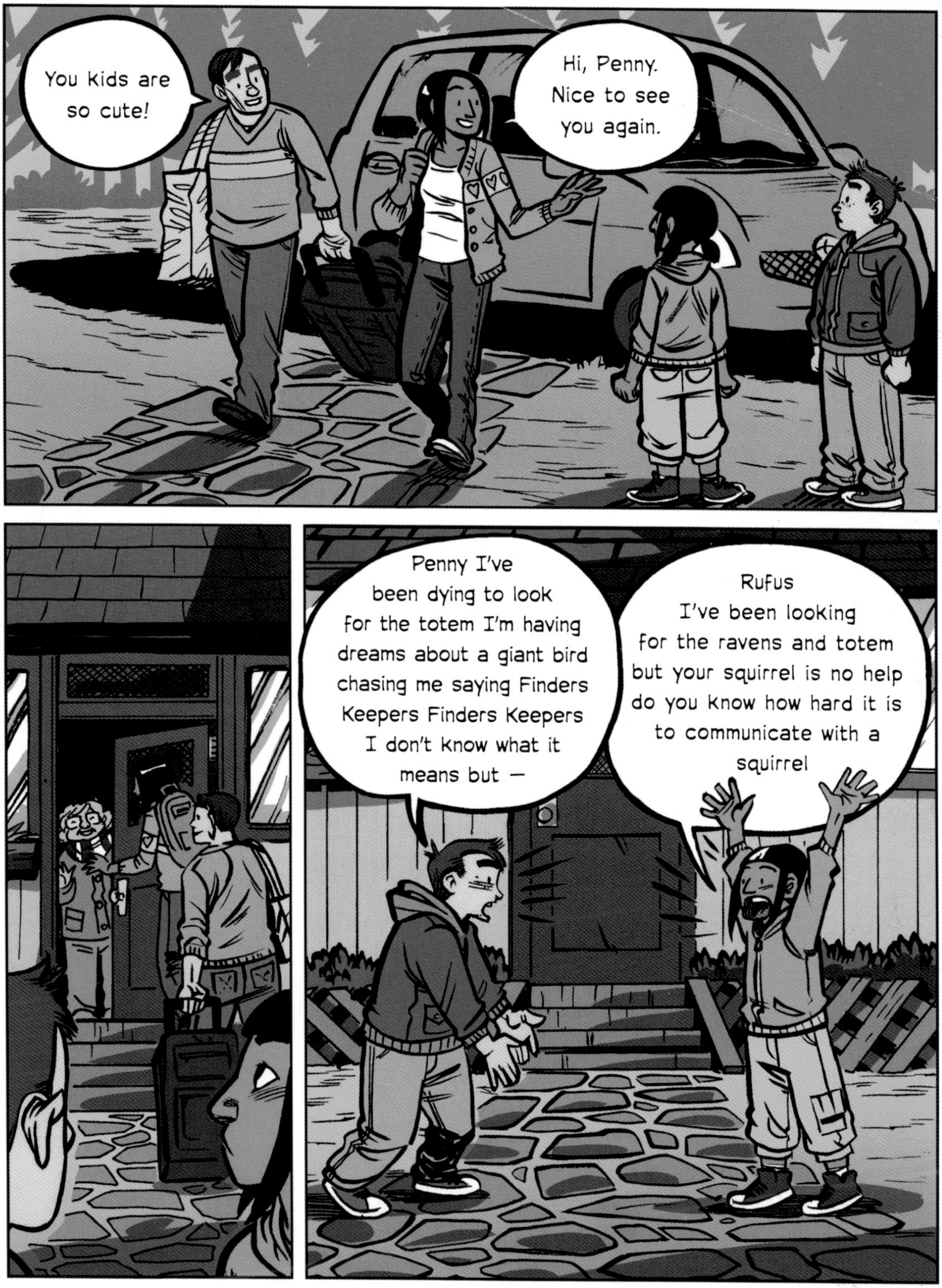
You kids are so cute!
Hi, Penny. Nice to see you again.
Penny I've been dying to look for the totem I'm having dreams about a giant bird chasing me saying Finders Keepers Finders Keepers I don't know what it means but —
Rufus I've been looking for the ravens and totem but your squirrel is no help do you know how hard it is to communicate with a squirrel

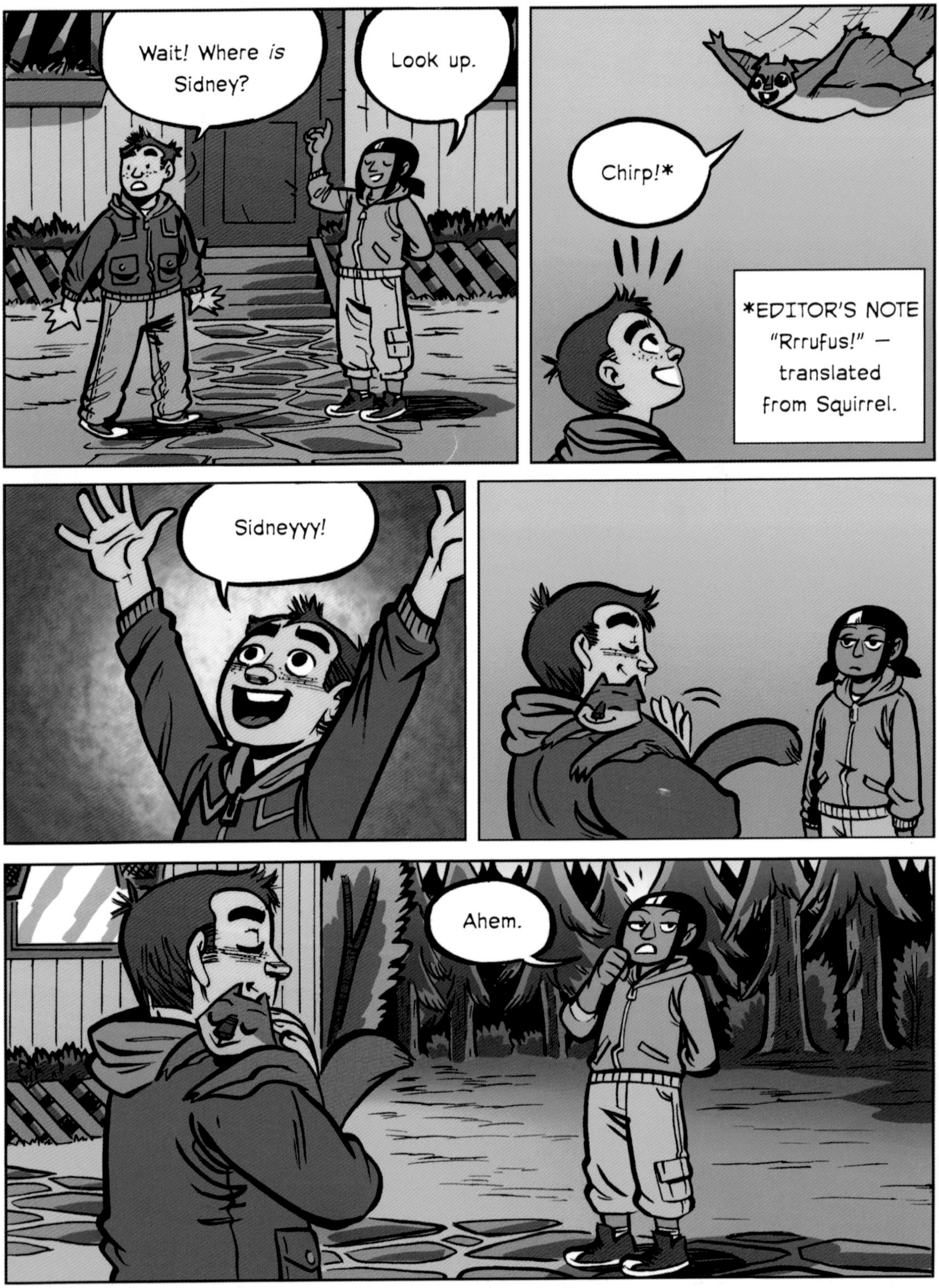
Wait! Where *is* Sidney?
Look up.
Chirp!*
*EDITOR'S NOTE "Rrrufus!" — translated from Squirrel.
Sidneyyy!
Ahem.

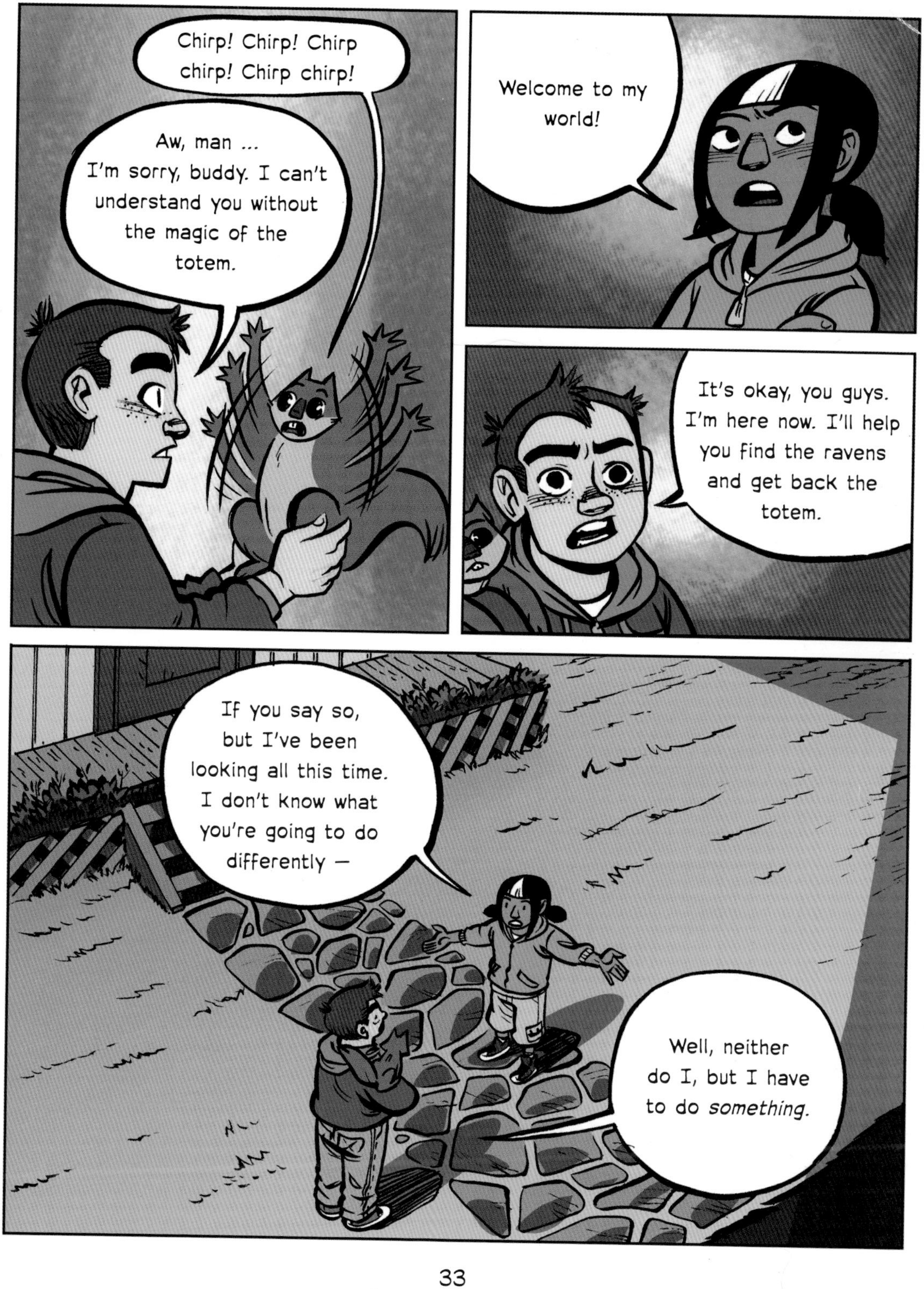
Aw, man ...
I'm sorry, buddy. I can't understand you without the magic of the totem.
Chirp! Chirp! Chirp chirp! Chirp chirp!
Welcome to my world!
It's okay, you guys. I'm here now. I'll help you find the ravens and get back the totem.
If you say so, but I've been looking all this time. I don't know what you're going to do differently —
Well, neither do I, but I have to do *something*.

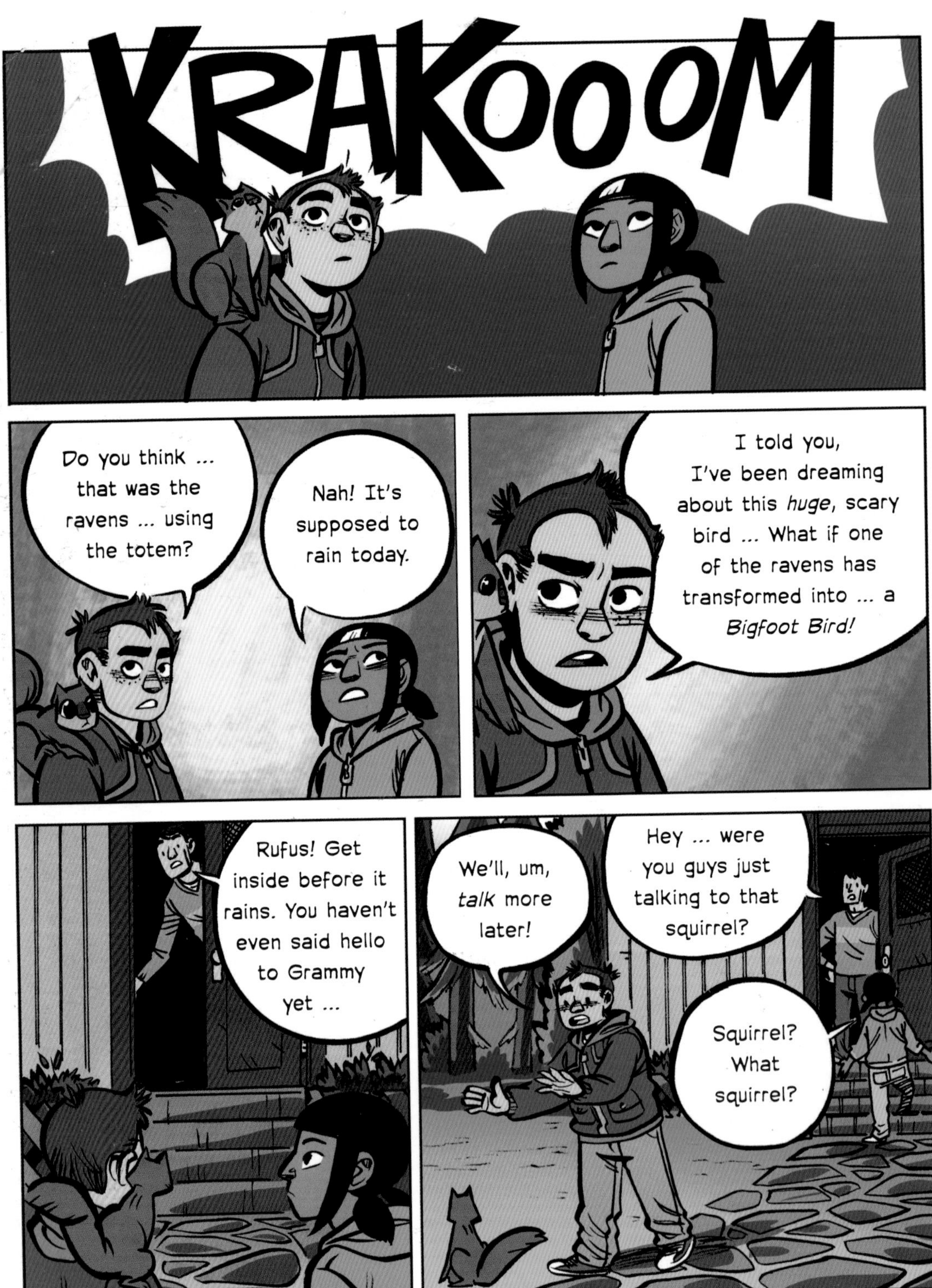
KRAKOOOM
Do you think ... that was the ravens ... using the totem?
Nah! It's supposed to rain today.
I told you, I've been dreaming about this *huge*, scary bird ... What if one of the ravens has transformed into ... a *Bigfoot Bird!*
Rufus! Get inside before it rains. You haven't even said hello to Grammy yet ...
We'll, um, *talk* more later!
Hey ... were you guys just talking to that squirrel?
Squirrel? What squirrel?

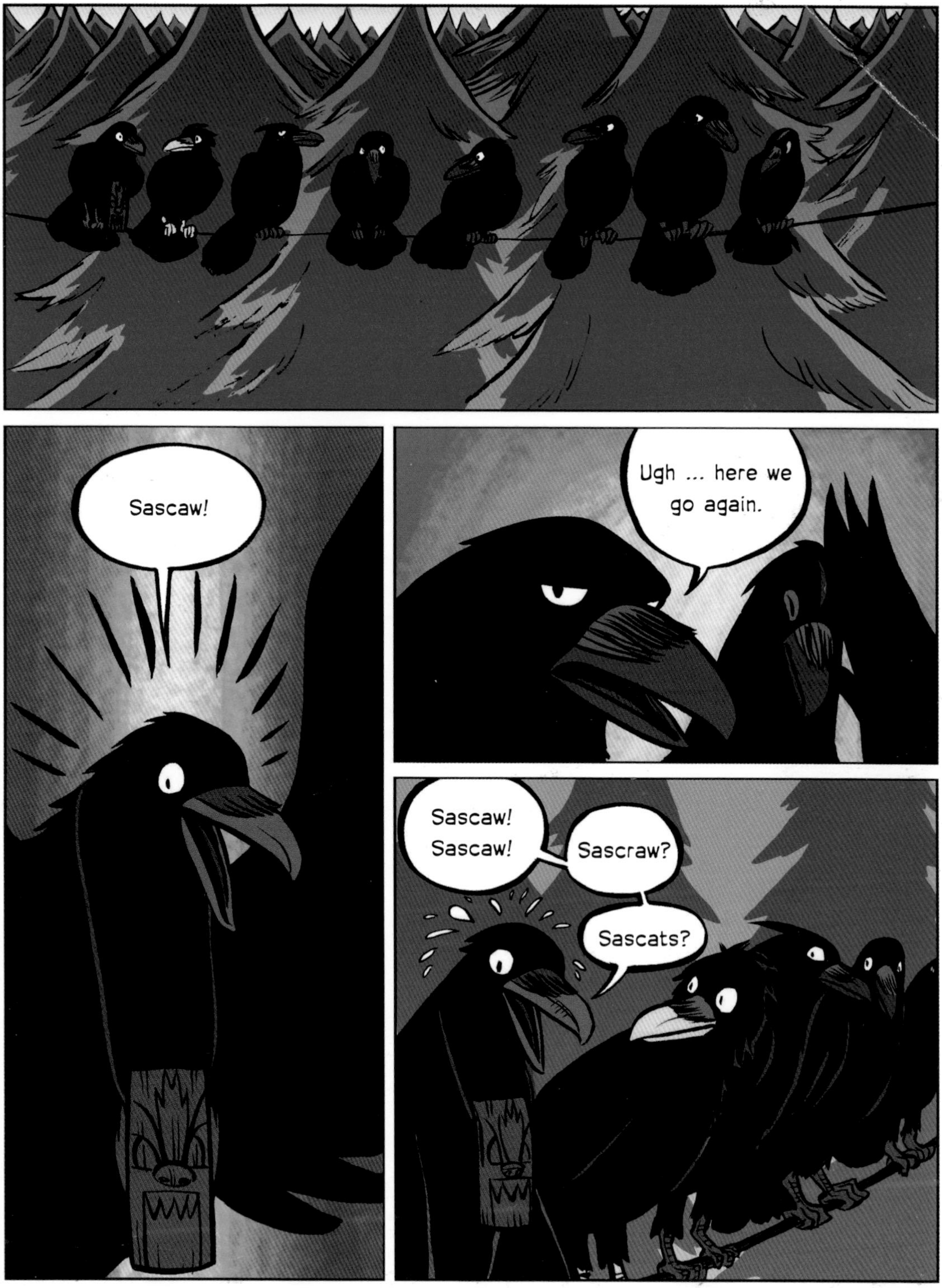
Sascaw!
Ugh ... here we go again.
Sascaw! Sascaw!
Sascraw?
Sascats?

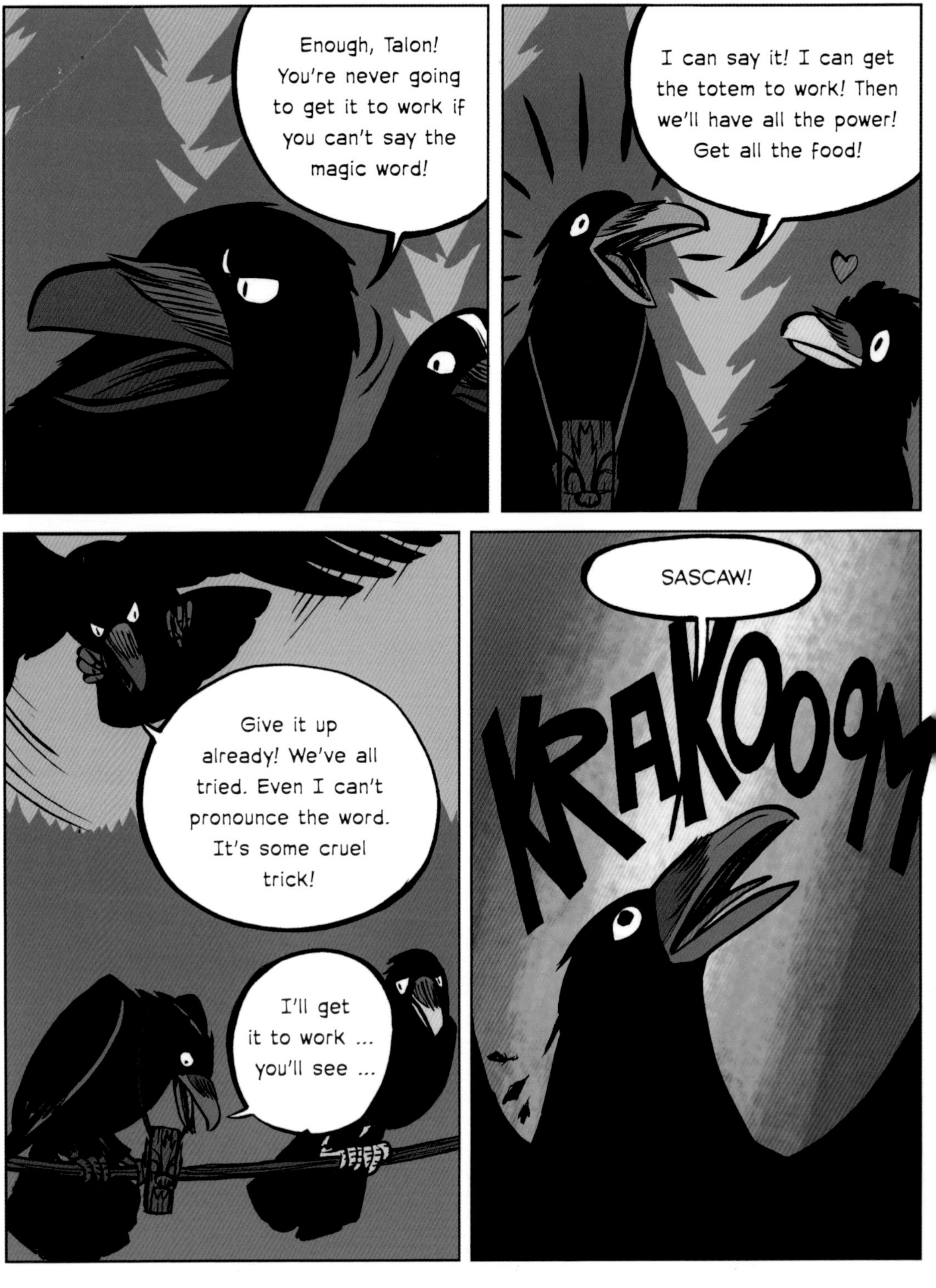
Enough, Talon! You're never going to get it to work if you can't say the magic word!
I can say it! I can get the totem to work! Then we'll have all the power! Get all the food!
Give it up already! We've all tried. Even I can't pronounce the word. It's some cruel trick!
I'll get it to work ... you'll see ...
SASCAW!
KRAKOOOM

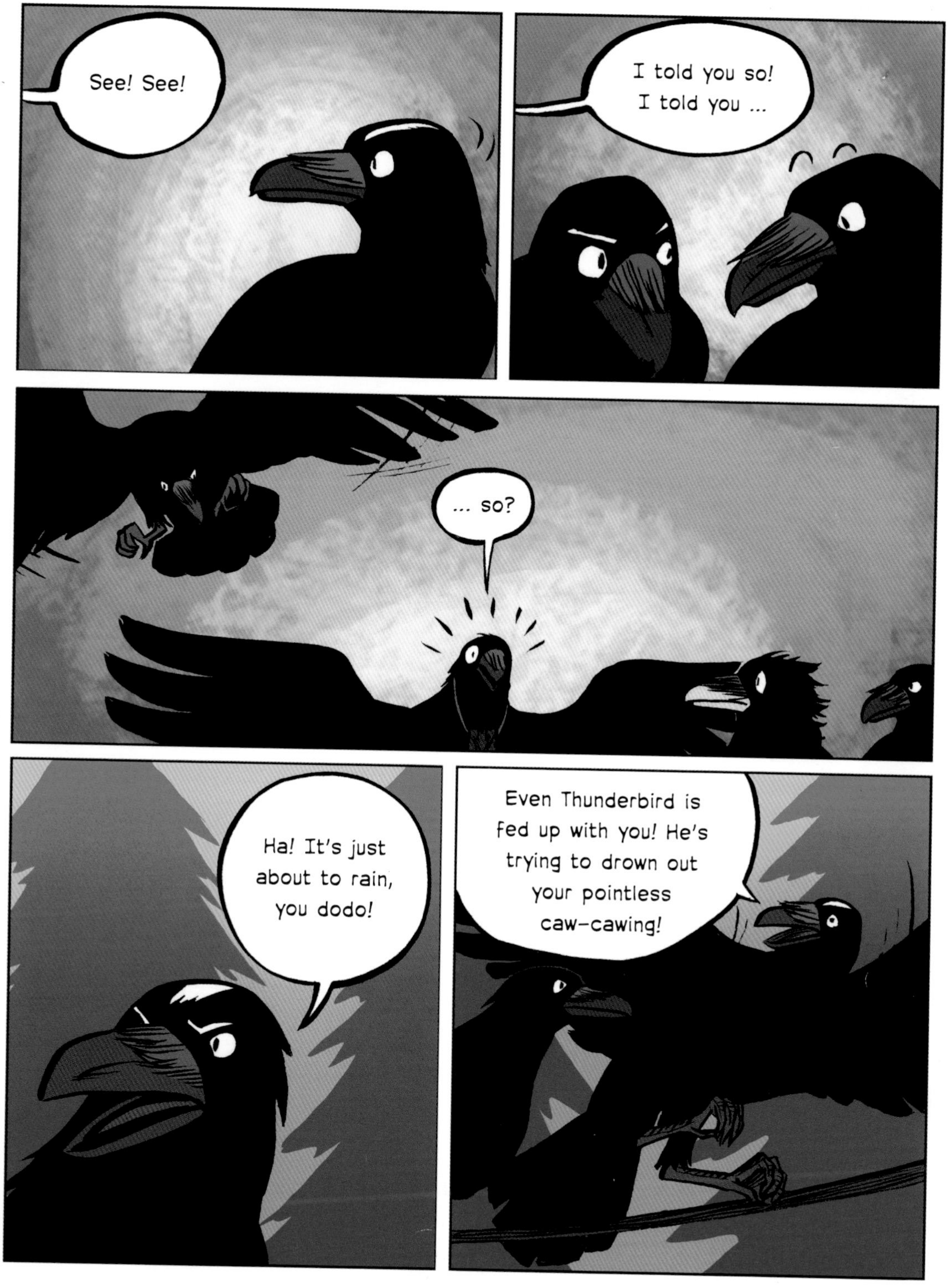
See! See!
I told you so! I told you ...
... so?
Ha! It's just about to rain, you dodo!
Even Thunderbird is fed up with you! He's trying to drown out your pointless caw-cawing!

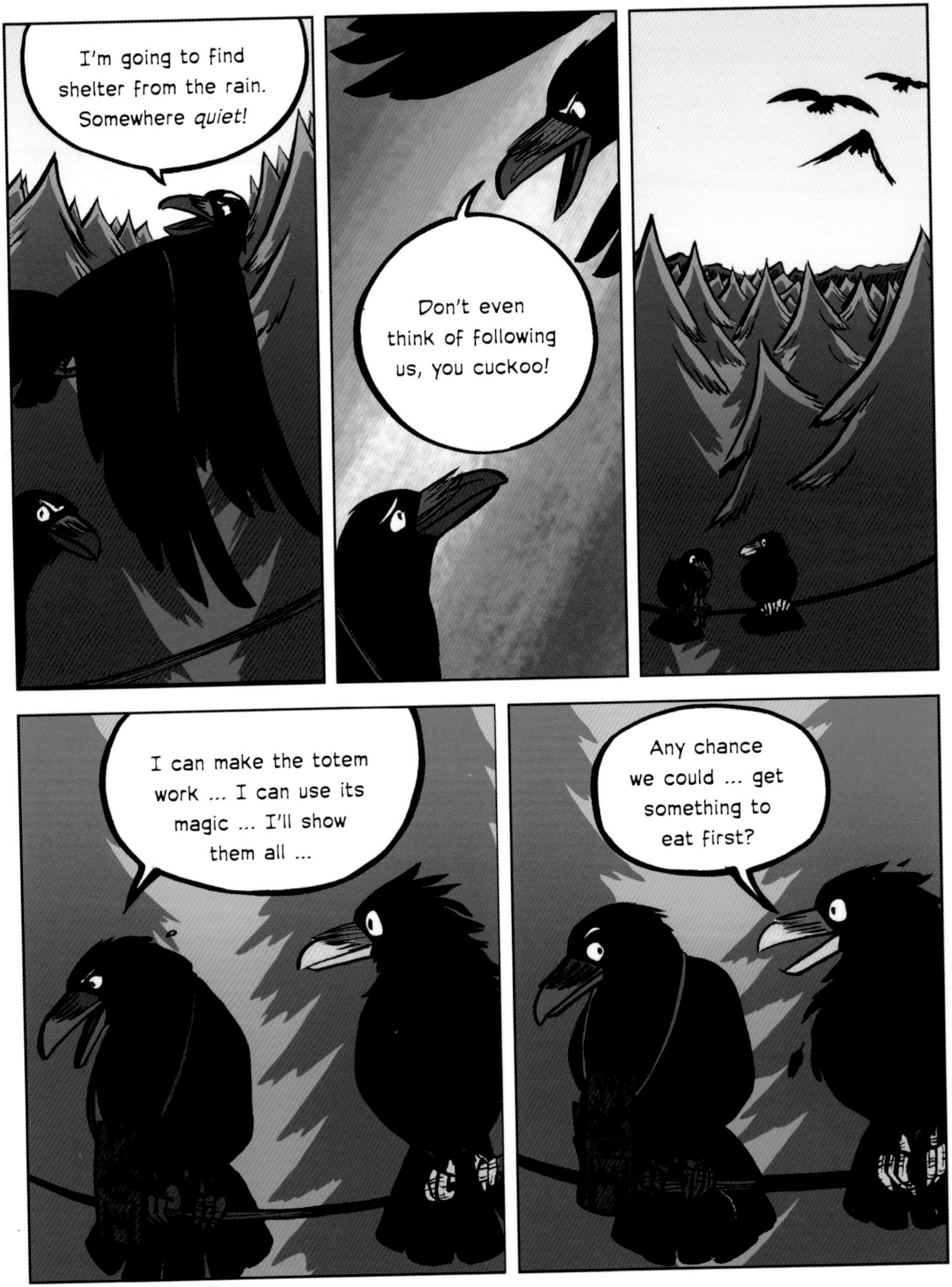

I'm going to find shelter from the rain. Somewhere *quiet*!
Don't even think of following us, you cuckoo!
I can make the totem work ... I can use its magic ... I'll show them all ...
Any chance we could ... get something to eat first?

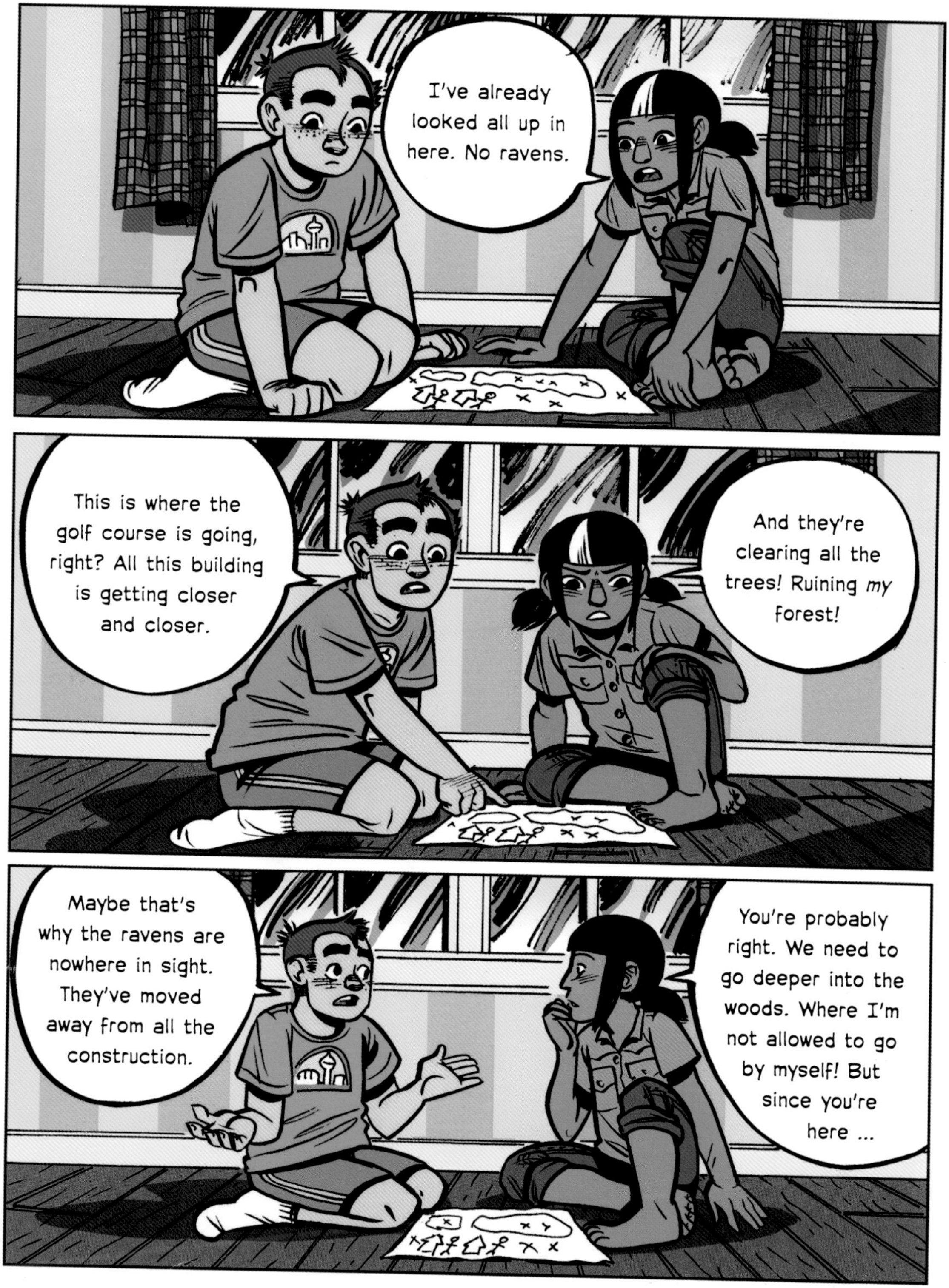
I've already looked all up in here. No ravens.
This is where the golf course is going, right? All this building is getting closer and closer.
And they're clearing all the trees! Ruining *my* forest!
Maybe that's why the ravens are nowhere in sight. They've moved away from all the construction.
You're probably right. We need to go deeper into the woods. Where I'm not allowed to go by myself! But since you're here ...

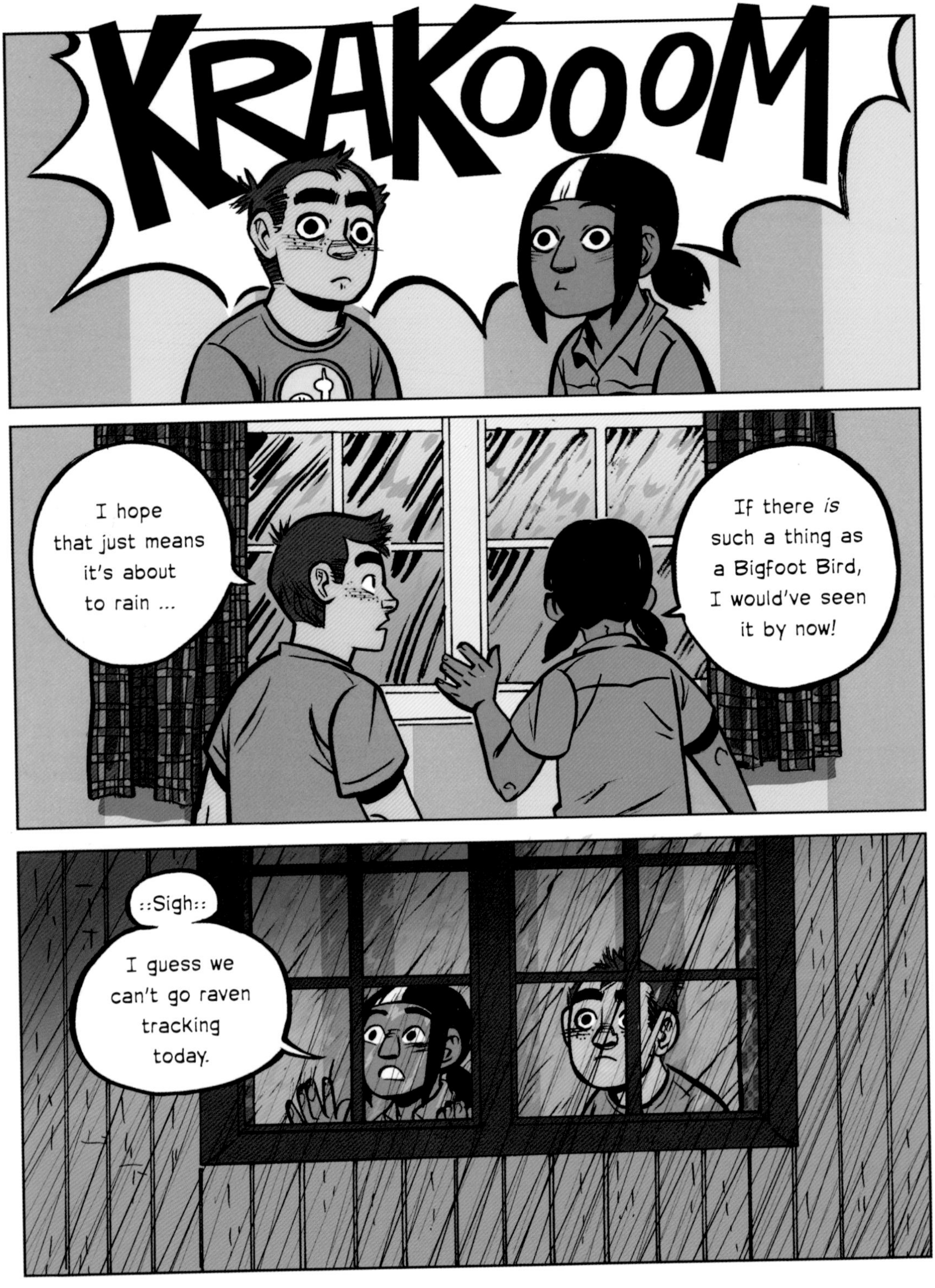
KRAKOOOM
I hope that just means it's about to rain ...
If there *is* such a thing as a Bigfoot Bird, I would've seen it by now!
::Sigh::
I guess we can't go raven tracking today.

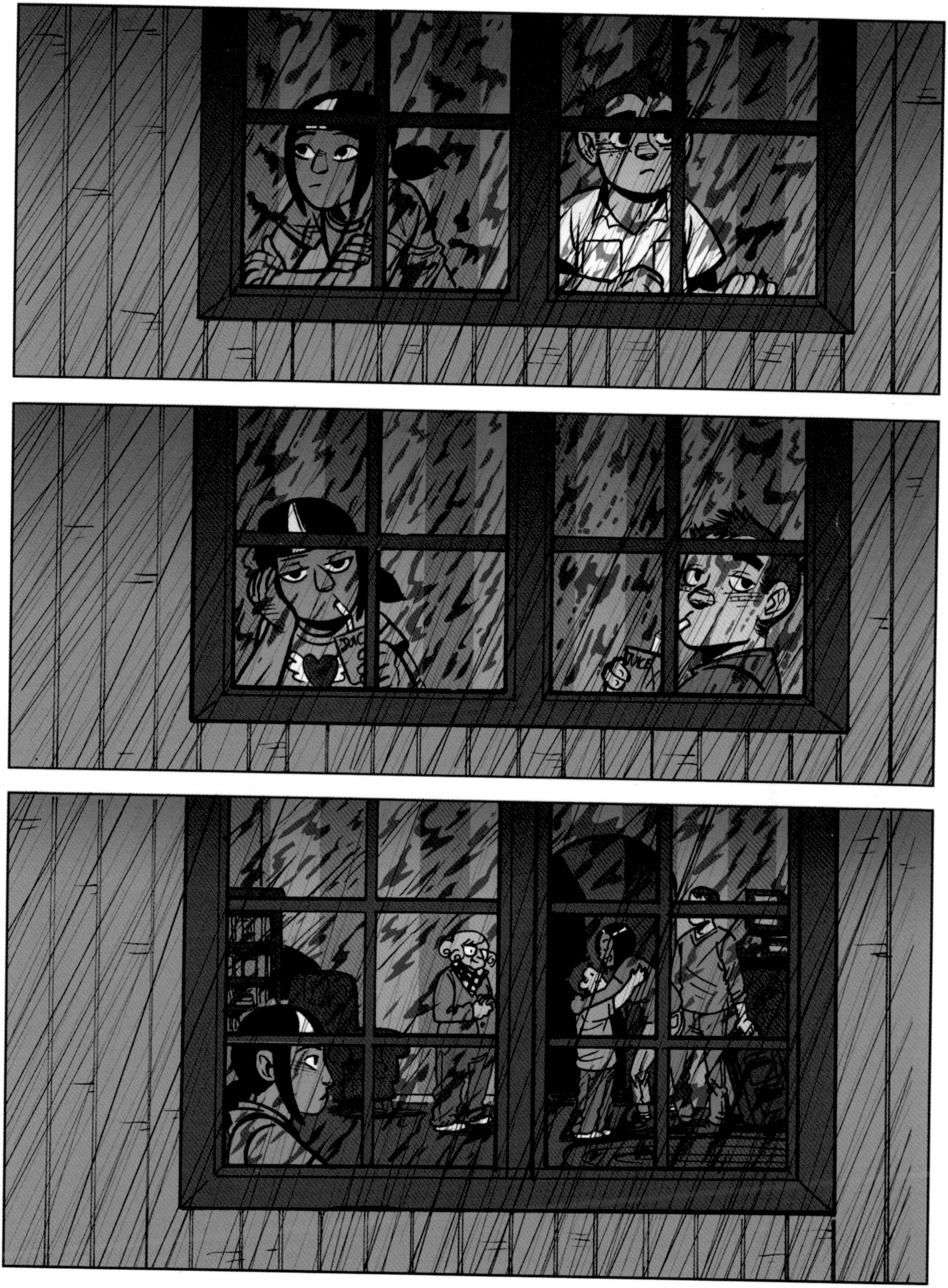
JUICE

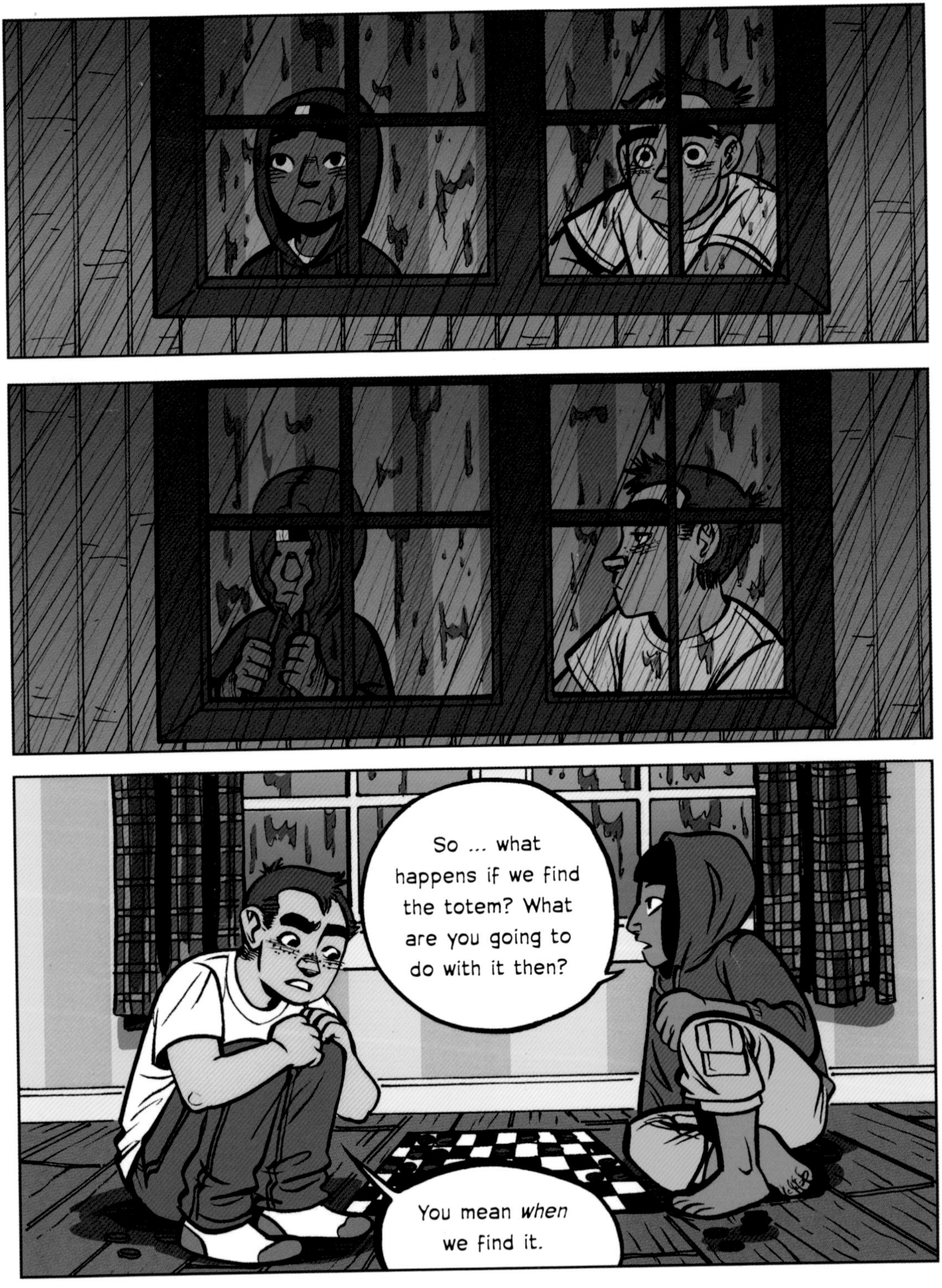
So ... what happens if we find the totem? What are you going to do with it then?
You mean *when* we find it.

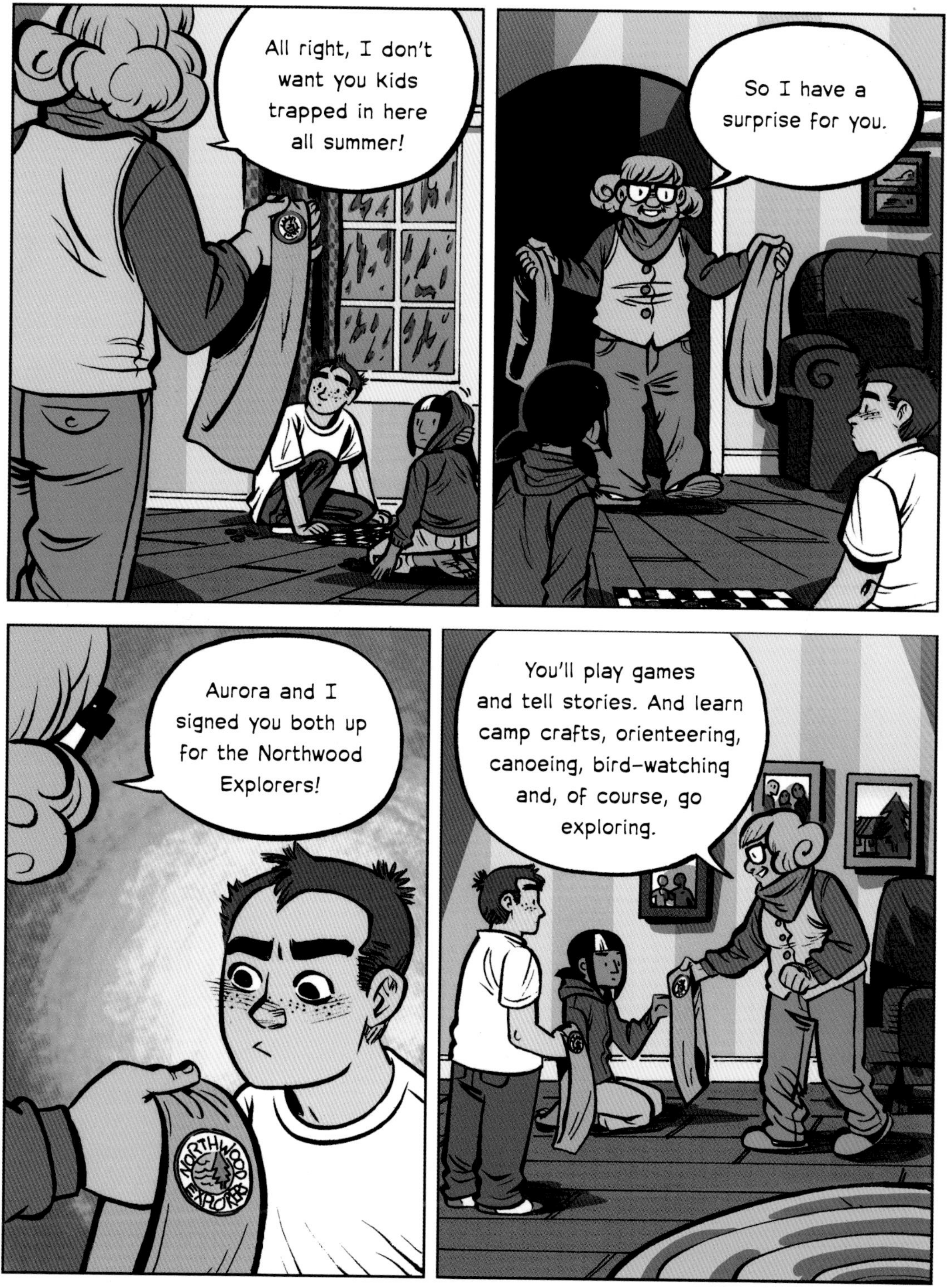
All right, I don't want you kids trapped in here all summer!
So I have a surprise for you.
Aurora and I signed you both up for the Northwood Explorers!
You'll play games and tell stories. And learn camp crafts, orienteering, canoeing, bird-watching and, of course, go exploring.

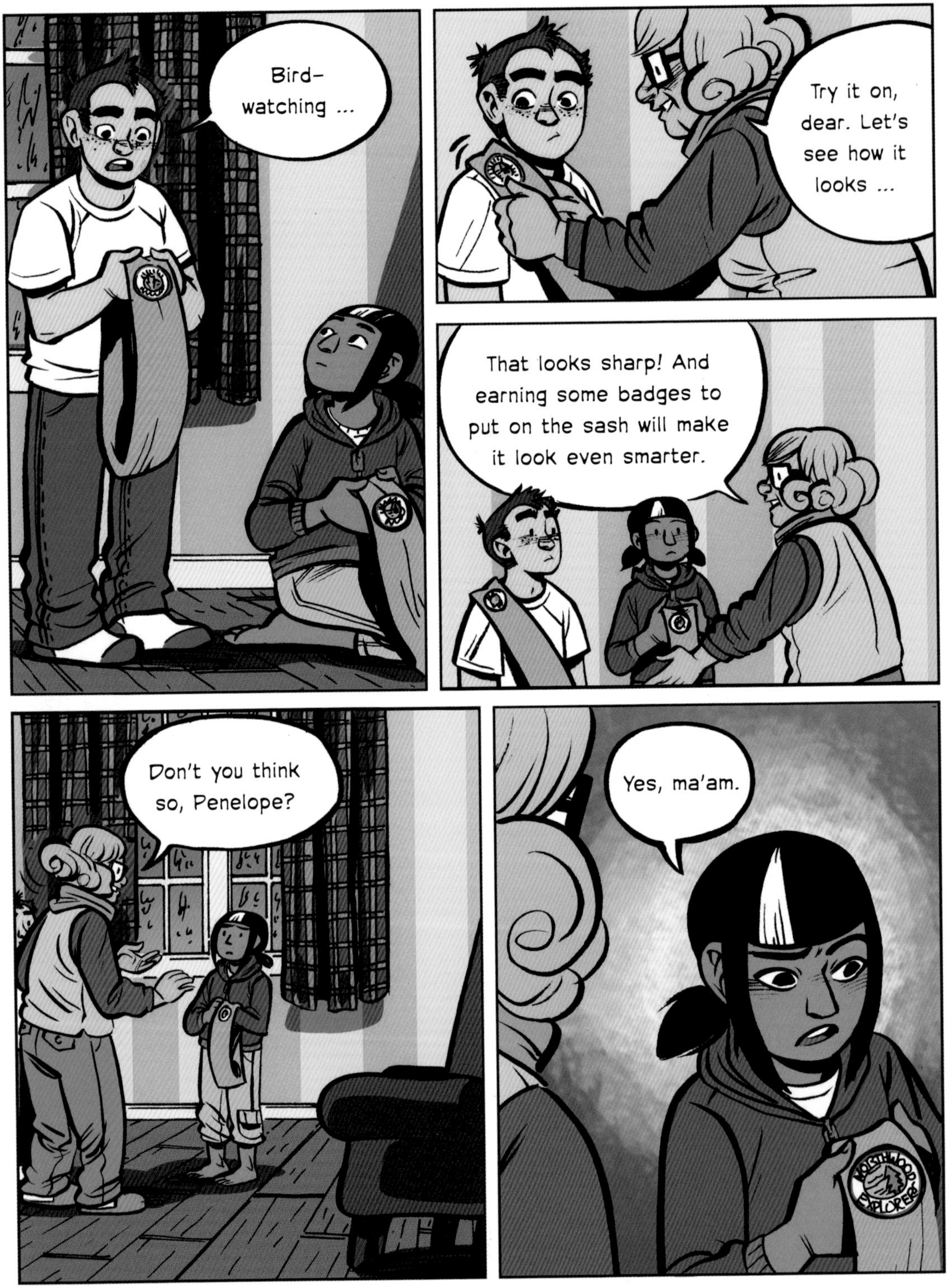

Bird-watching ...
Try it on, dear. Let's see how it looks ...
That looks sharp! And earning some badges to put on the sash will make it look even smarter.
Don't you think so, Penelope?
Yes, ma'am.
NORTHWOOD EXPLORERS

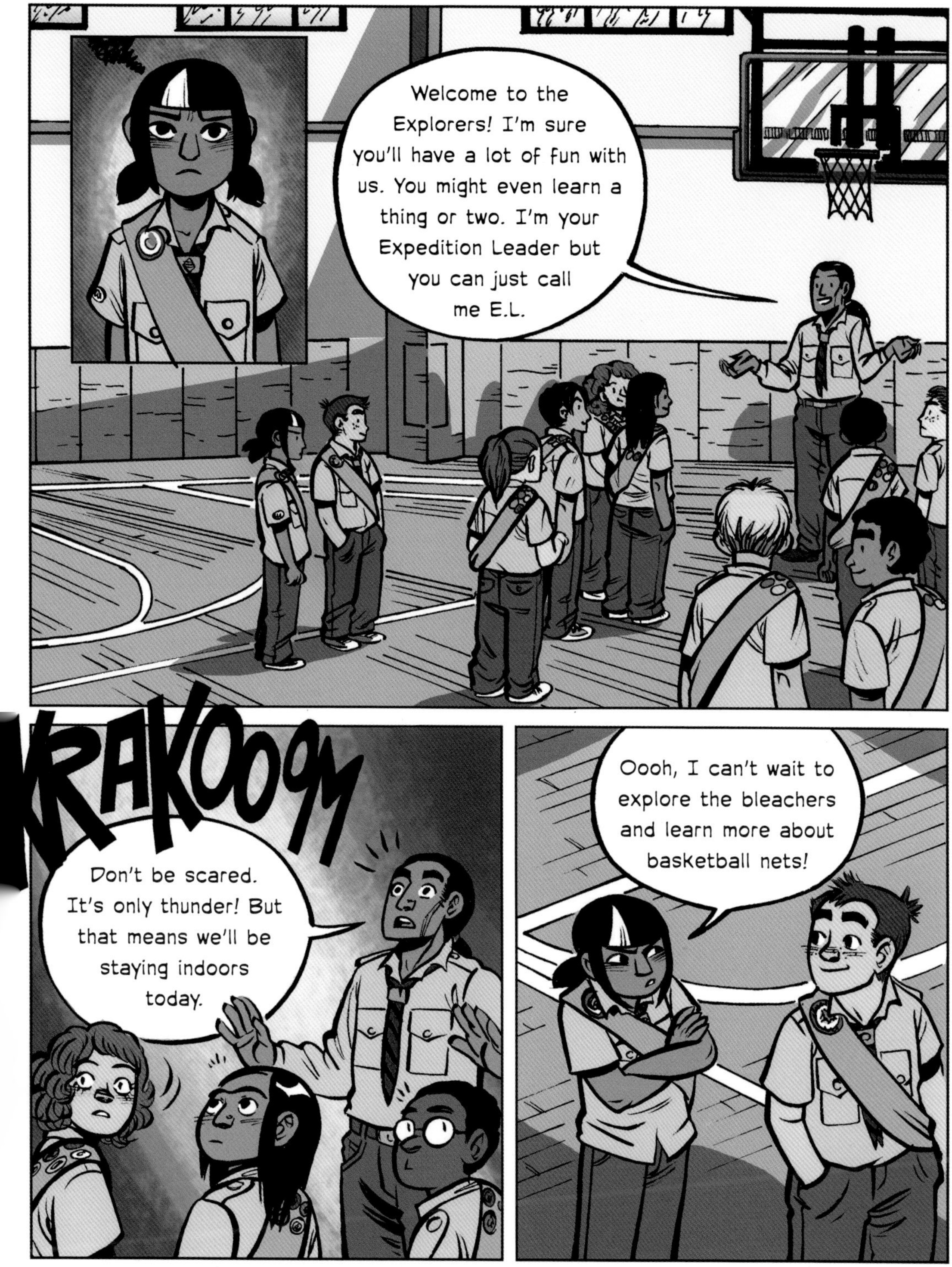
Welcome to the Explorers! I'm sure you'll have a lot of fun with us. You might even learn a thing or two. I'm your Expedition Leader but you can just call me E.L.
KRAKOOOM
Don't be scared. It's only thunder! But that means we'll be staying indoors today.
Oooh, I can't wait to explore the bleachers and learn more about basketball nets!

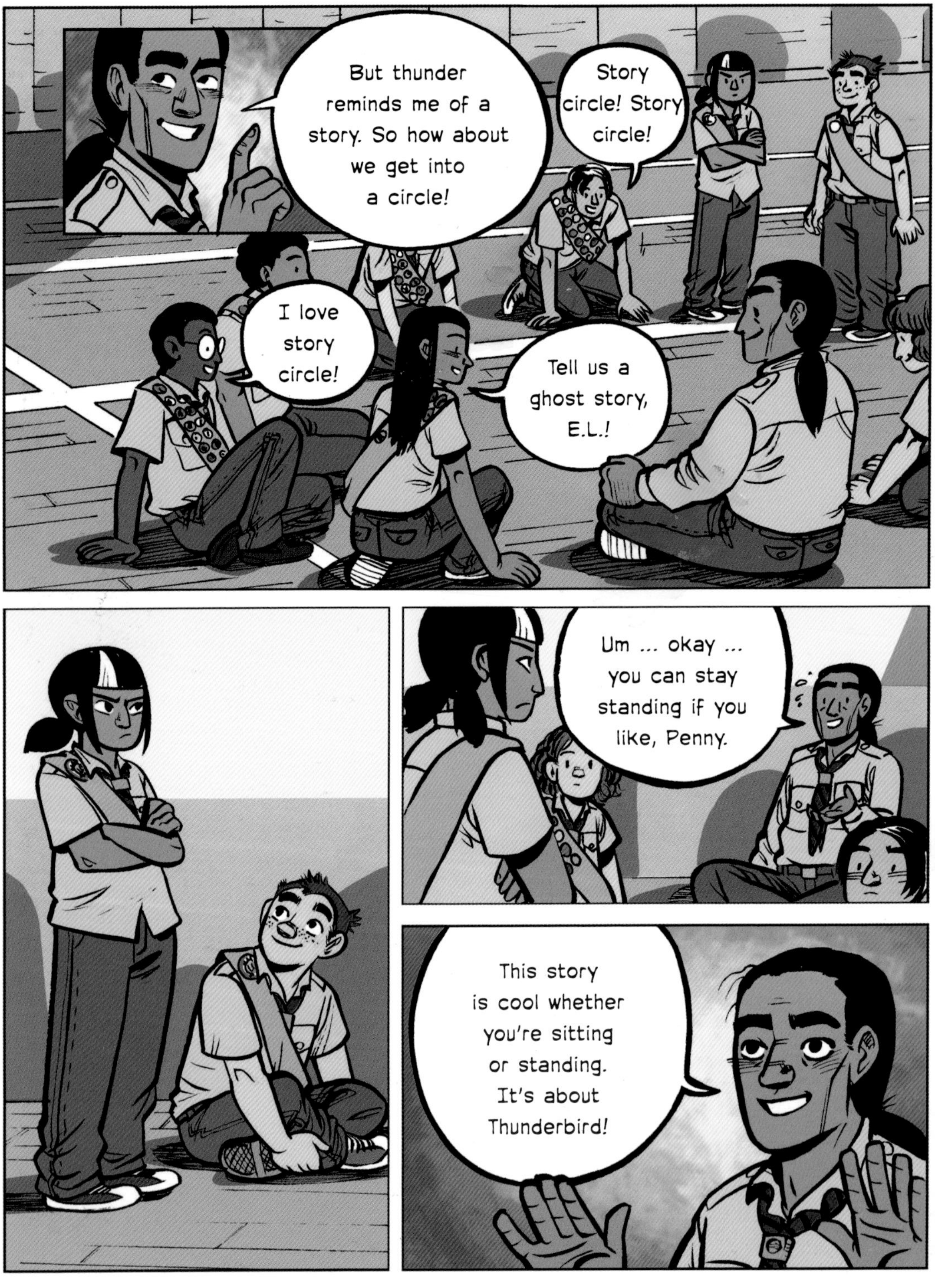
But thunder reminds me of a story. So how about we get into a circle!
Story circle! Story circle!
I love story circle!
Tell us a ghost story, E.L.!
Um ... okay ... you can stay standing if you like, Penny.
This story is cool whether you're sitting or standing. It's about Thunderbird!

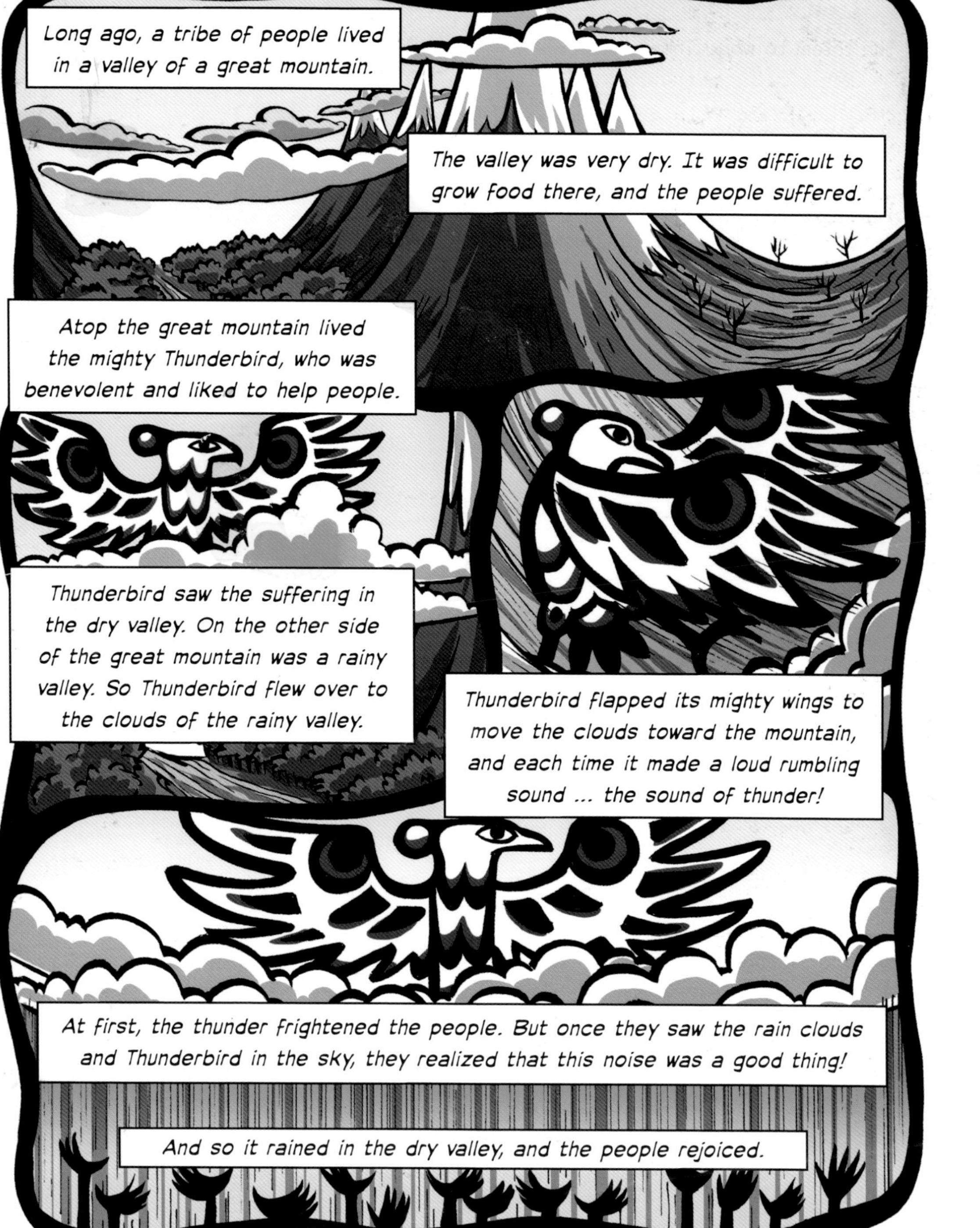
Long ago, a tribe of people lived in a valley of a great mountain.
The valley was very dry. It was difficult to grow food there, and the people suffered.
Atop the great mountain lived the mighty Thunderbird, who was benevolent and liked to help people.
Thunderbird saw the suffering in the dry valley. On the other side of the great mountain was a rainy valley. So Thunderbird flew over to the clouds of the rainy valley.
Thunderbird flapped its mighty wings to move the clouds toward the mountain, and each time it made a loud rumbling sound ... the sound of thunder!
At first, the thunder frightened the people. But once they saw the rain clouds and Thunderbird in the sky, they realized that this noise was a good thing!
And so it rained in the dry valley, and the people rejoiced.

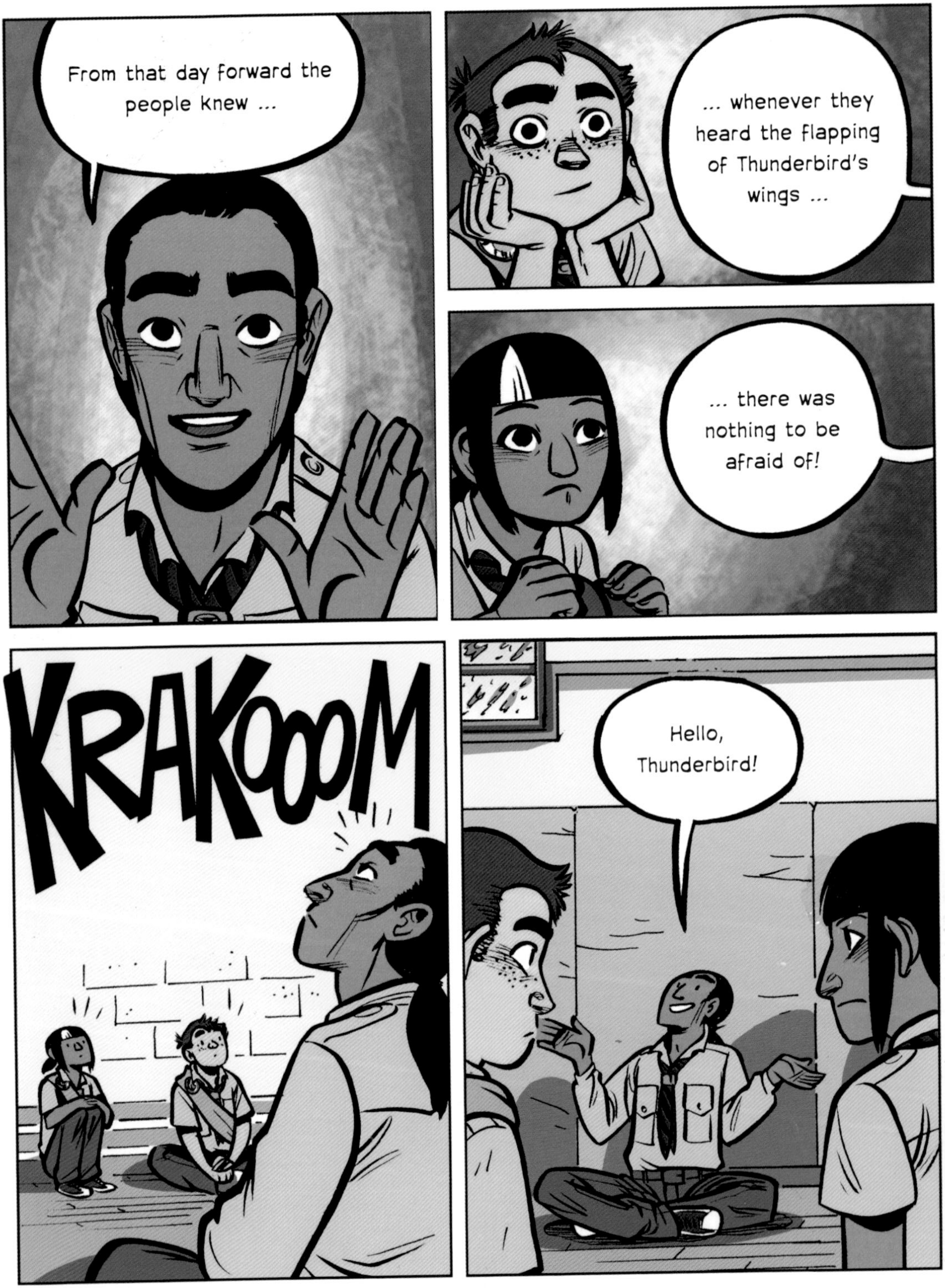
From that day forward the people knew ...
... whenever they heard the flapping of Thunderbird's wings ...
... there was nothing to be afraid of!
KRAKOOOM
Hello, Thunderbird!

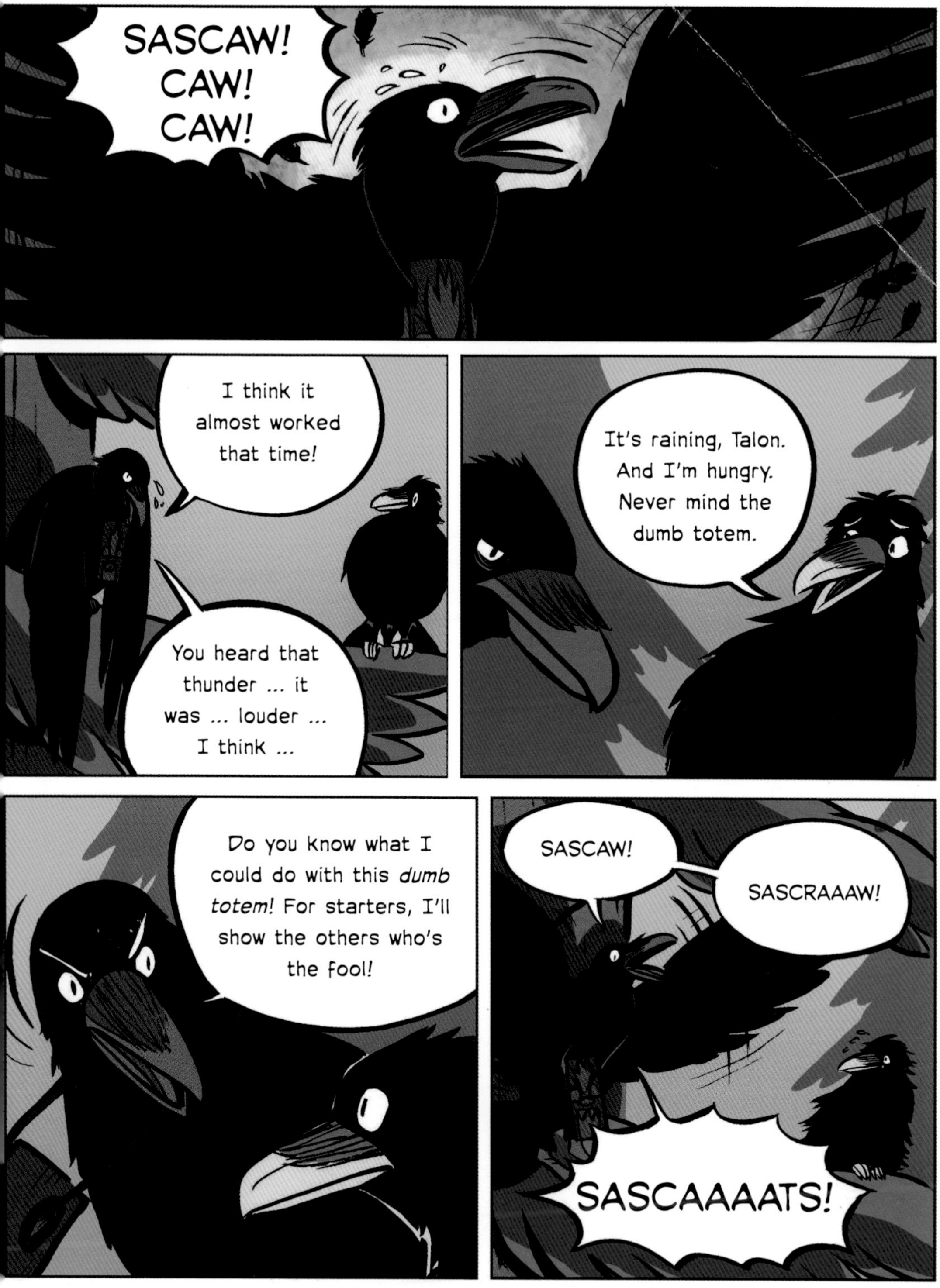

SASCAW! CAW! CAW!
I think it almost worked that time!
You heard that thunder ... it was ... louder ... I think ...
It's raining, Talon. And I'm hungry. Never mind the dumb totem.
Do you know what I could do with this *dumb totem!* For starters, I'll show the others who's the fool!
SASCAW!
SASCRAAAW!
SASCAAAATS!

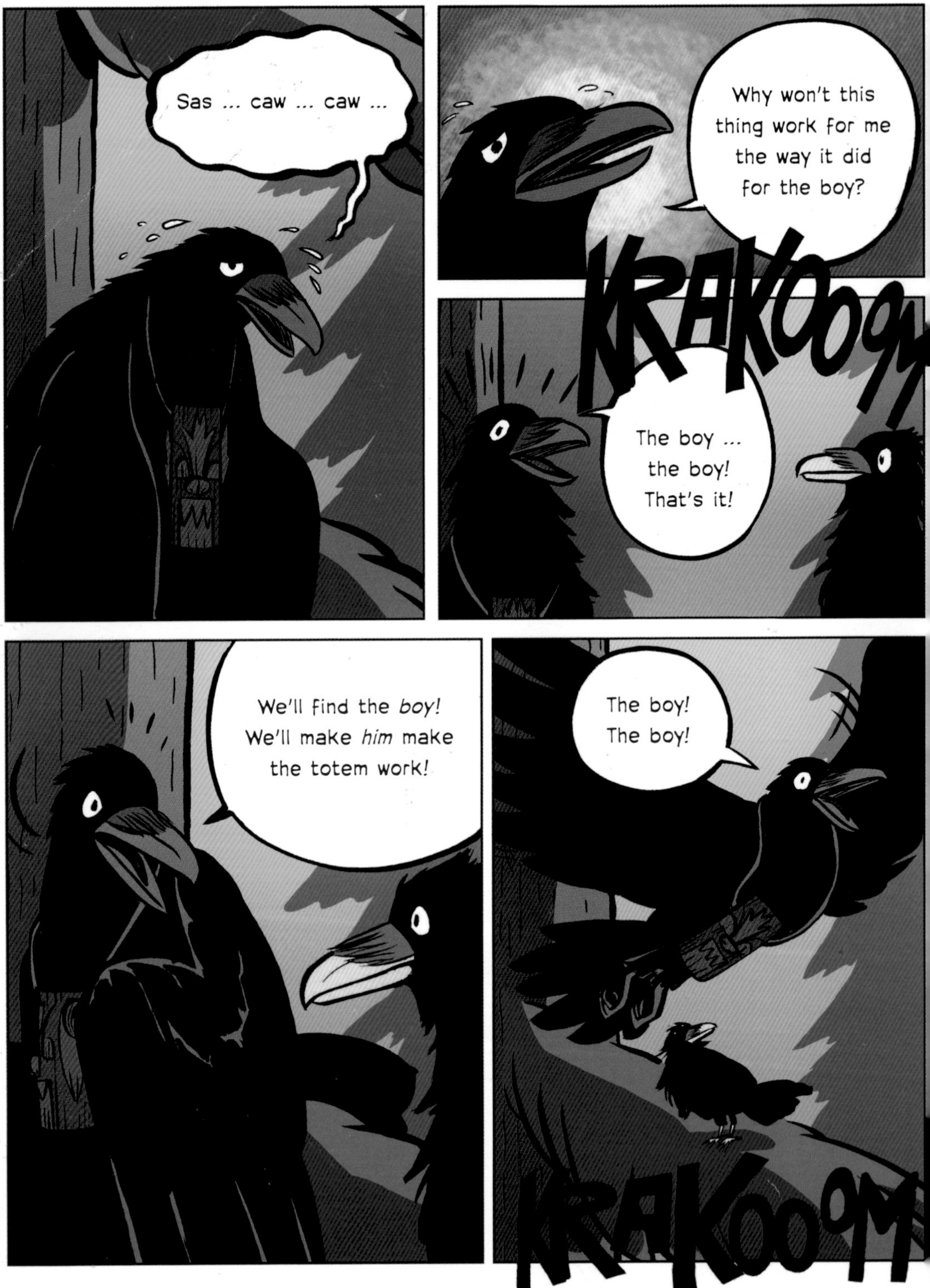

Sas ... caw ... caw ...
Why won't this thing work for me the way it did for the boy?
KRAKOOOM
The boy ... the boy! That's it!
We'll find the *boy*! We'll make *him* make the totem work!
The boy! The boy!
KRAKOOOM

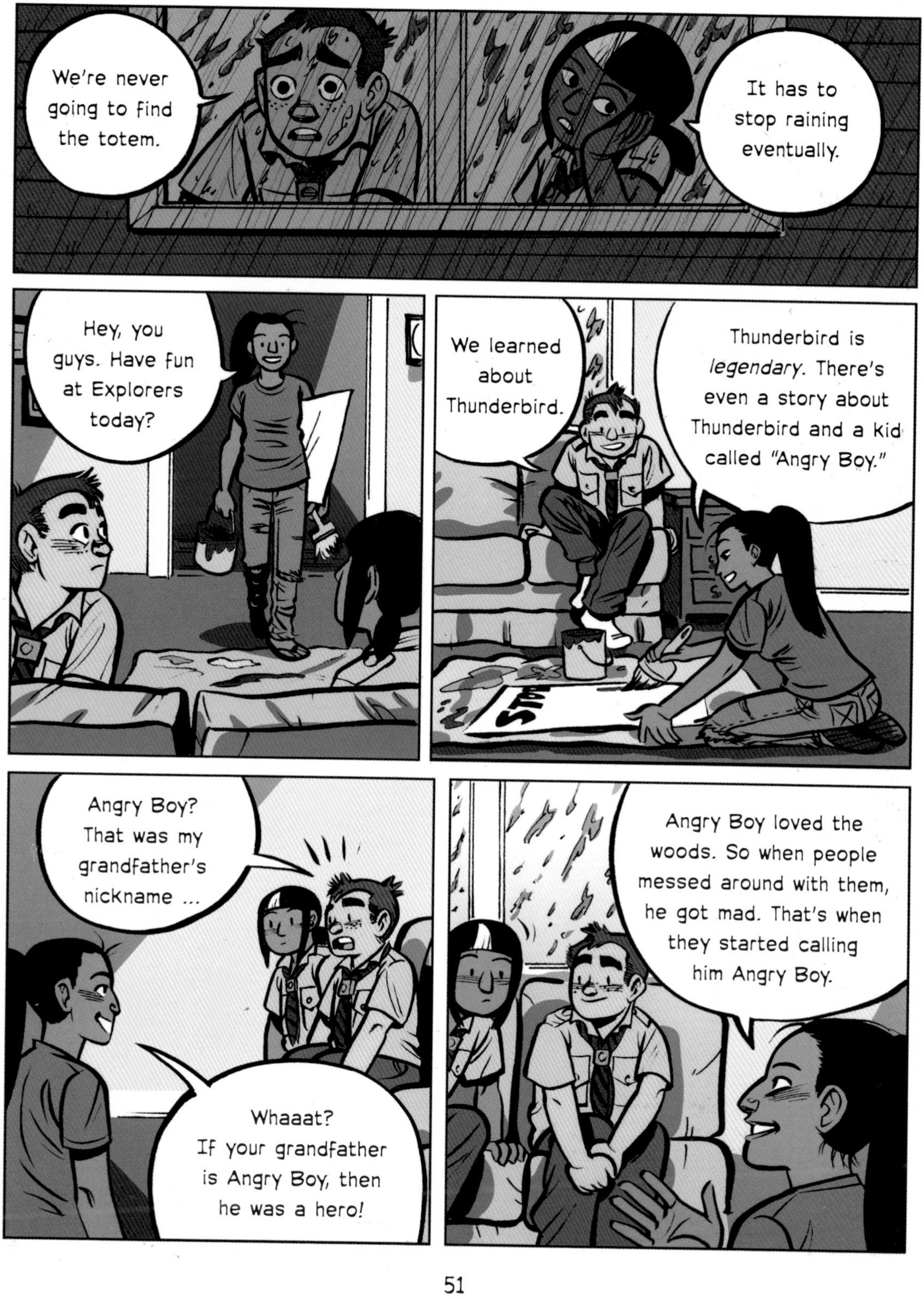
We're never going to find the totem.
It has to stop raining eventually.
Hey, you guys. Have fun at Explorers today?
We learned about Thunderbird.
Thunderbird is *legendary*. There's even a story about Thunderbird and a kid called "Angry Boy."
Angry Boy? That was my grandfather's nickname ...
Whaaat? If your grandfather is Angry Boy, then he was a hero!
Angry Boy loved the woods. So when people messed around with them, he got mad. That's when they started calling him Angry Boy.

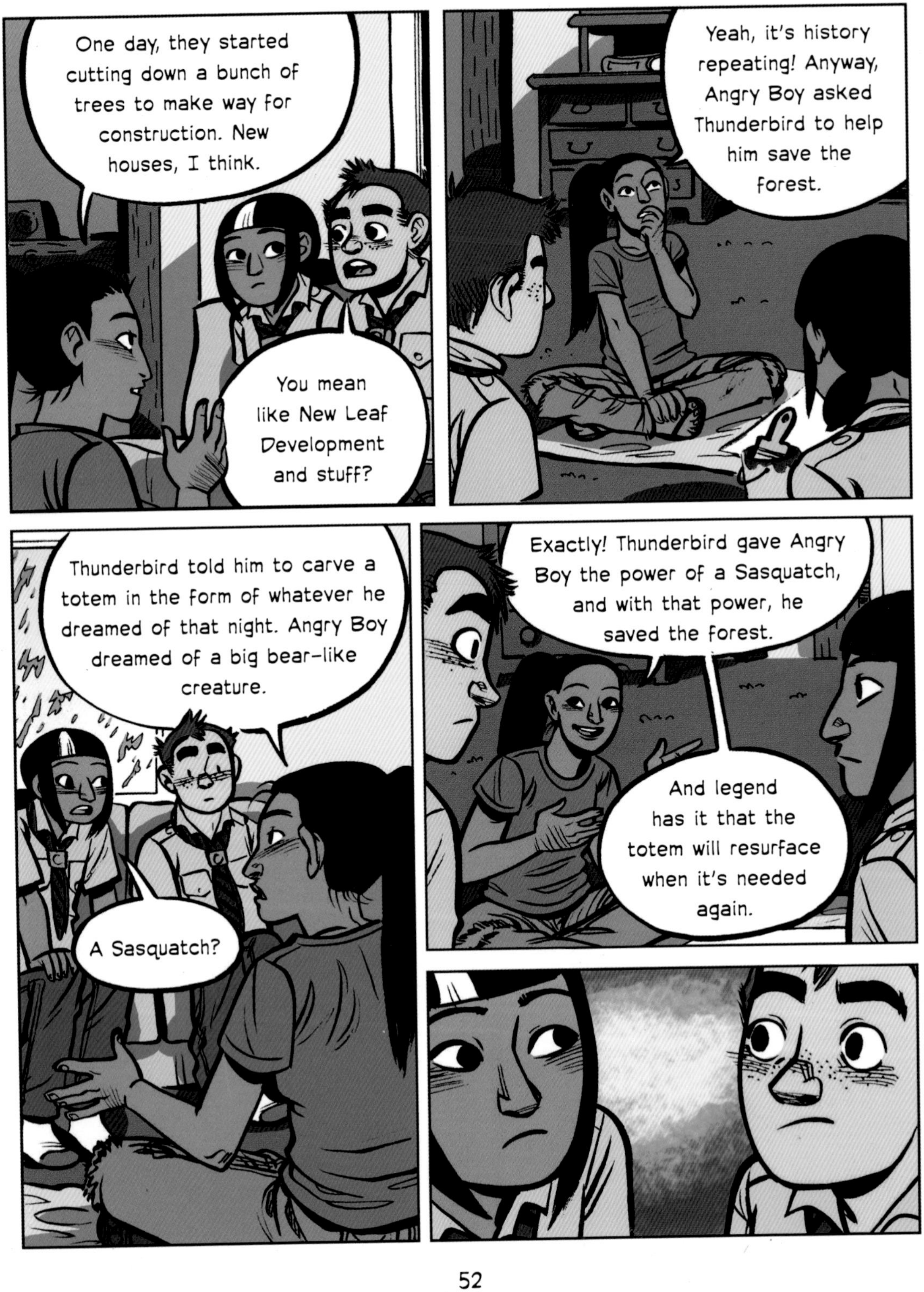

One day, they started cutting down a bunch of trees to make way for construction. New houses, I think.
You mean like New Leaf Development and stuff?
Yeah, it's history repeating! Anyway, Angry Boy asked Thunderbird to help him save the forest.
Thunderbird told him to carve a totem in the form of whatever he dreamed of that night. Angry Boy dreamed of a big bear-like creature.
A Sasquatch?
Exactly! Thunderbird gave Angry Boy the power of a Sasquatch, and with that power, he saved the forest.
And legend has it that the totem will resurface when it's needed again.

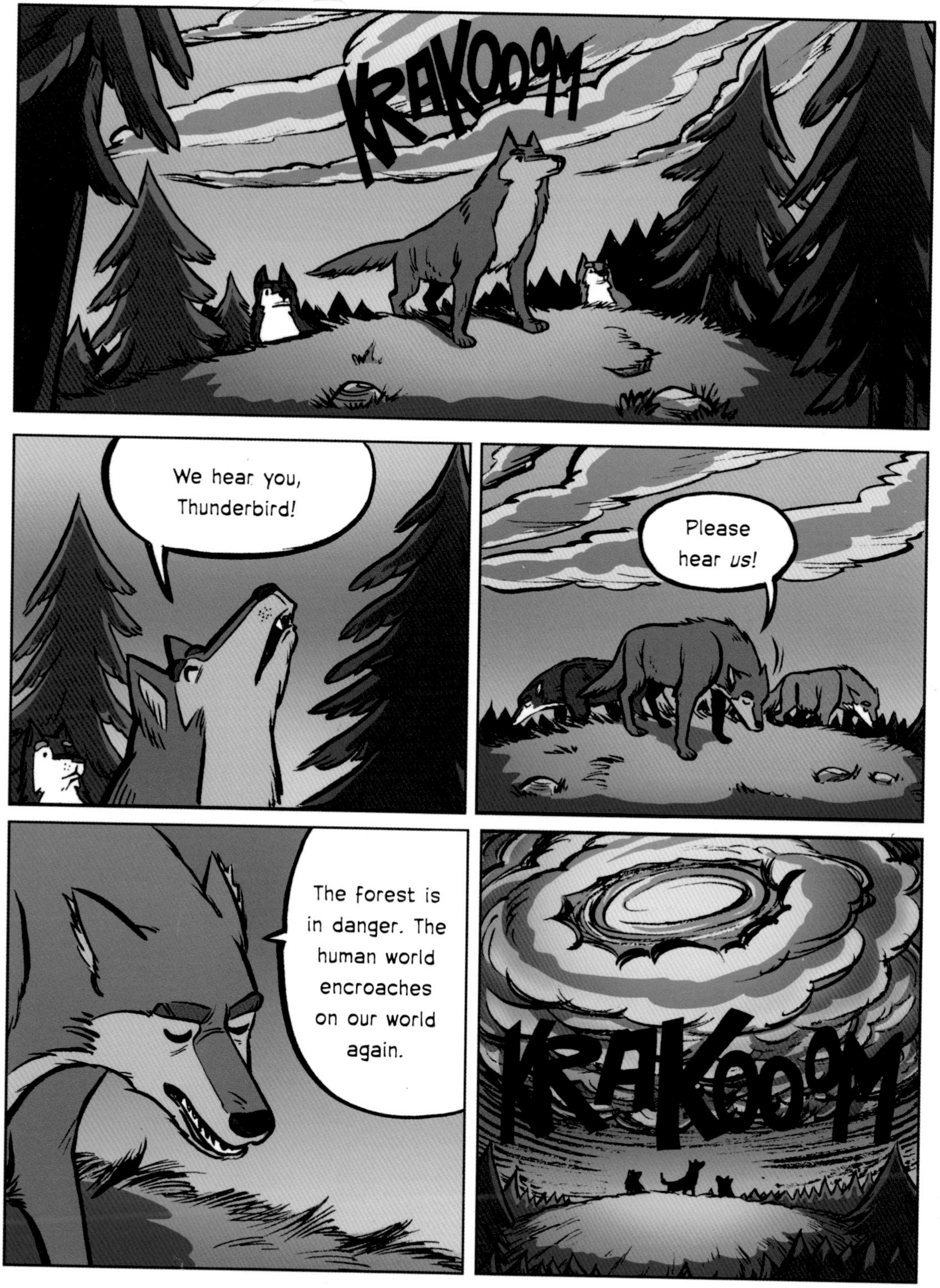
KRAKOOOM
We hear you, Thunderbird!
Please hear us!
The forest is in danger. The human world encroaches on our world again.
KRAKOOOM

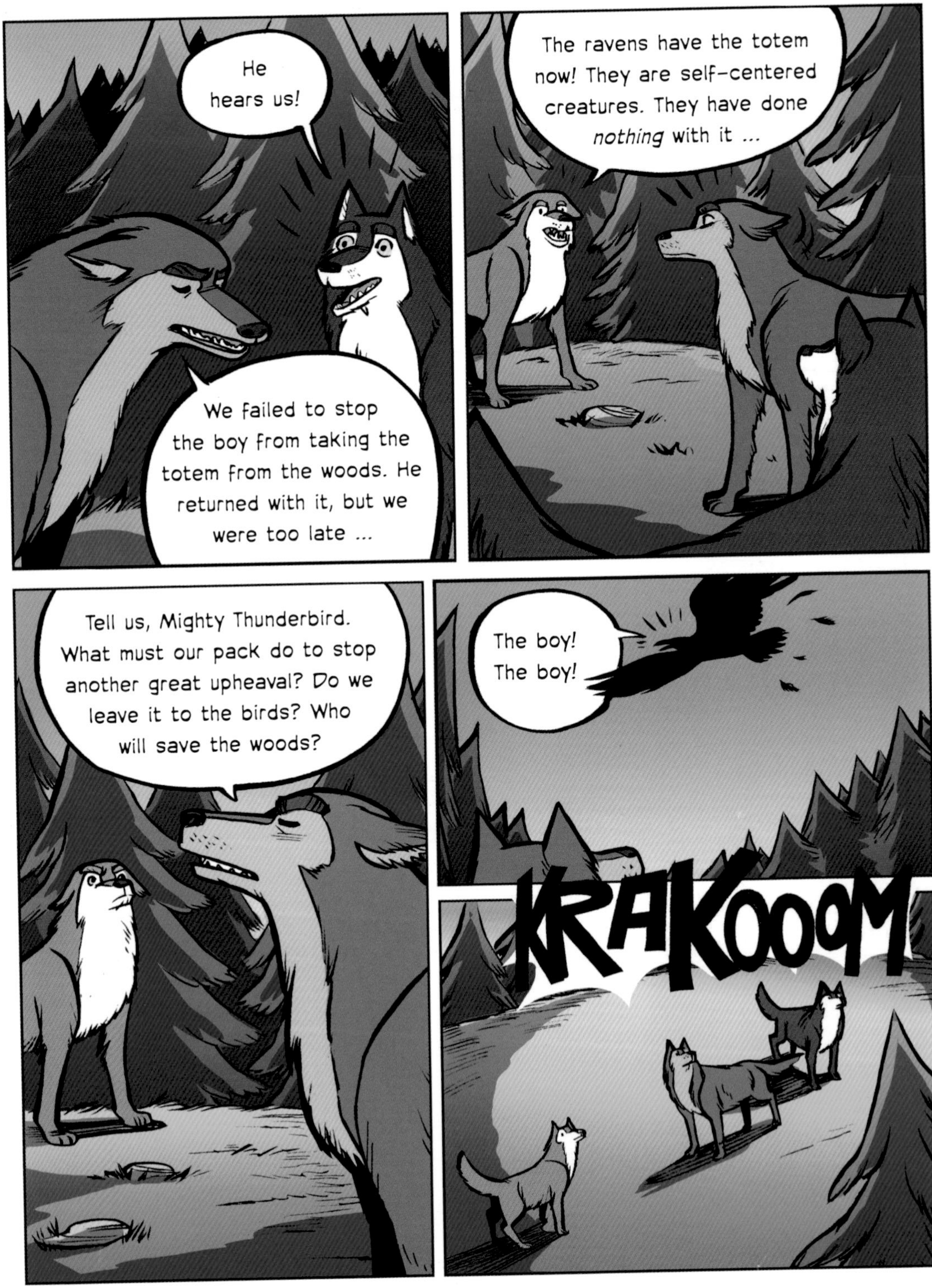
He hears us!
We failed to stop the boy from taking the totem from the woods. He returned with it, but we were too late ...
The ravens have the totem now! They are self-centered creatures. They have done *nothing* with it ...
Tell us, Mighty Thunderbird. What must our pack do to stop another great upheaval? Do we leave it to the birds? Who will save the woods?
The boy! The boy!
KRAKOOOM

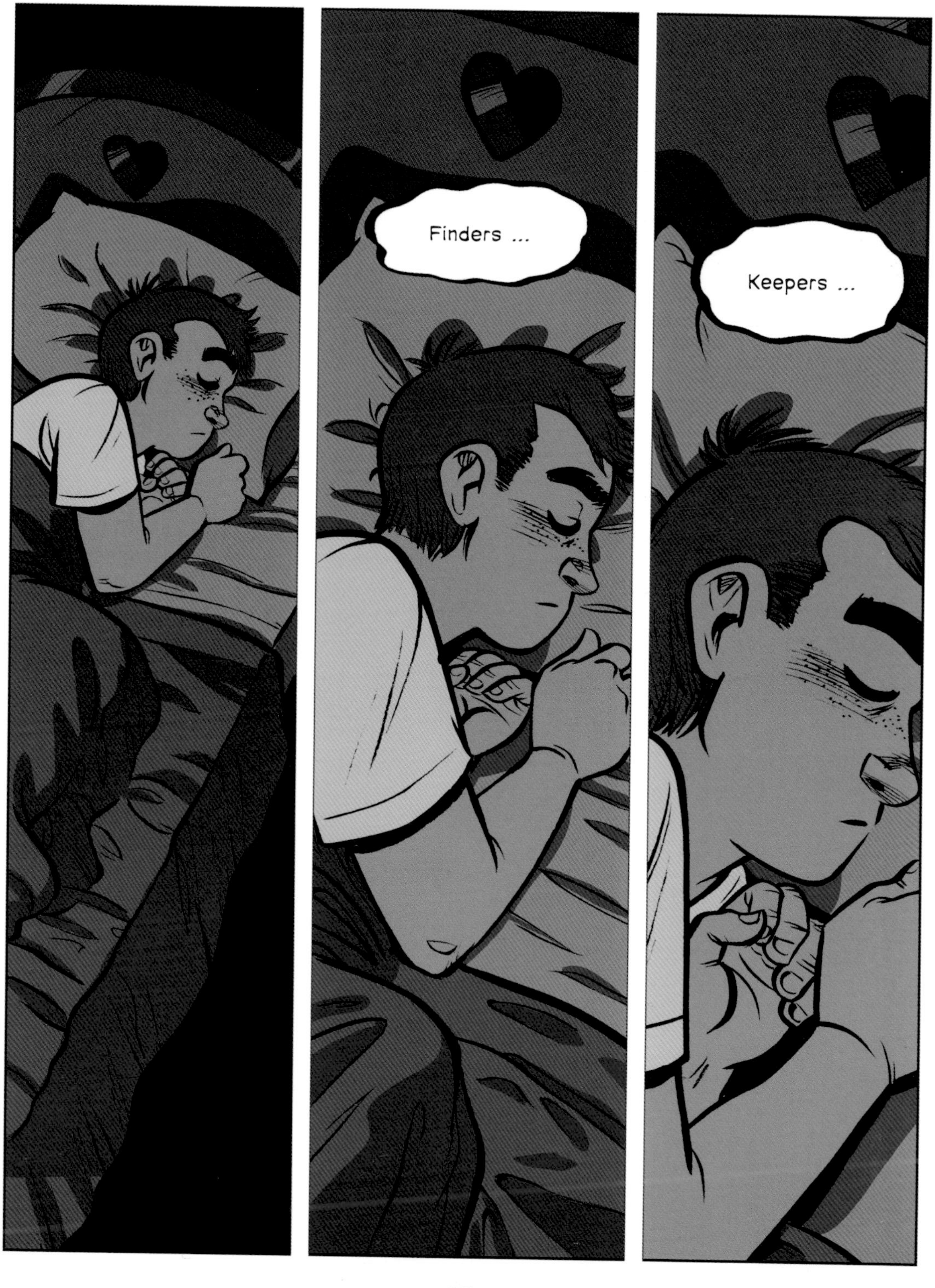
Finders ...
Keepers ...

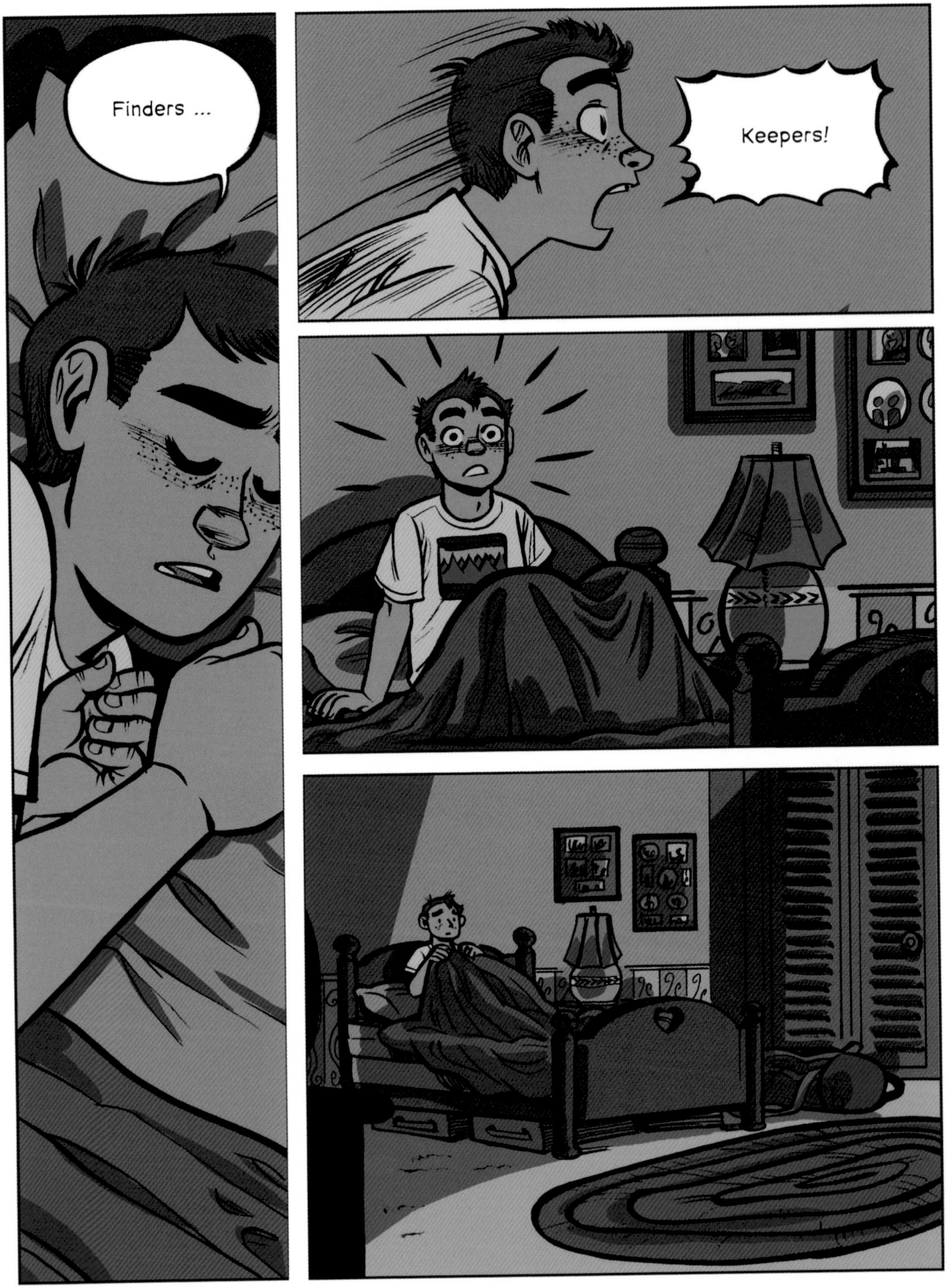
Finders ...
Keepers!

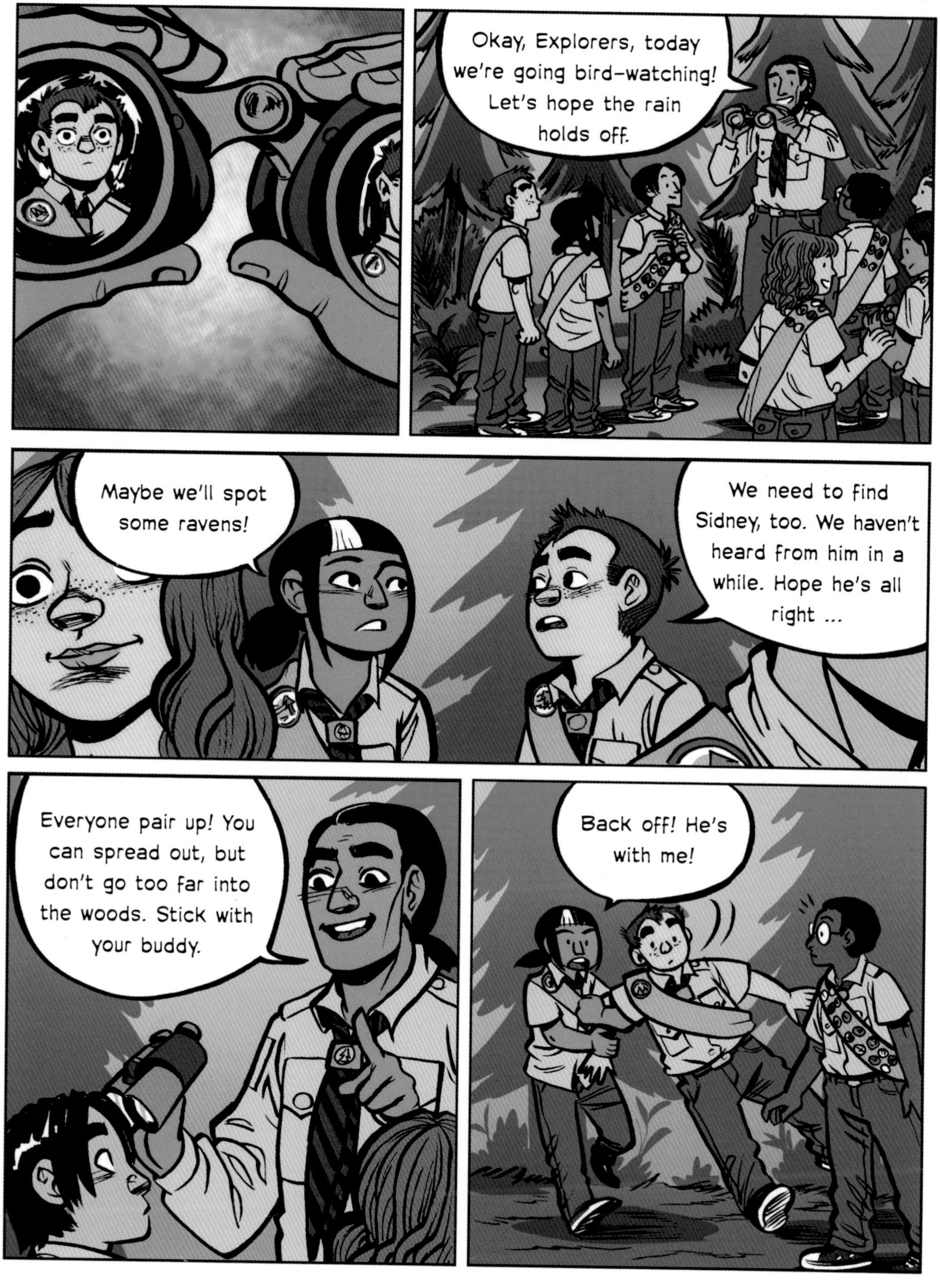
Okay, Explorers, today we're going bird-watching! Let's hope the rain holds off.
Maybe we'll spot some ravens!
We need to find Sidney, too. We haven't heard from him in a while. Hope he's all right ...
Everyone pair up! You can spread out, but don't go too far into the woods. Stick with your buddy.
Back off! He's with me!

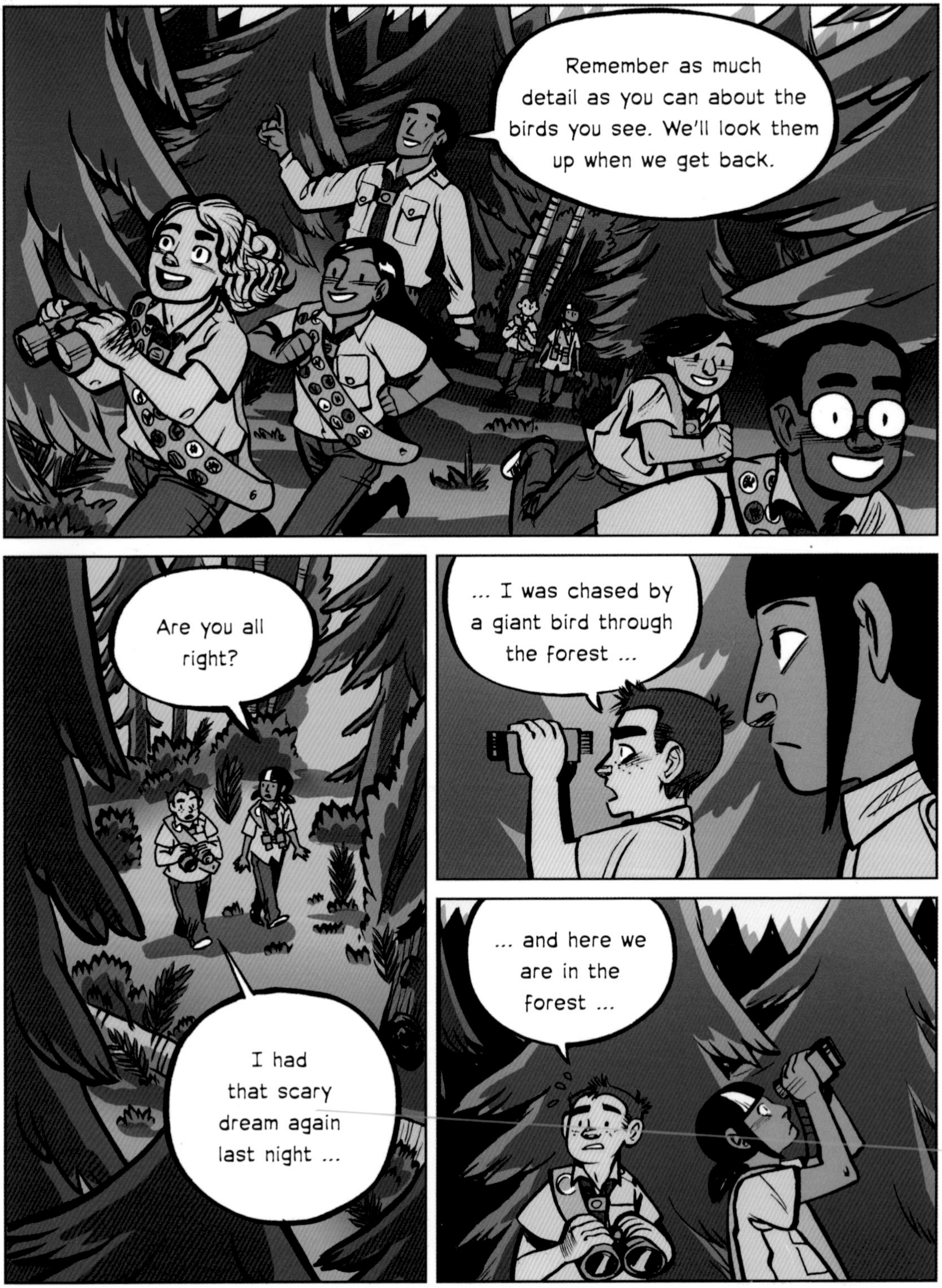
Remember as much detail as you can about the birds you see. We'll look them up when we get back.
Are you all right?
I had that scary dream again last night ...
... I was chased by a giant bird through the forest ...
... and here we are in the forest ...

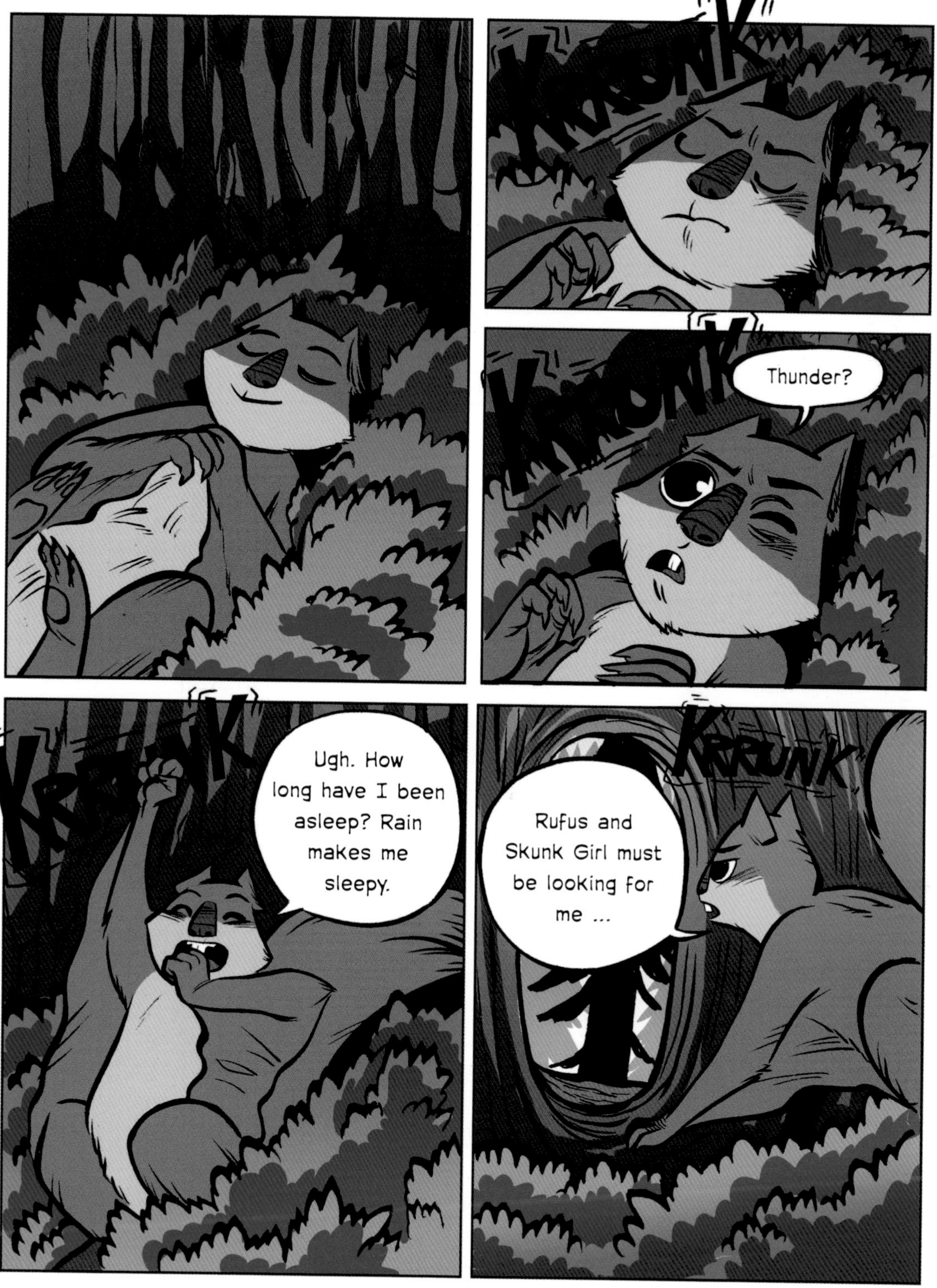
KRRONK
KRRONK
Thunder?
Ugh. How long have I been asleep? Rain makes me sleepy.
KRRUNK
Rufus and Skunk Girl must be looking for me ...

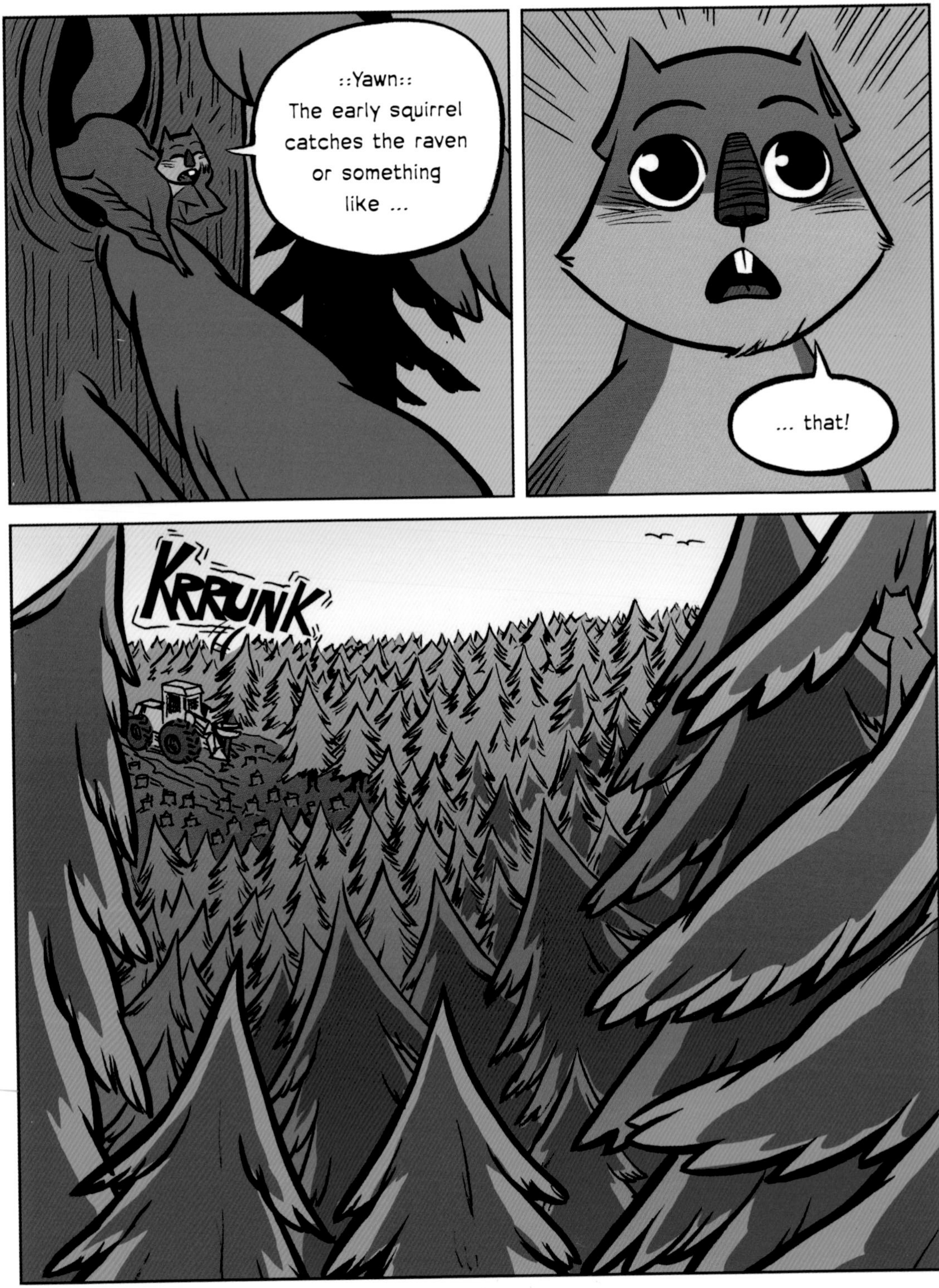
::Yawn::
The early squirrel catches the raven or something like ...
... that!
KRRUNK

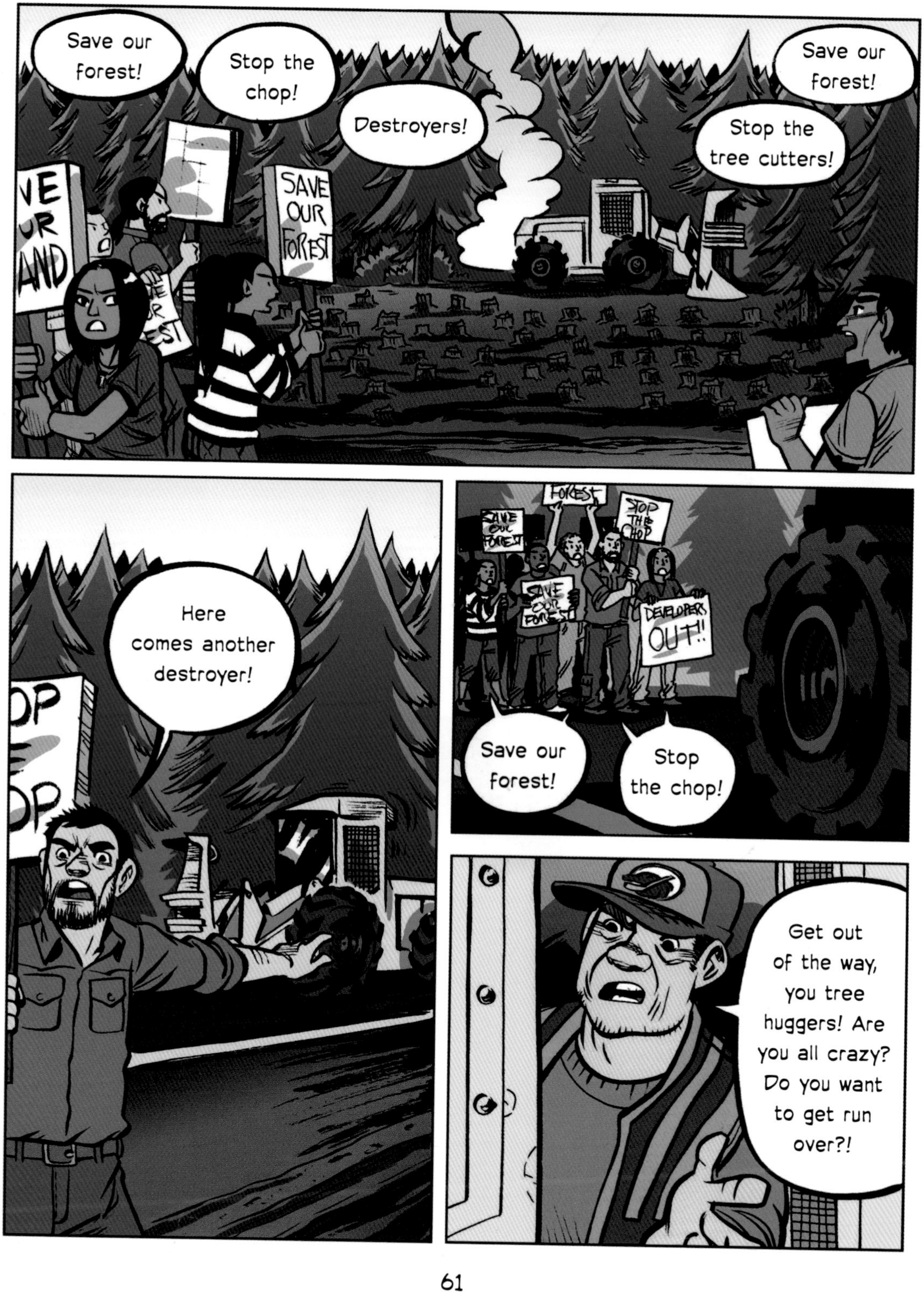
Save our forest!
Stop the chop!
Destroyers!
Save our forest!
Stop the tree cutters!
SAVE OUR FOREST
Here comes another destroyer!
FOREST
SAVE OUR FOREST
STOP THE CHOP
SAVE OUR FOREST
DEVELOPERS OUT!!
Save our forest!
Stop the chop!
Get out of the way, you tree huggers! Are you all crazy? Do you want to get run over?!

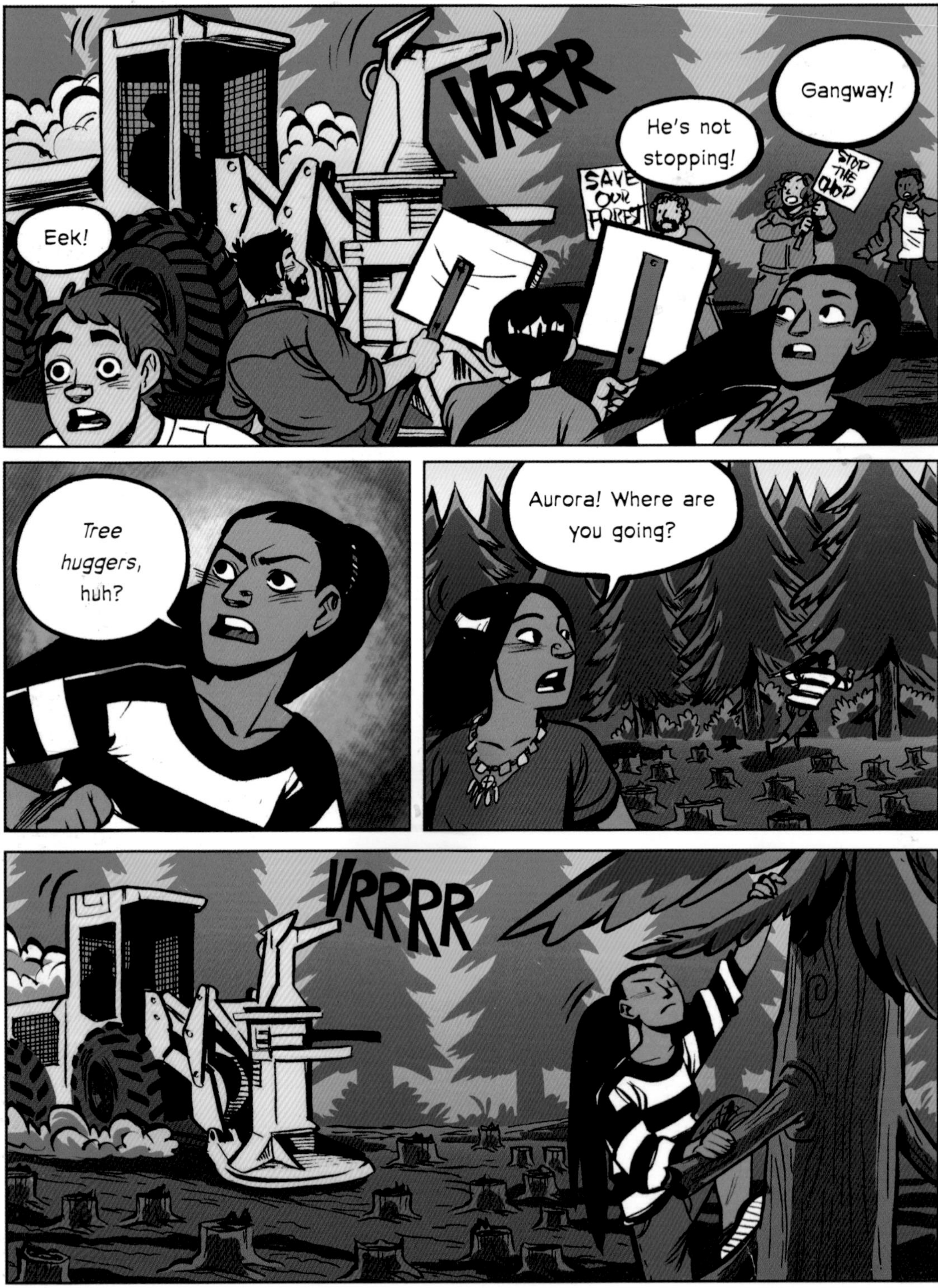
VRRR
Gangway!
He's not stopping!
SAVE OUR FOREST
STOP THE CHOP
Eek!
Tree huggers, huh?
Aurora! Where are you going?
VRRRR

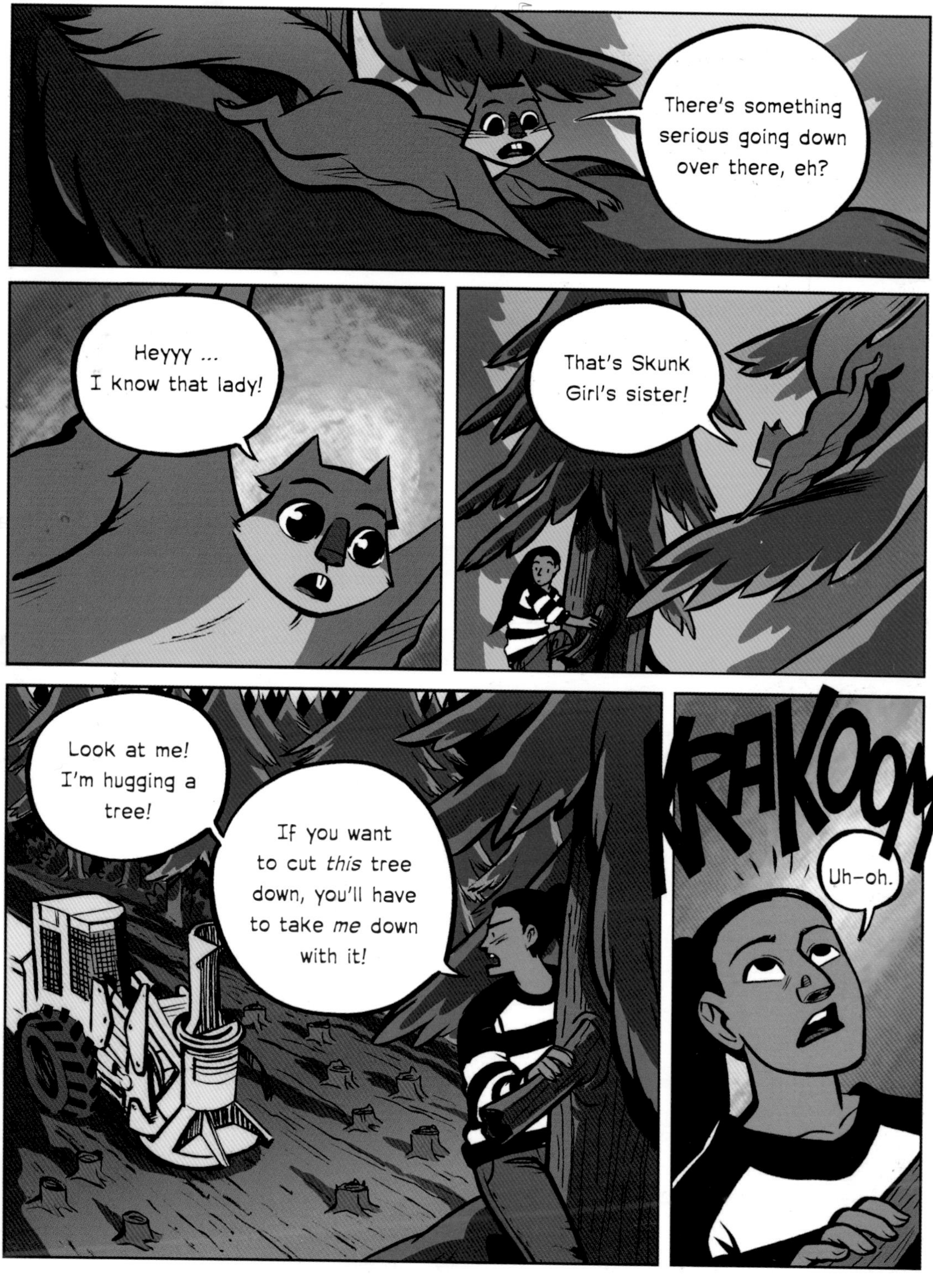
There's something serious going down over there, eh?
Heyyy ... I know that lady!
That's Skunk Girl's sister!
Look at me! I'm hugging a tree!
If you want to cut *this* tree down, you'll have to take *me* down with it!
KRAKOOM
Uh-oh.

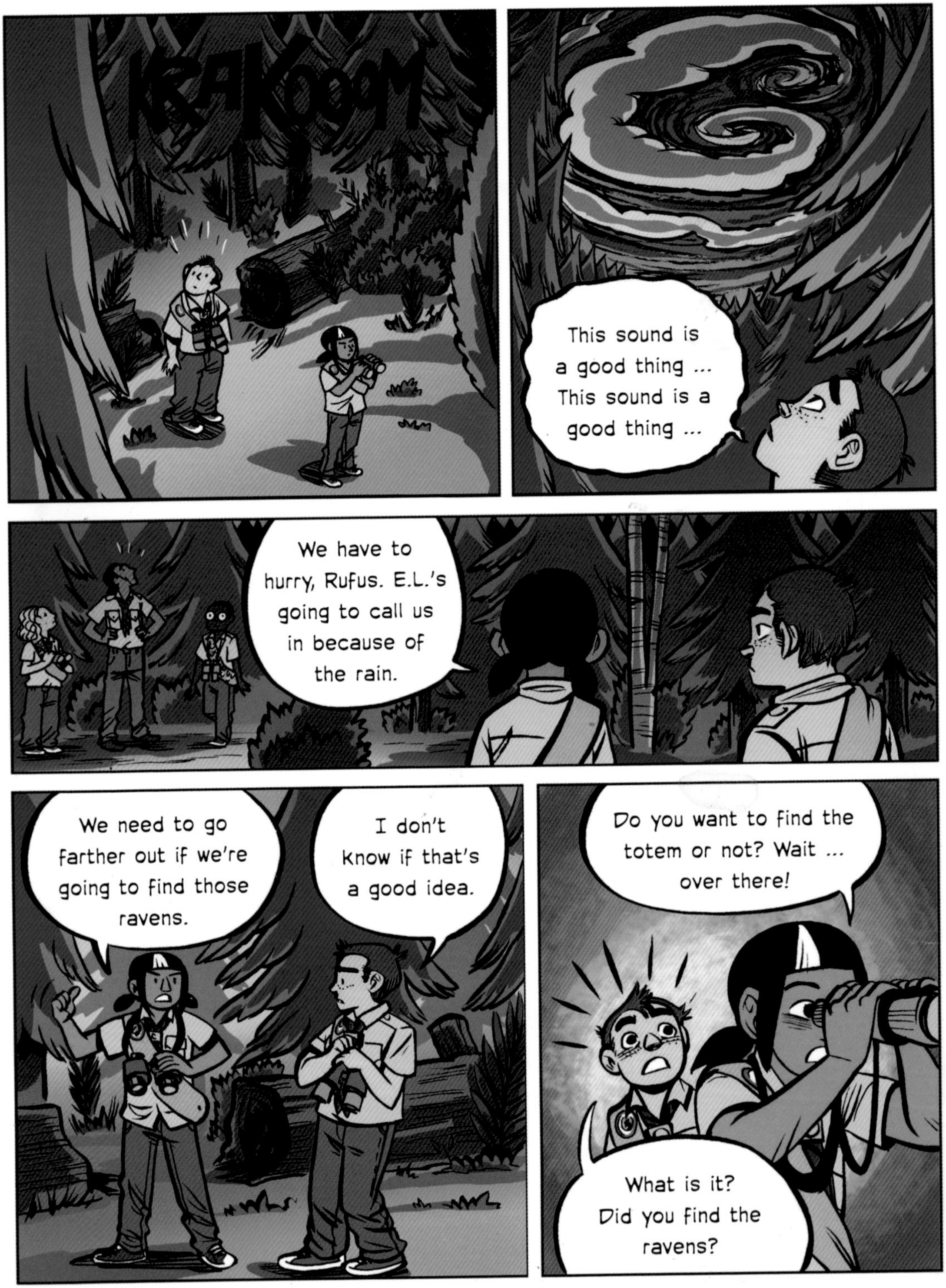
KRAKOOOM
This sound is a good thing ... This sound is a good thing ...
We have to hurry, Rufus. E.L.'s going to call us in because of the rain.
We need to go farther out if we're going to find those ravens.
I don't know if that's a good idea.
Do you want to find the totem or not? Wait ... over there!
What is it? Did you find the ravens?

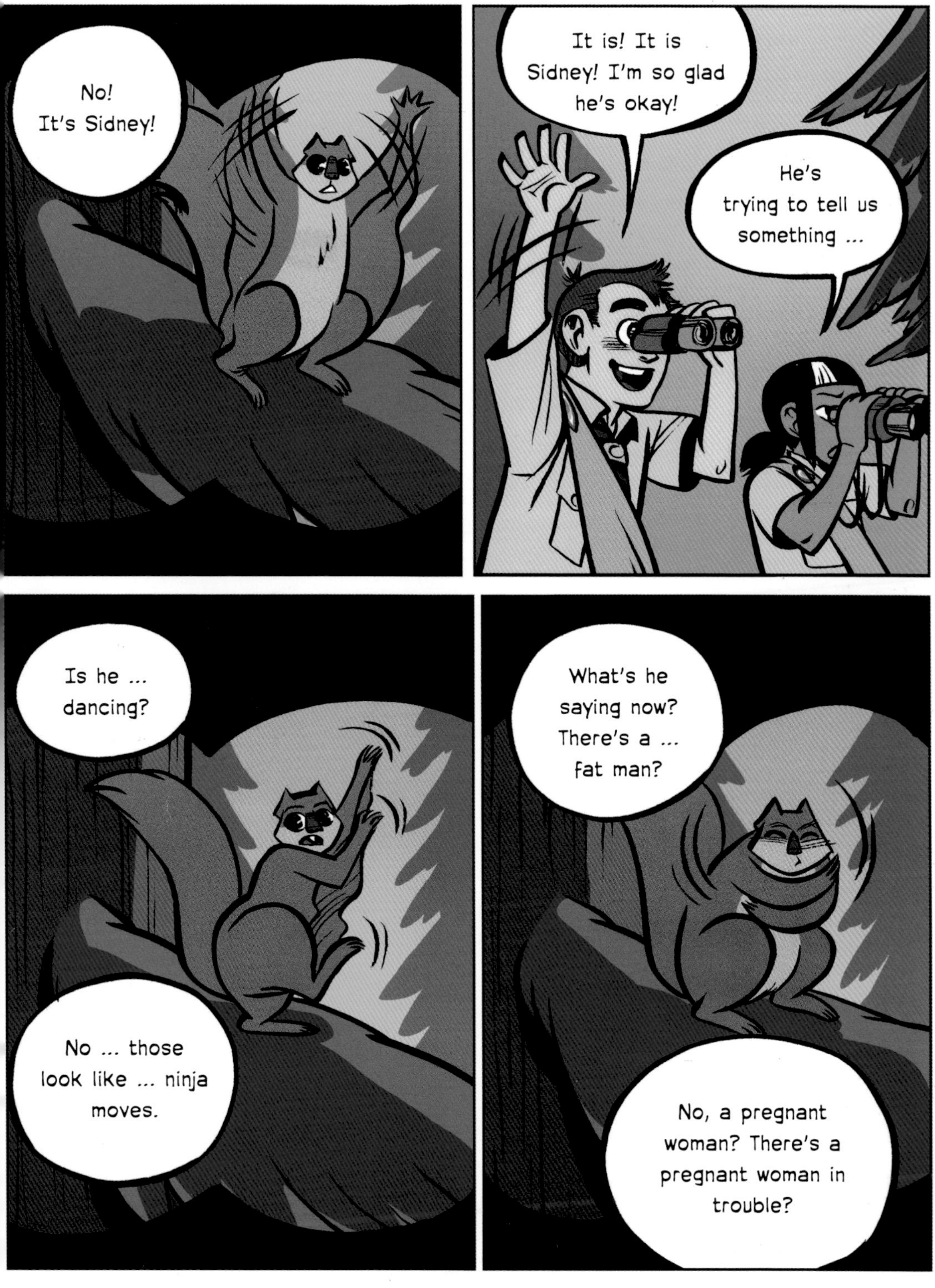
No! It's Sidney!
It is! It is Sidney! I'm so glad he's okay!
He's trying to tell us something ...
Is he ... dancing?
No ... those look like ... ninja moves.
What's he saying now? There's a ... fat man?
No, a pregnant woman? There's a pregnant woman in trouble?

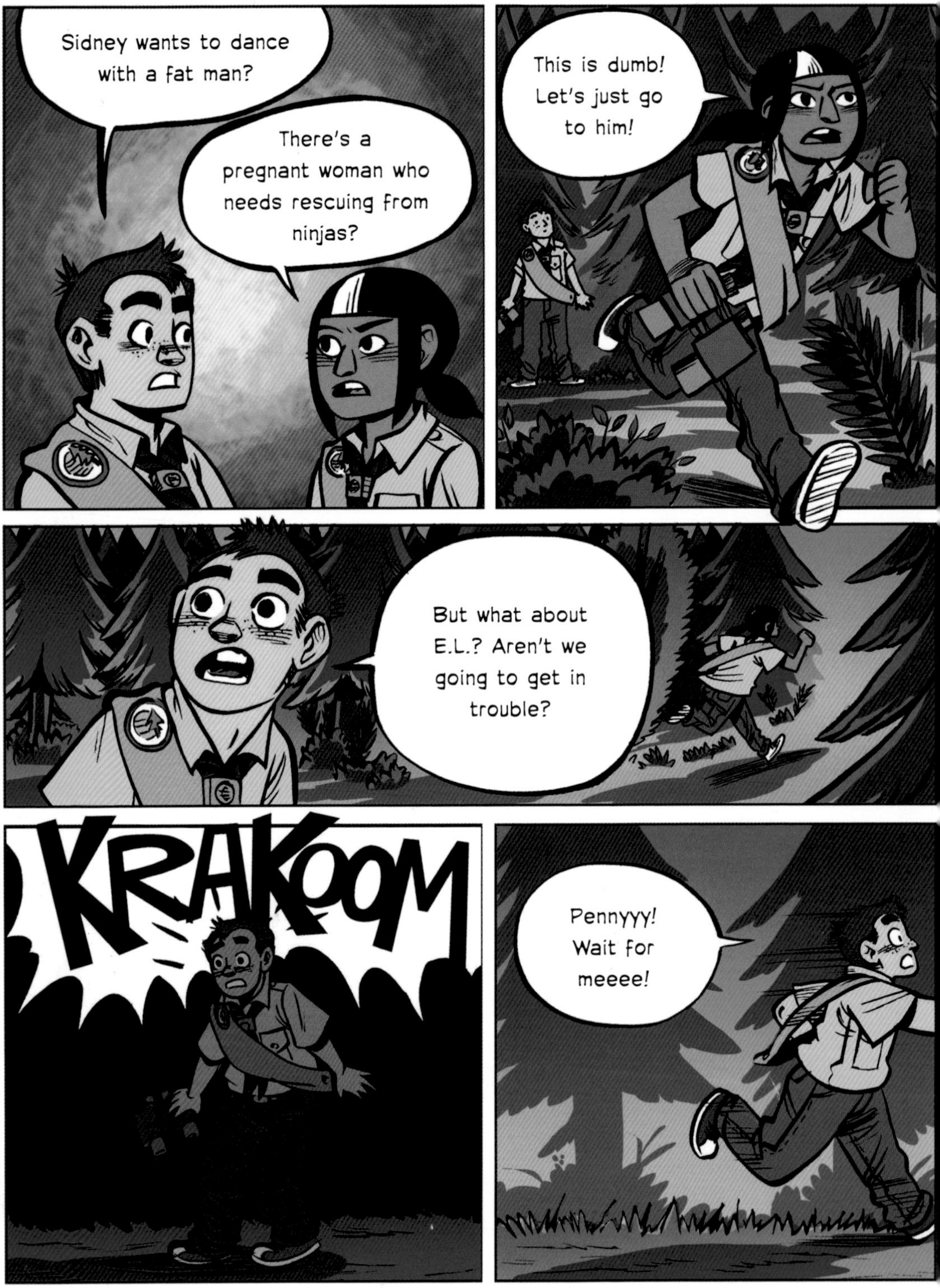

Sidney wants to dance with a fat man?
There's a pregnant woman who needs rescuing from ninjas?
This is dumb! Let's just go to him!
But what about E.L.? Aren't we going to get in trouble?
KRAKOOM
Pennyyy! Wait for meeee!

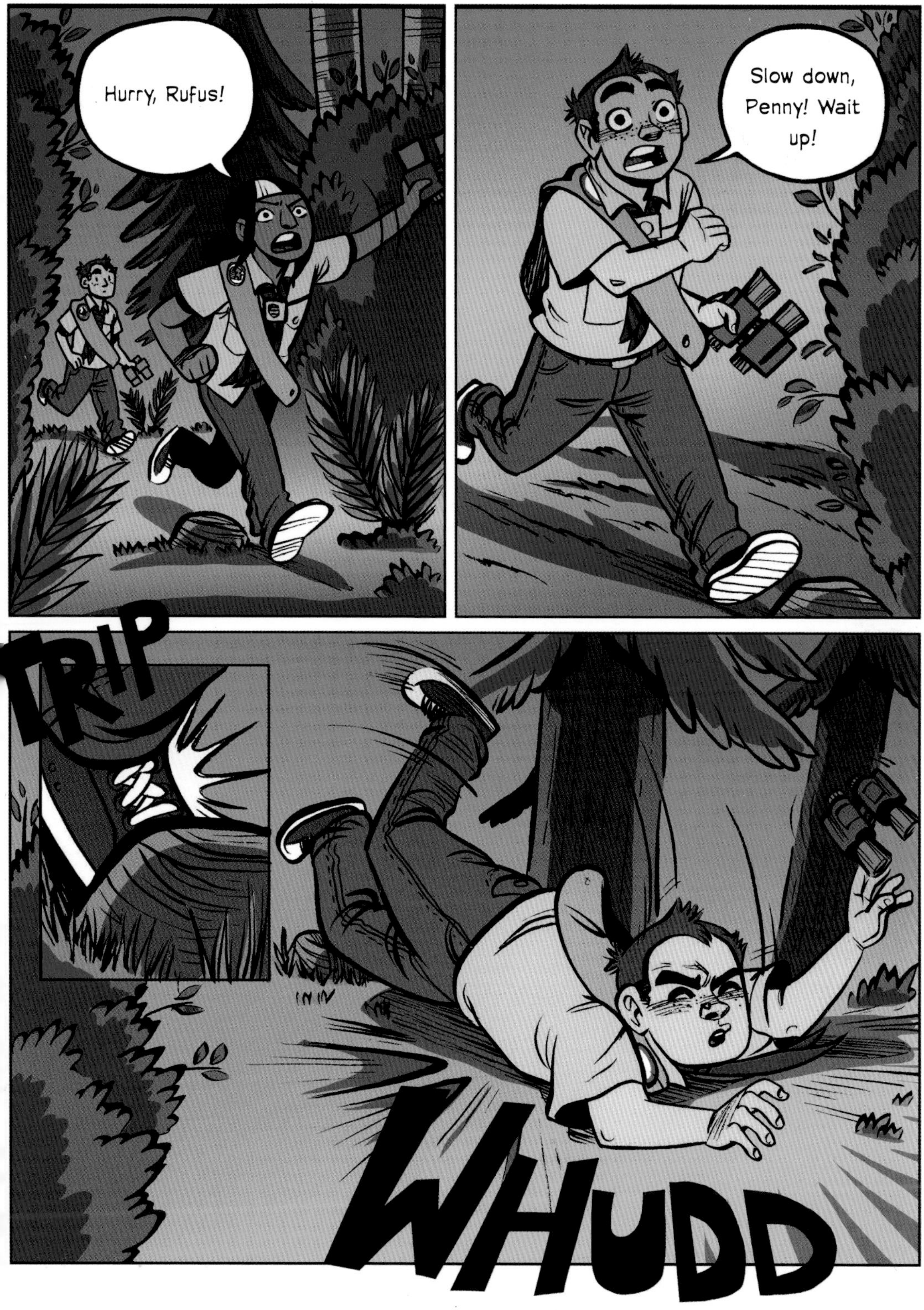
Hurry, Rufus!
Slow down, Penny! Wait up!
TRIP
WHUDD

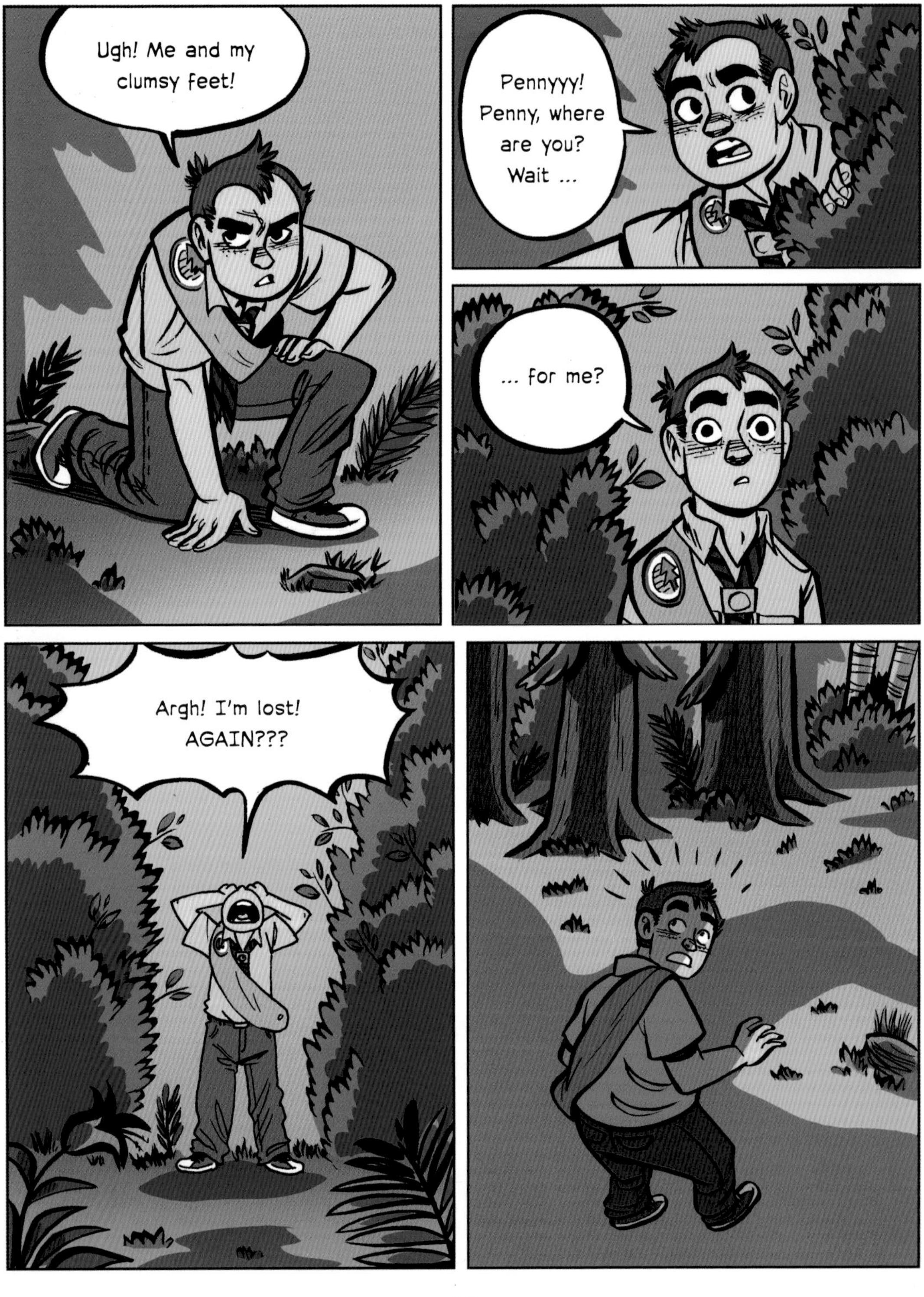
Ugh! Me and my clumsy feet!
Pennyyy! Penny, where are you? Wait ...
... for me?
Argh! I'm lost! AGAIN???

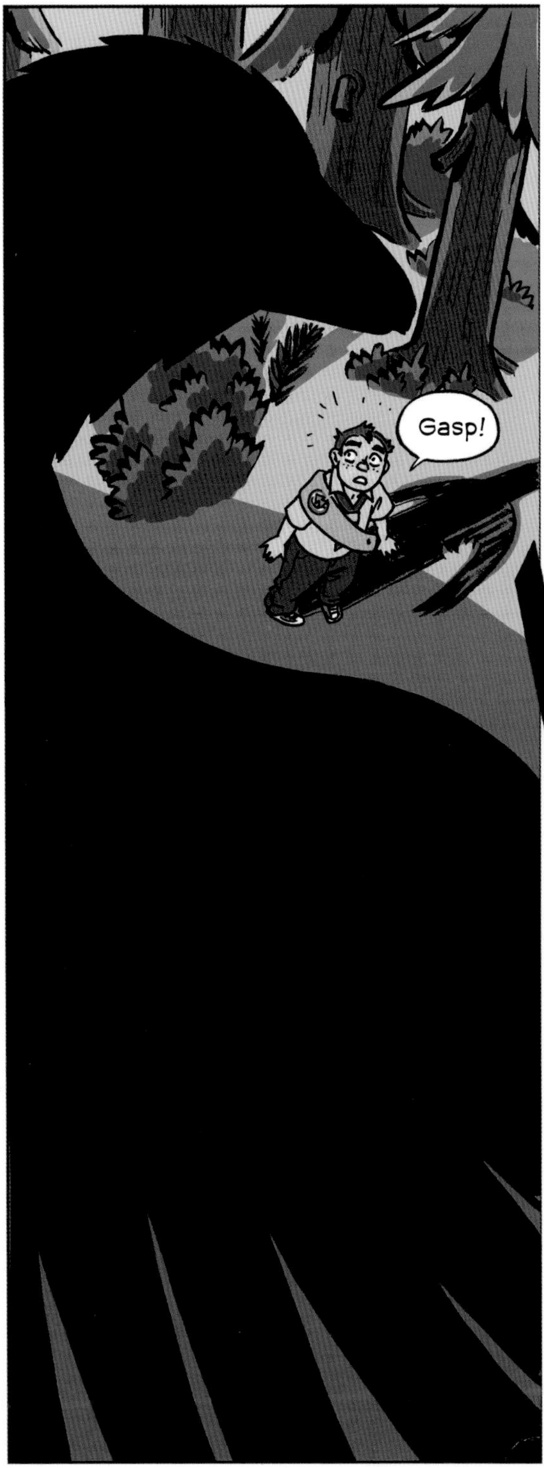
Gasp!

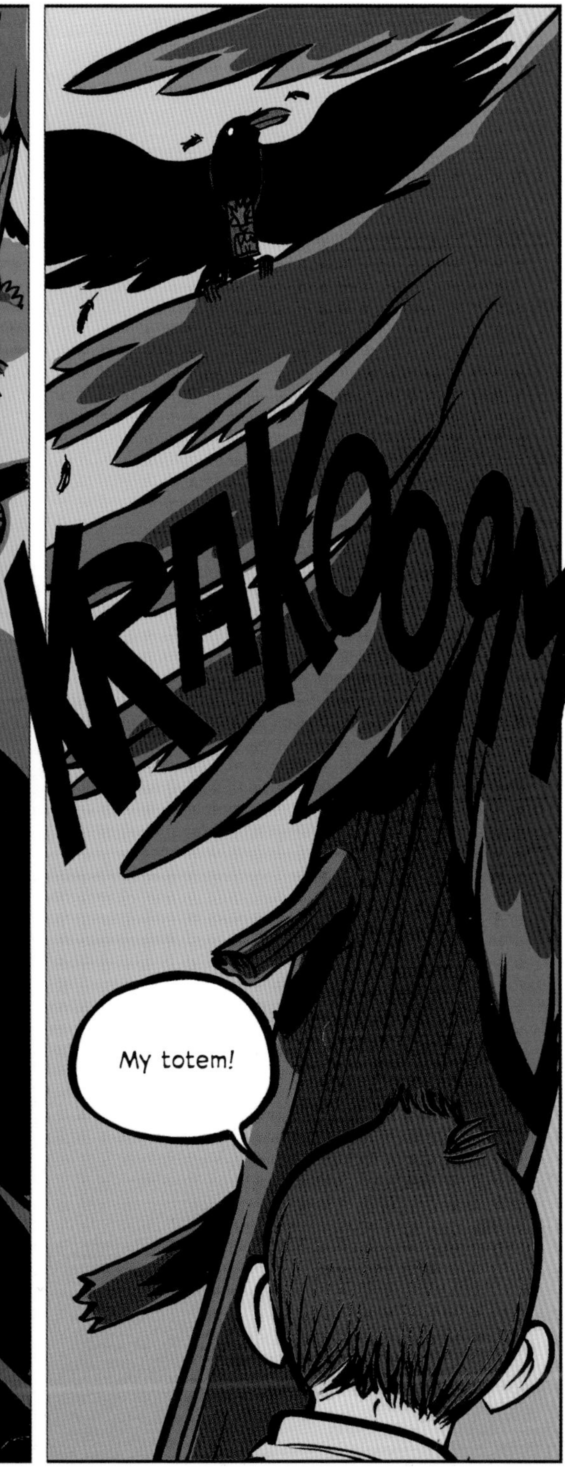
KRAKOOOM
My totem!

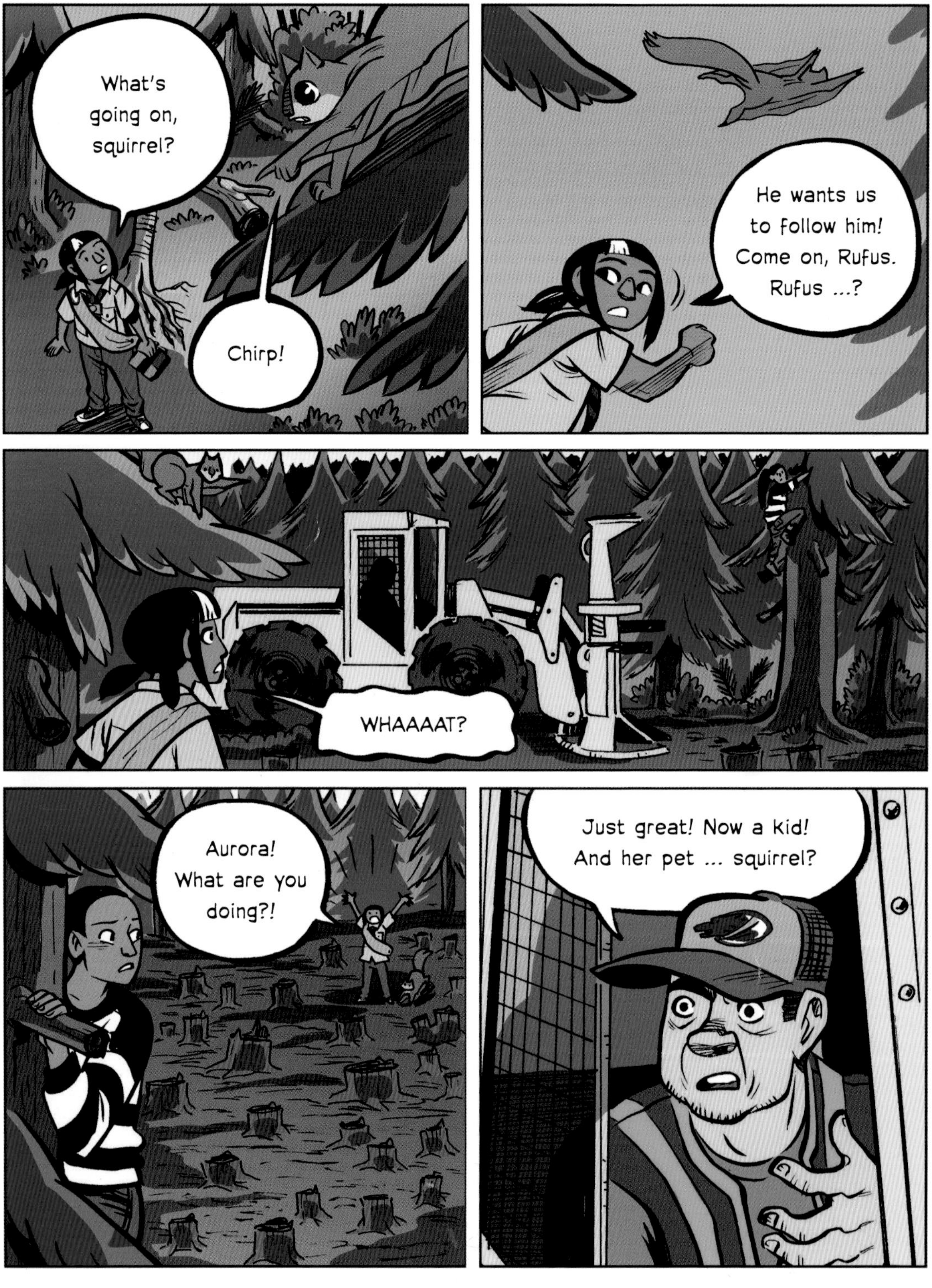
What's going on, squirrel?
Chirp!
He wants us to follow him! Come on, Rufus. Rufus ...?
WHAAAAT?
Aurora! What are you doing?!
Just great! Now a kid! And her pet ... squirrel?

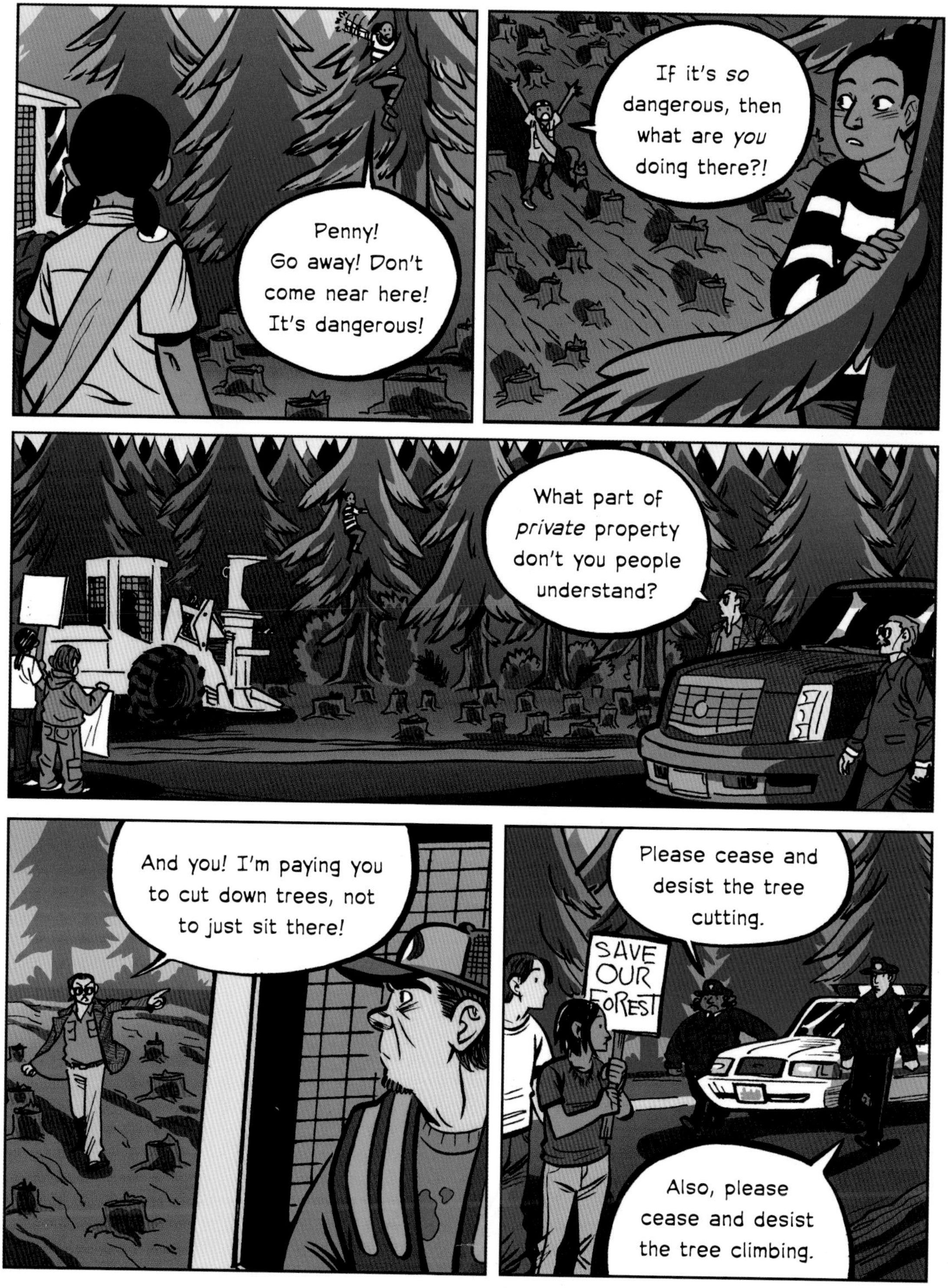
Penny! Go away! Don't come near here! It's dangerous!
If it's *so* dangerous, then what are *you* doing there?!
What part of *private* property don't you people understand?
And you! I'm paying you to cut down trees, not to just sit there!
SAVE OUR FOREST
Please cease and desist the tree cutting.
Also, please cease and desist the tree climbing.

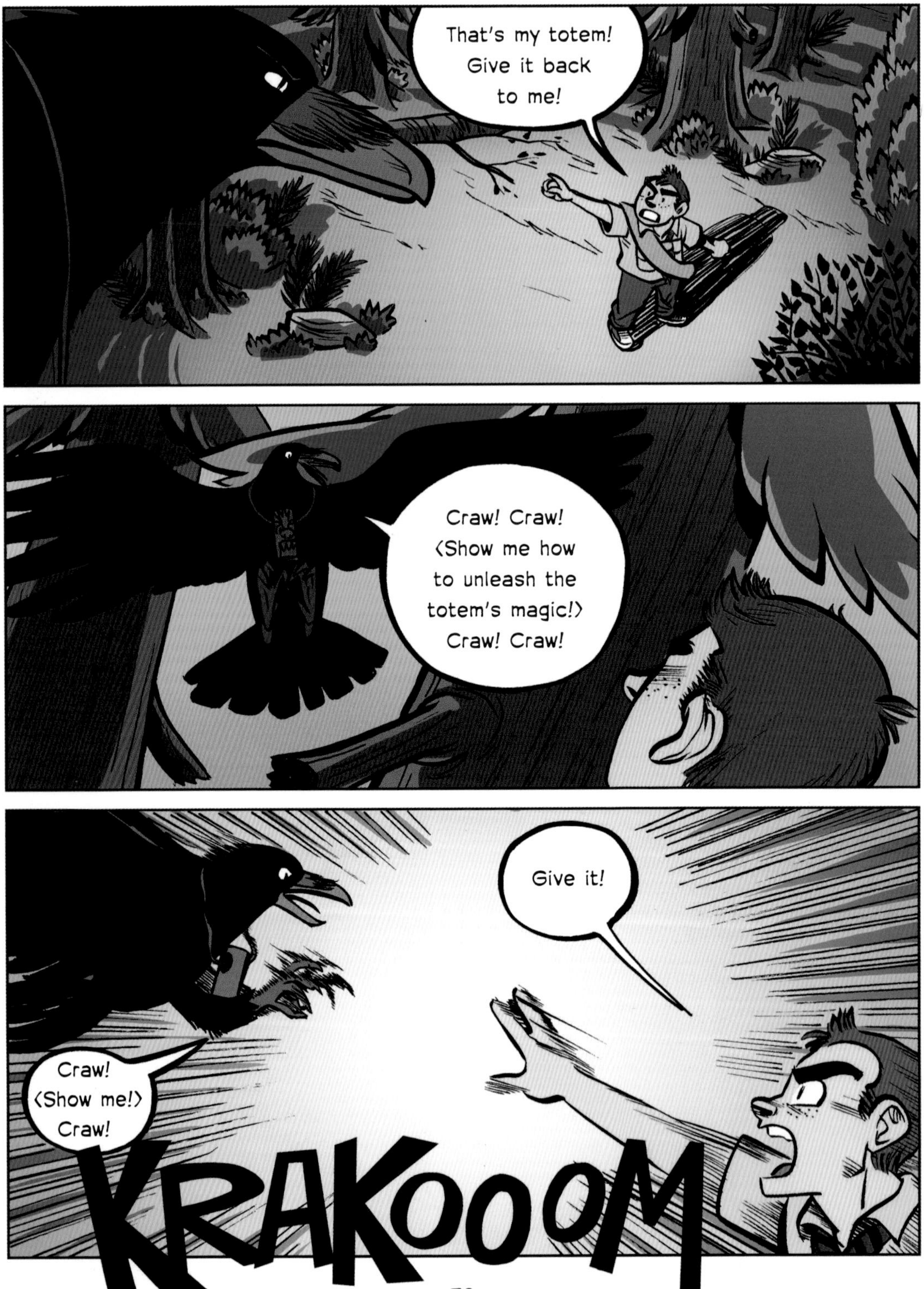
That's my totem! Give it back to me!
Craw! Craw! <Show me how to unleash the totem's magic!> Craw! Craw!
Give it!
Craw! <Show me!> Craw!
KRAKOOOM

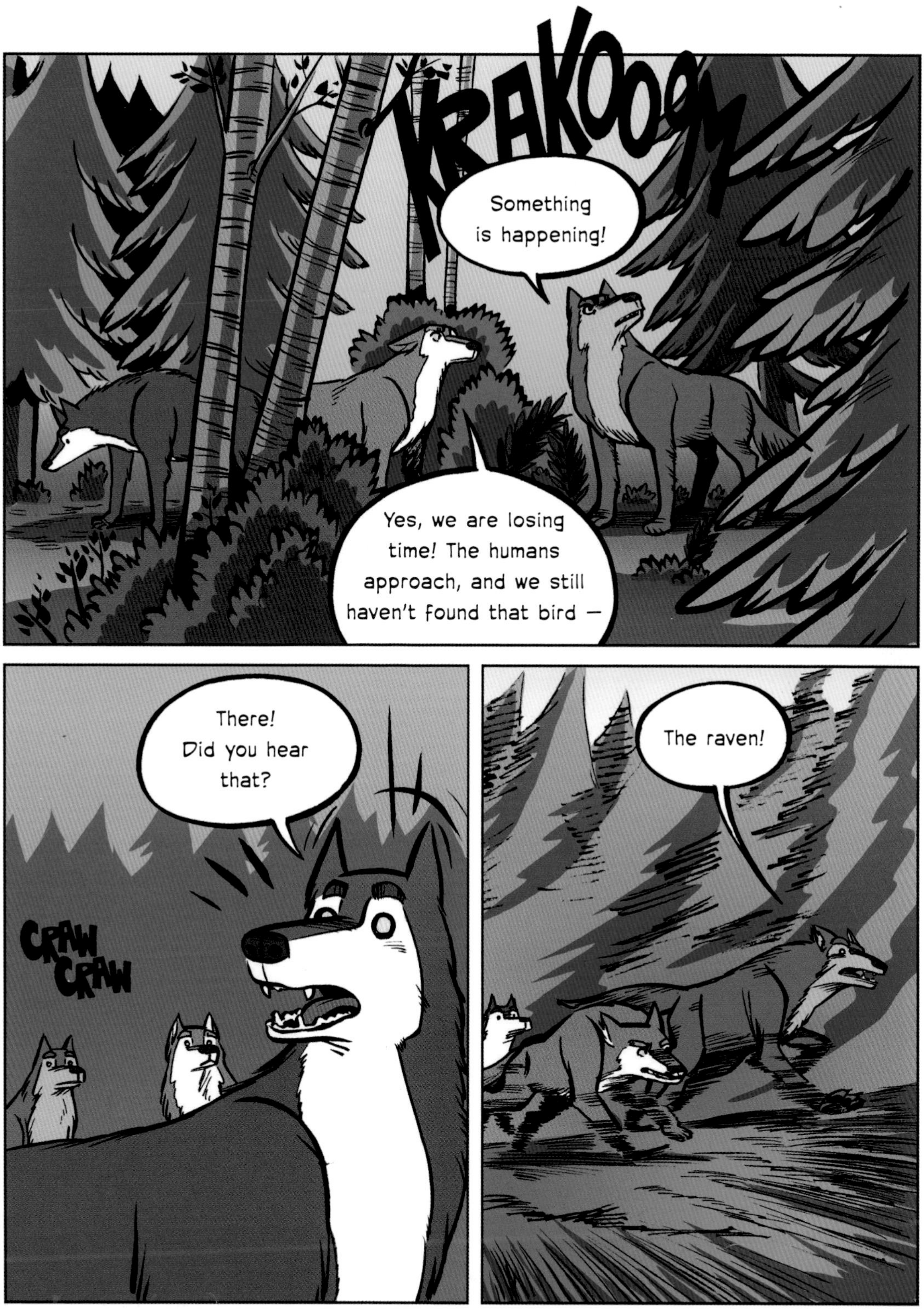
KRAKOOOM
Something is happening!
Yes, we are losing time! The humans approach, and we still haven't found that bird —
There! Did you hear that?
CRAW CRAW
The raven!

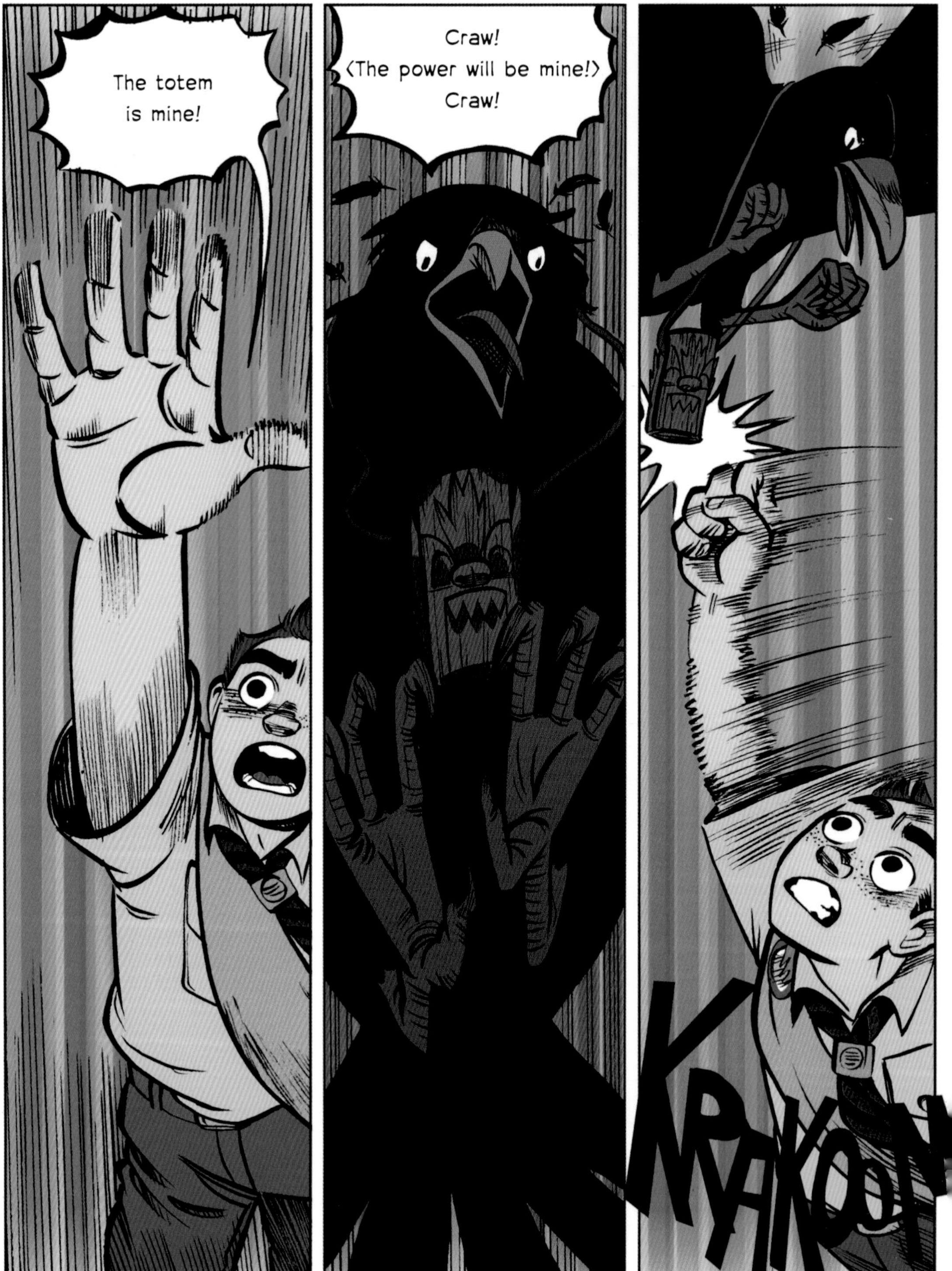
The totem
is mine!
Craw!
<The power will be mine!>
Craw!
KRAKOOM

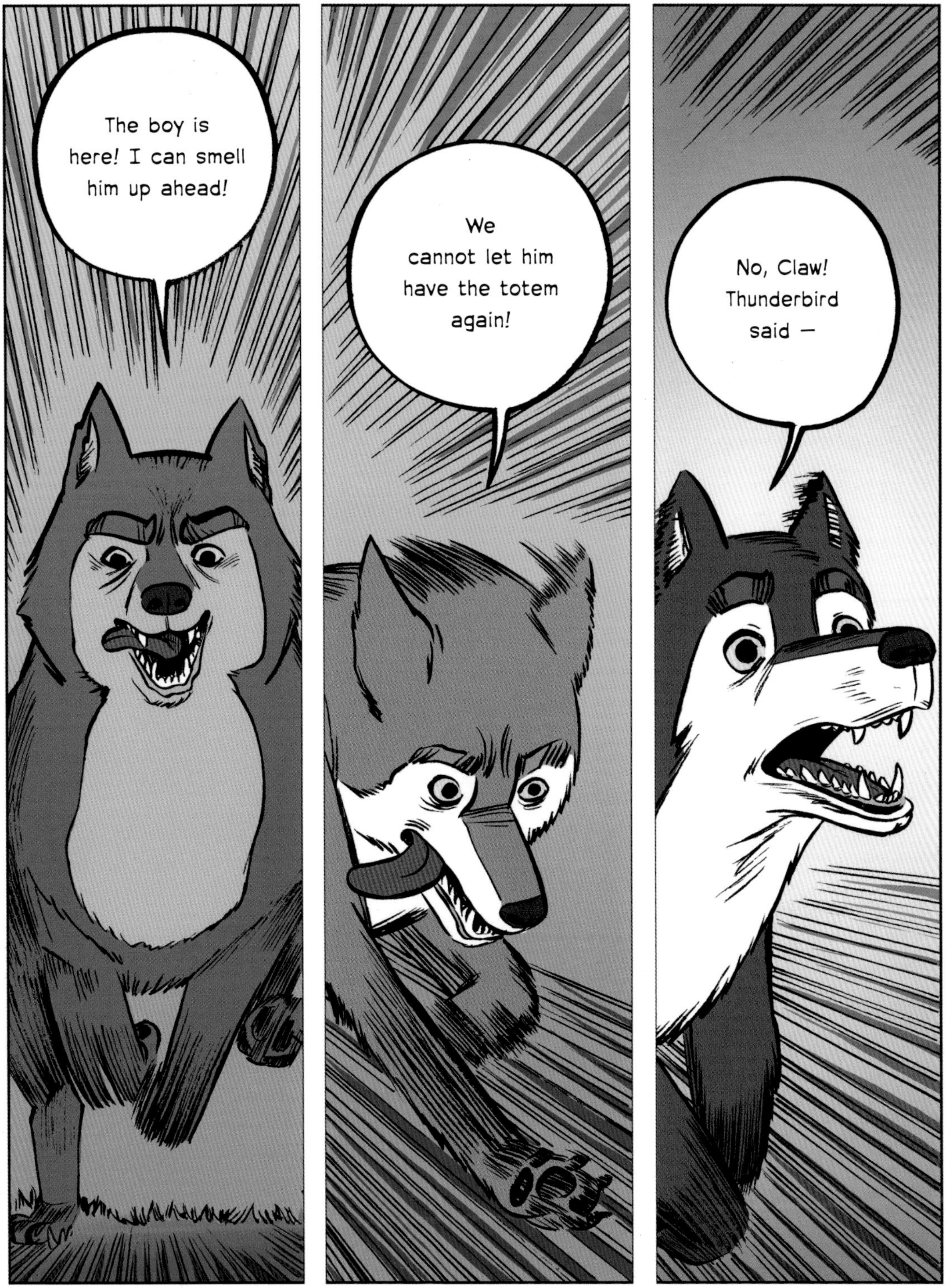
The boy is here! I can smell him up ahead!
We cannot let him have the totem again!
No, Claw! Thunderbird said —

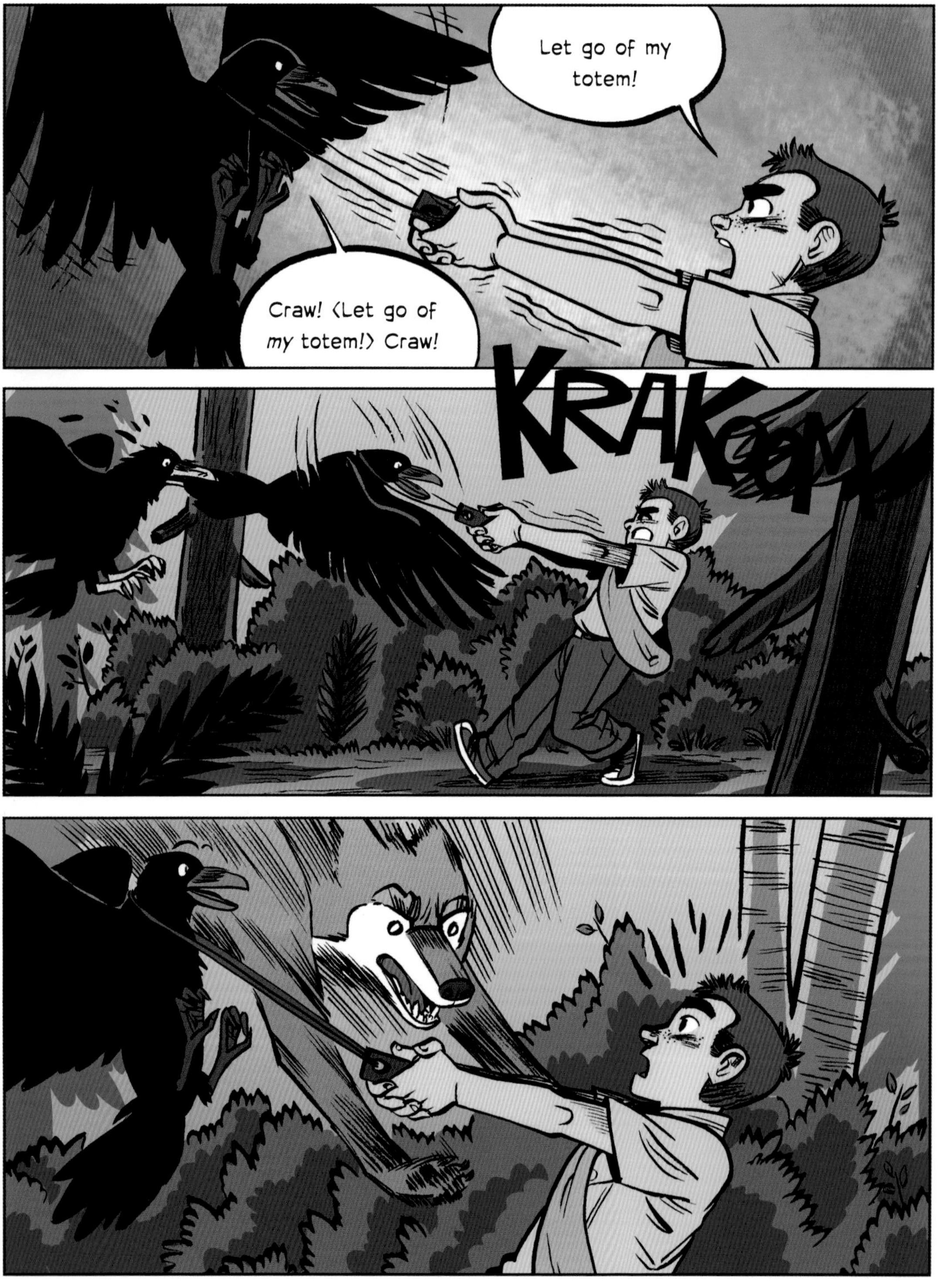
Let go of my totem!
Craw! ‹Let go of *my* totem!› Craw!
KRAKOOM

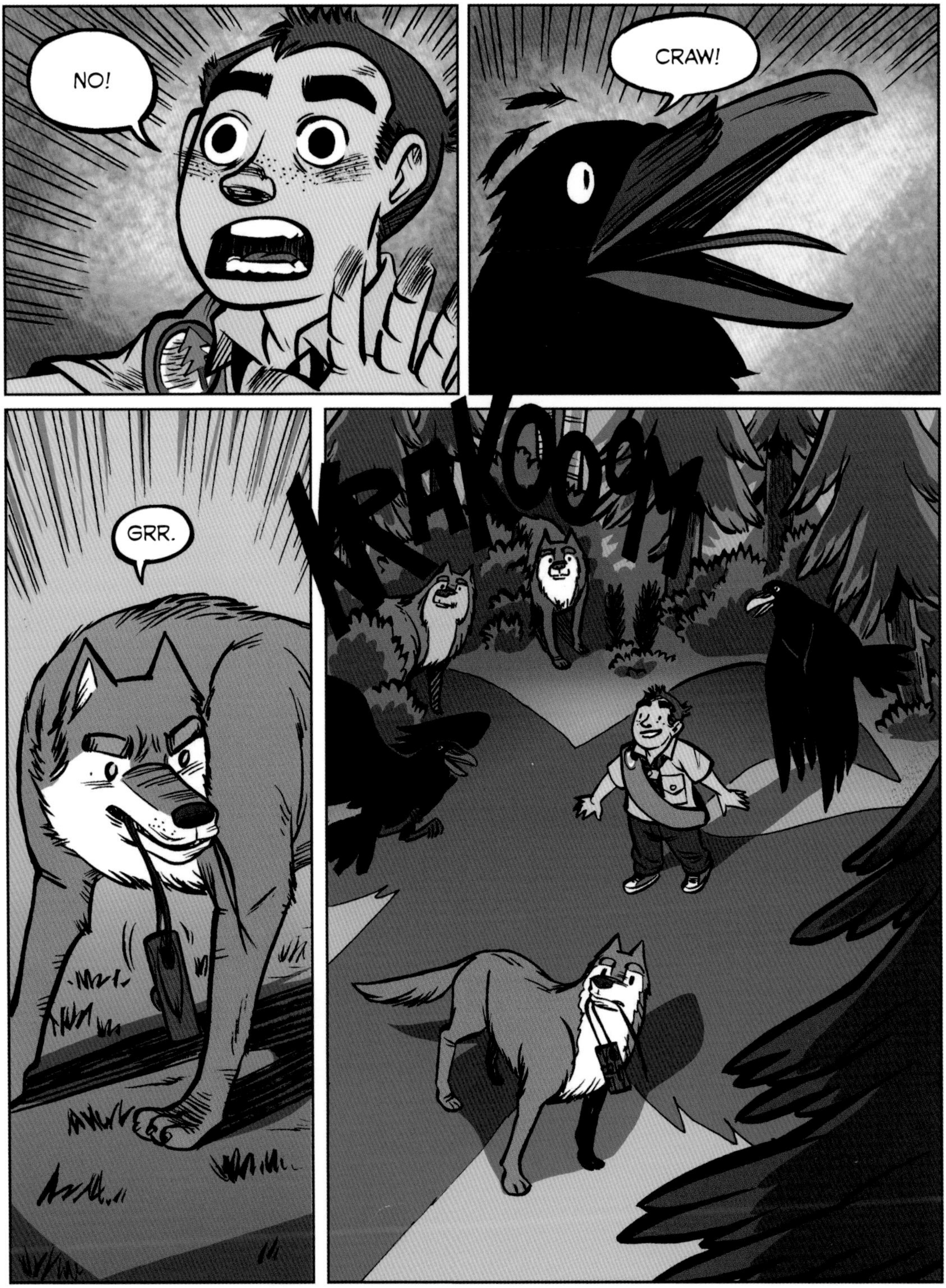
NO!
CRAW!
GRR.
KRAKOOOM

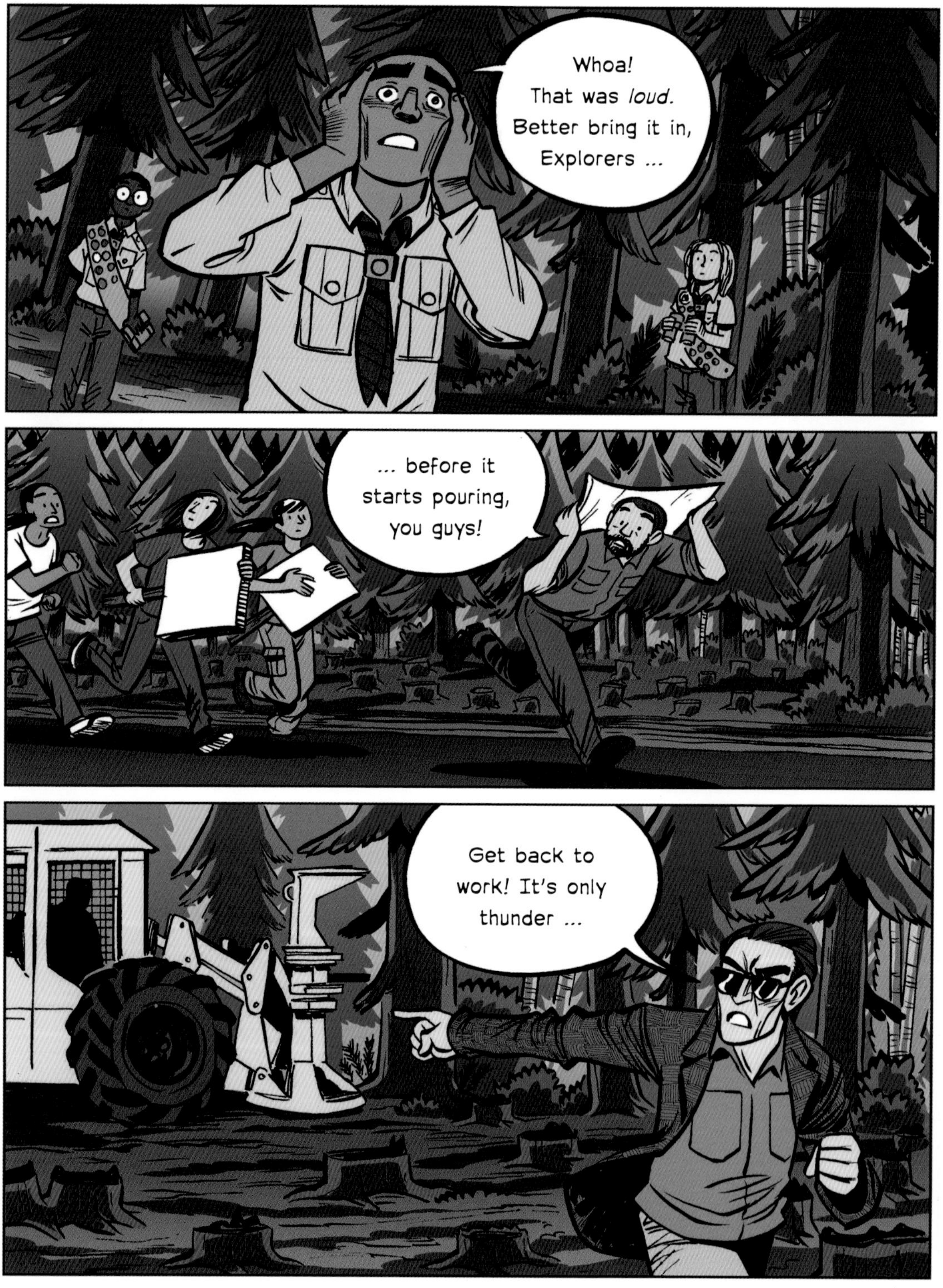
Whoa! That was *loud.* Better bring it in, Explorers ...
... before it starts pouring, you guys!
Get back to work! It's only thunder ...

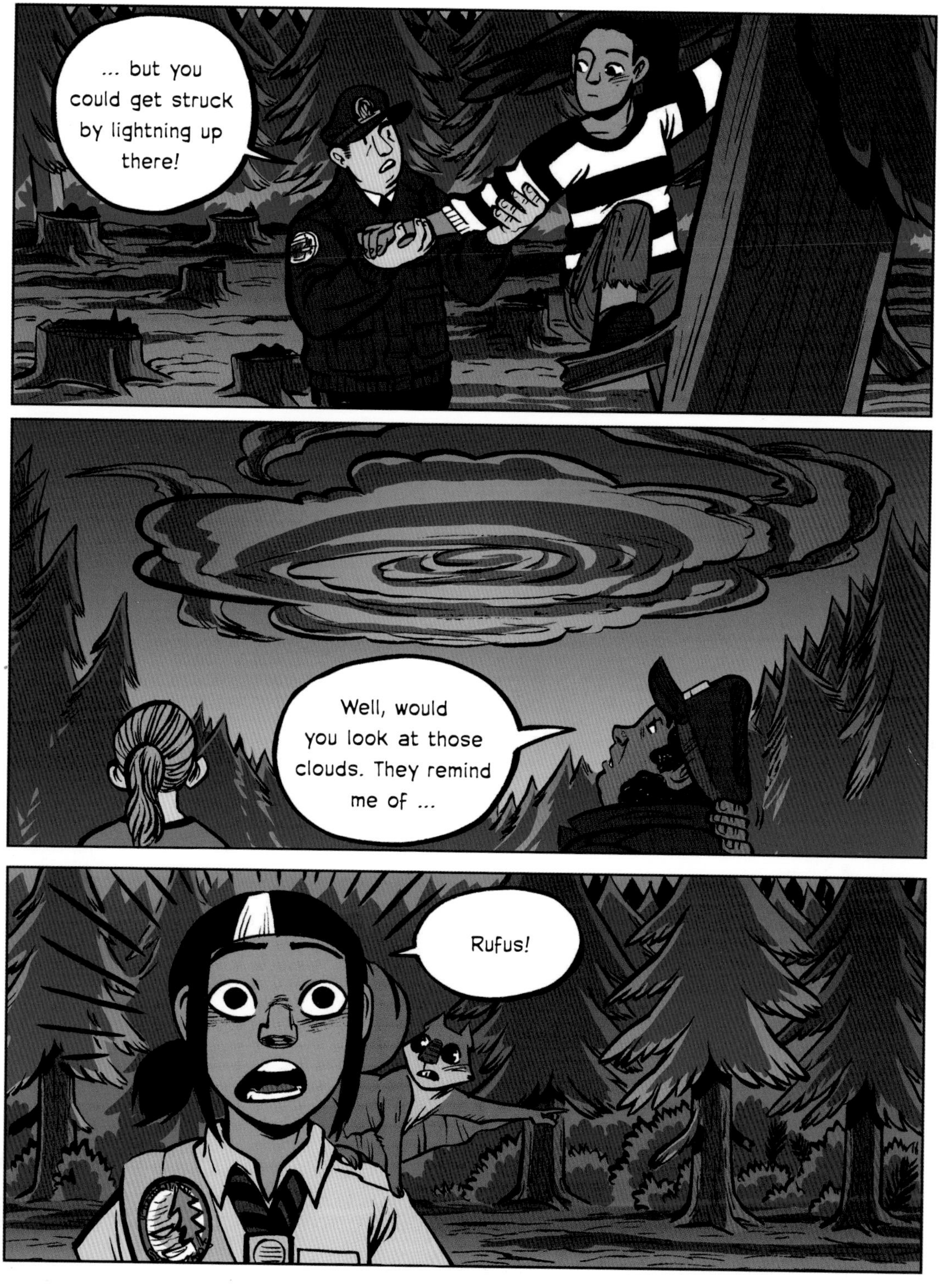
... but you could get struck by lightning up there!
Well, would you look at those clouds. They remind me of ...
Rufus!

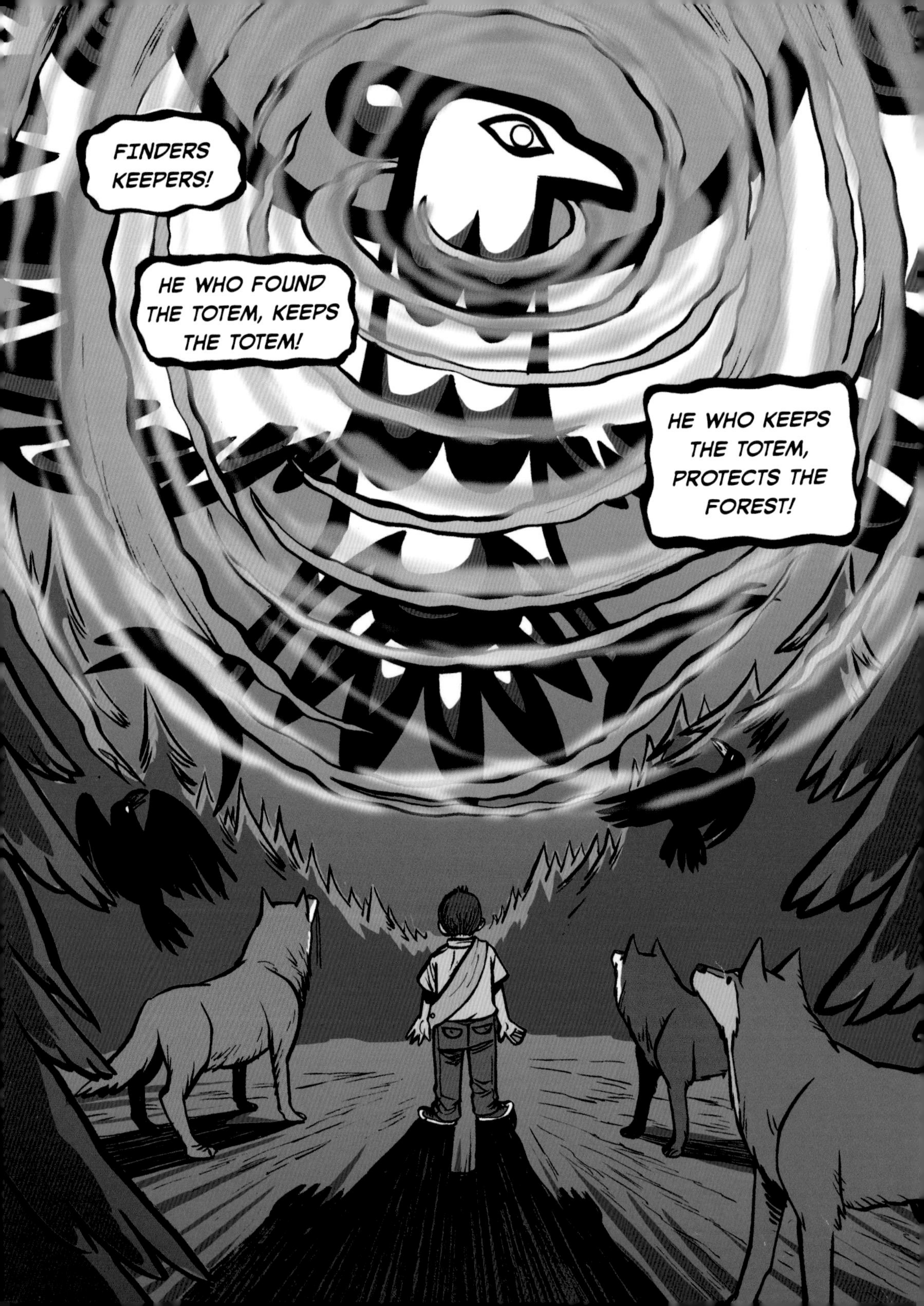
FINDERS KEEPERS!
HE WHO FOUND THE TOTEM, KEEPS THE TOTEM!
HE WHO KEEPS THE TOTEM, PROTECTS THE FOREST!

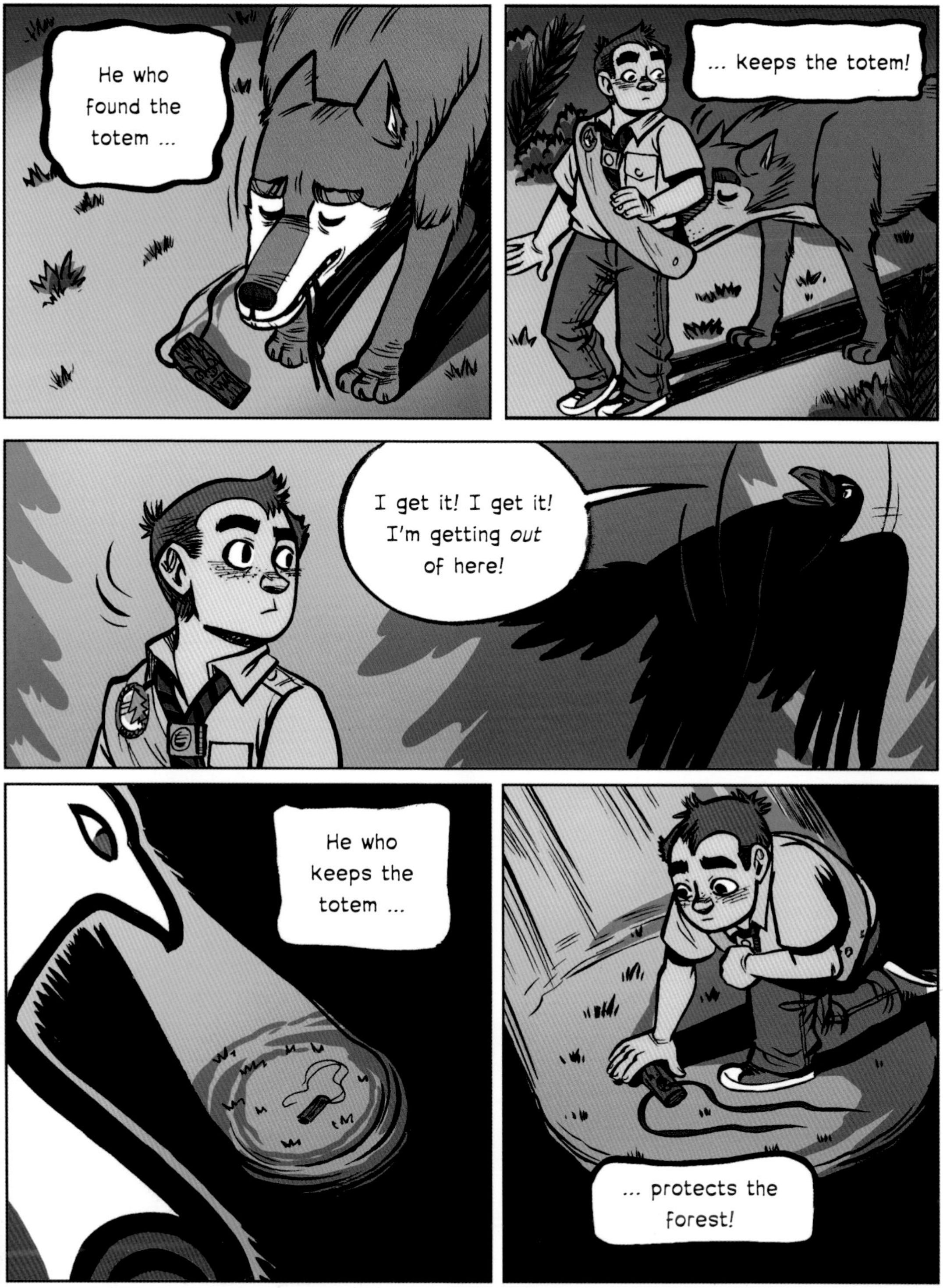
He who found the totem ...
... keeps the totem!
I get it! I get it! I'm getting *out* of here!
He who keeps the totem ...
... protects the forest!

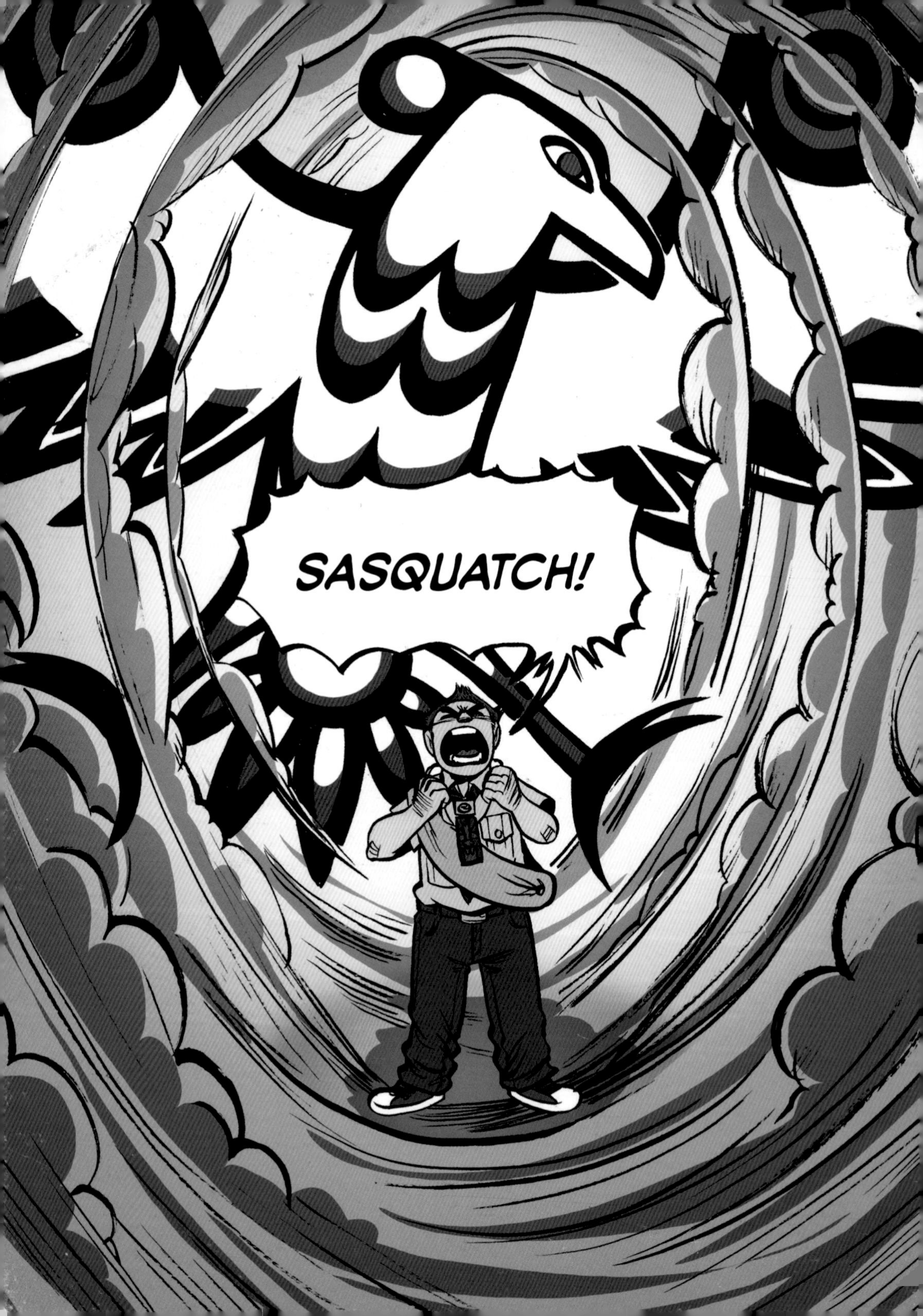
SASQUATCH!

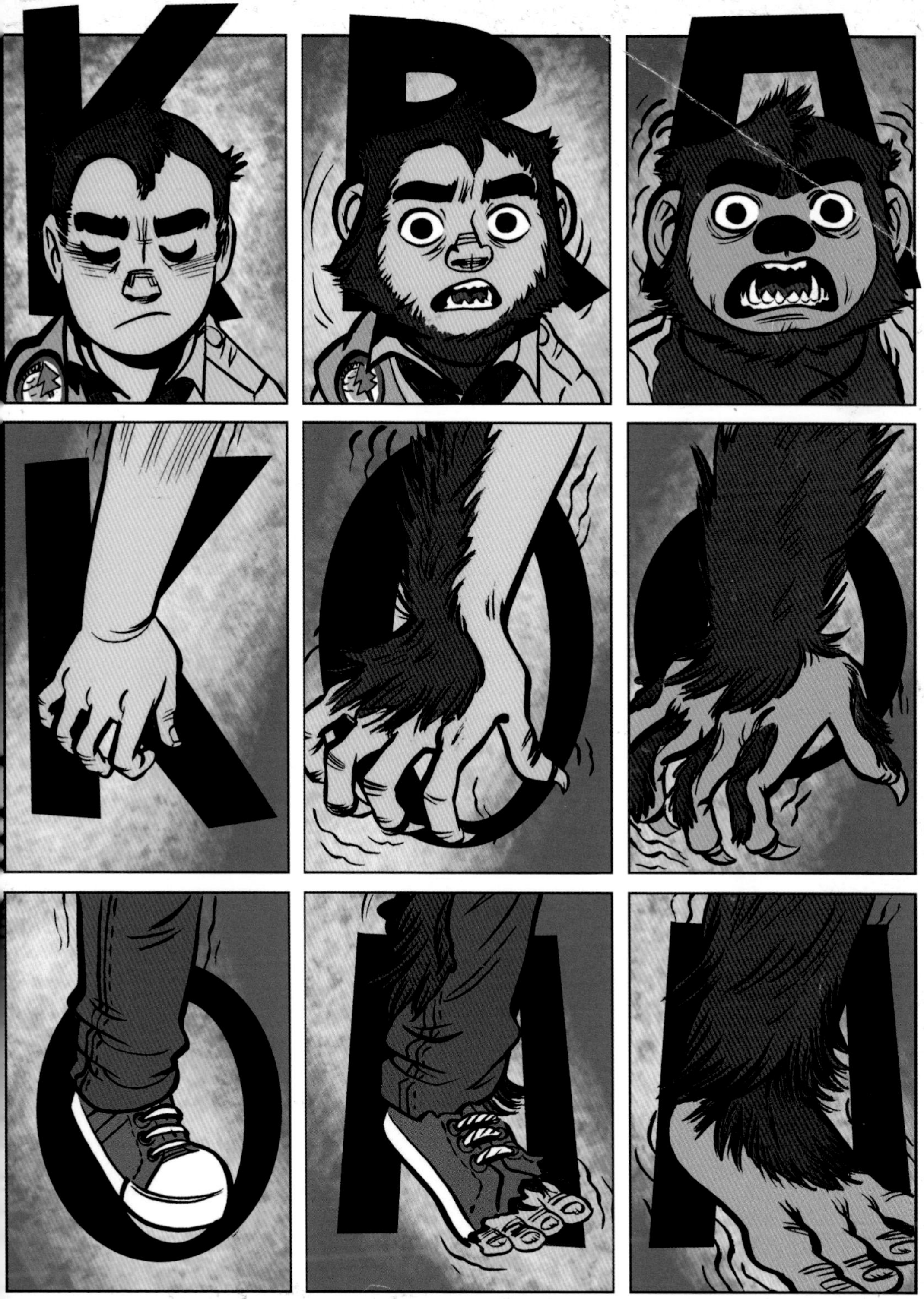
KRA
KOO
O

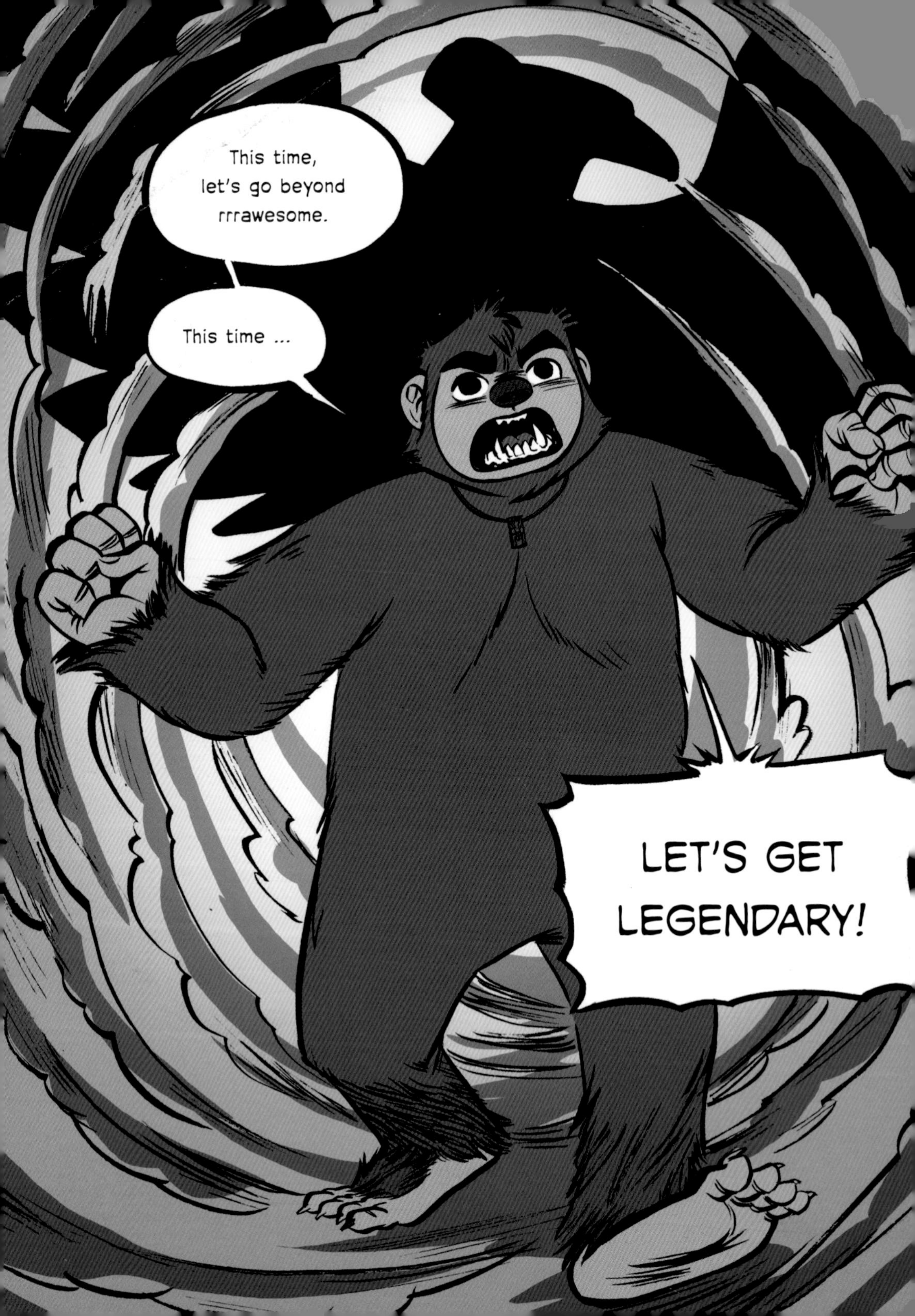
This time, let's go beyond rrrawesome.
This time ...
LET'S GET LEGENDARY!

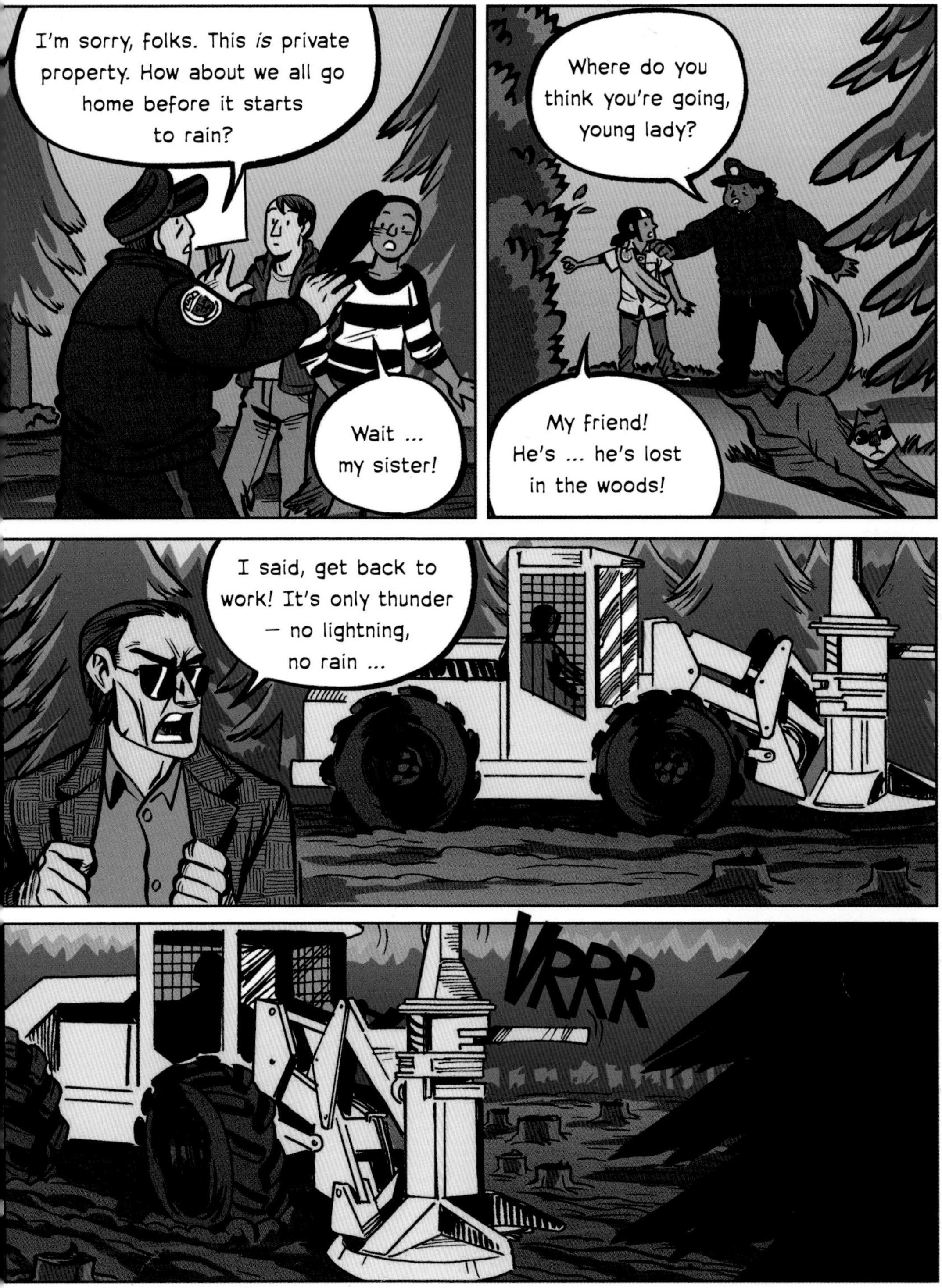
I'm sorry, folks. This *is* private property. How about we all go home before it starts to rain?
Wait ... my sister!
Where do you think you're going, young lady?
My friend! He's ... he's lost in the woods!
I said, get back to work! It's only thunder — no lightning, no rain ...
VRRR

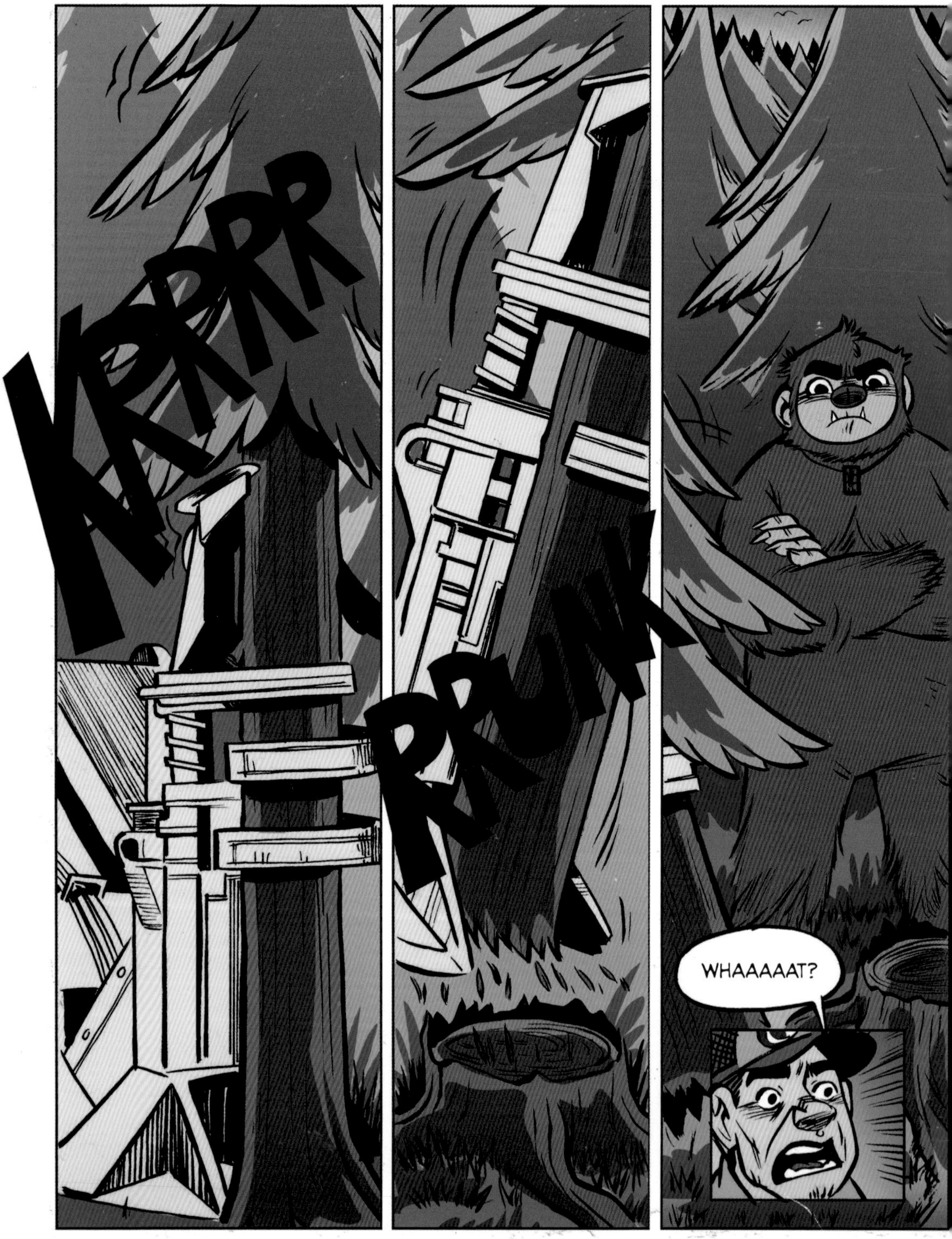
KRRRR
RRRUNK
WHAAAAAT?

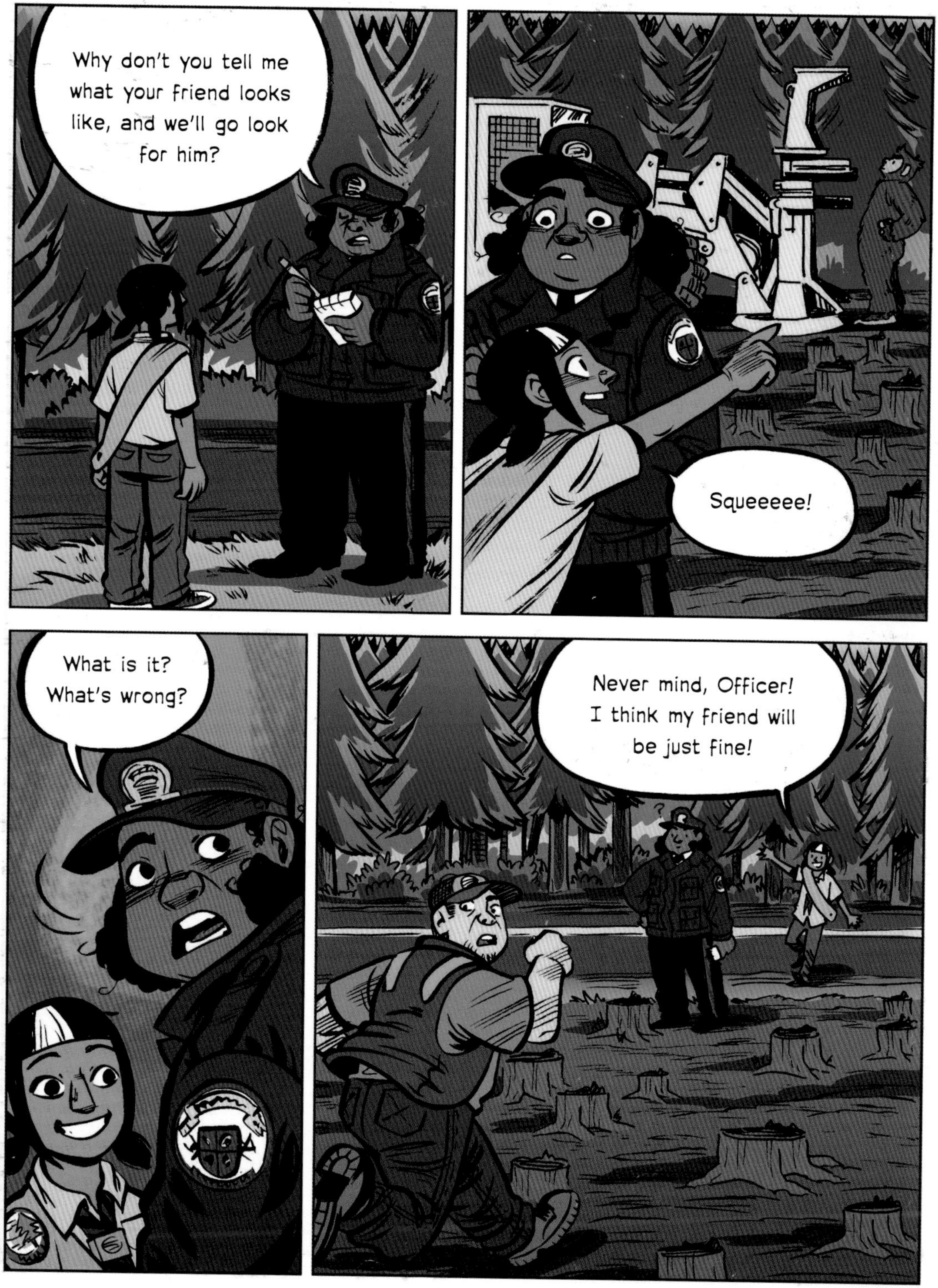
Why don't you tell me what your friend looks like, and we'll go look for him?
Squeeeee!
What is it? What's wrong?
Never mind, Officer! I think my friend will be just fine!

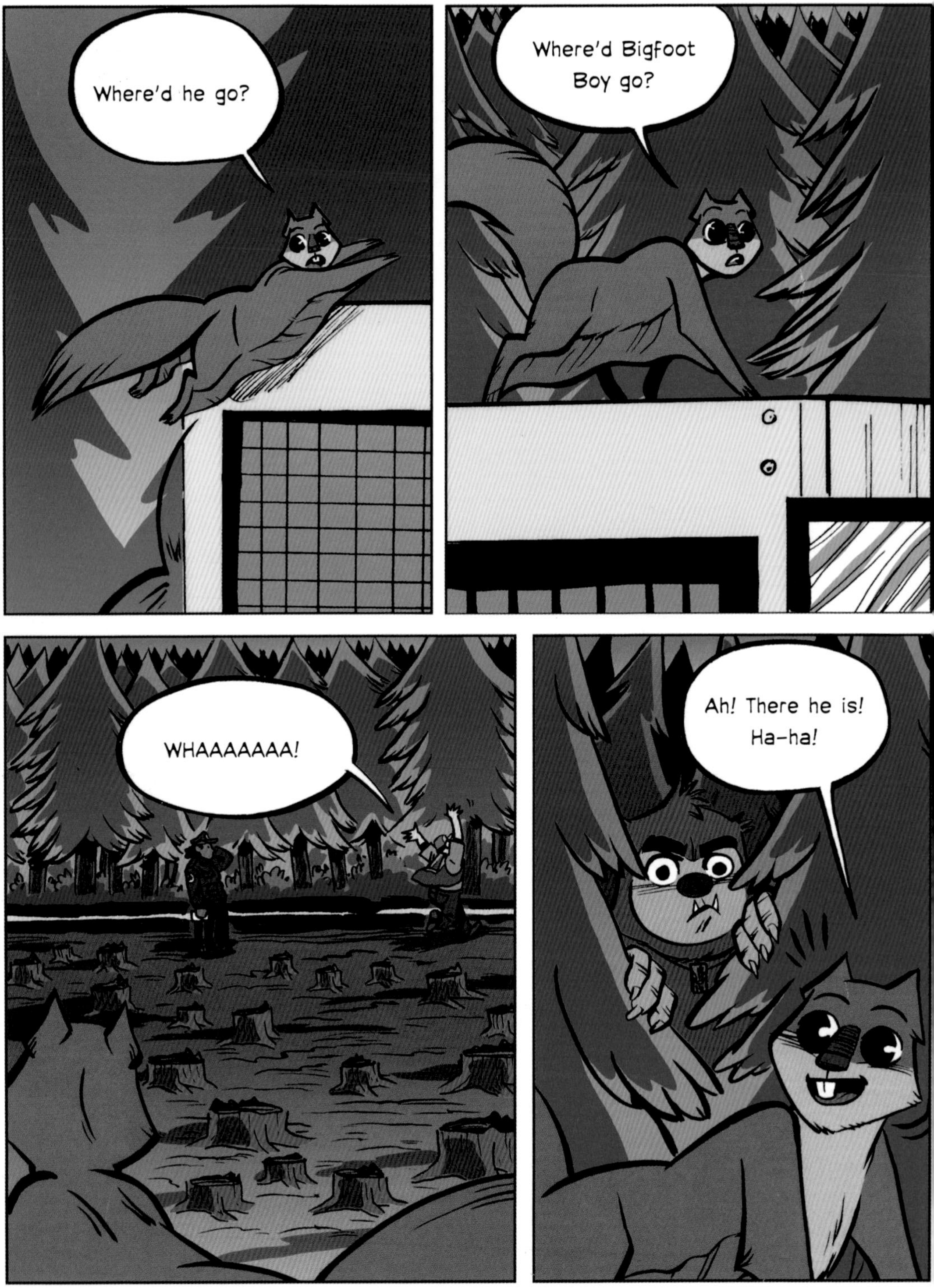
Where'd he go?
Where'd Bigfoot Boy go?
WHAAAAAAA!
Ah! There he is! Ha-ha!

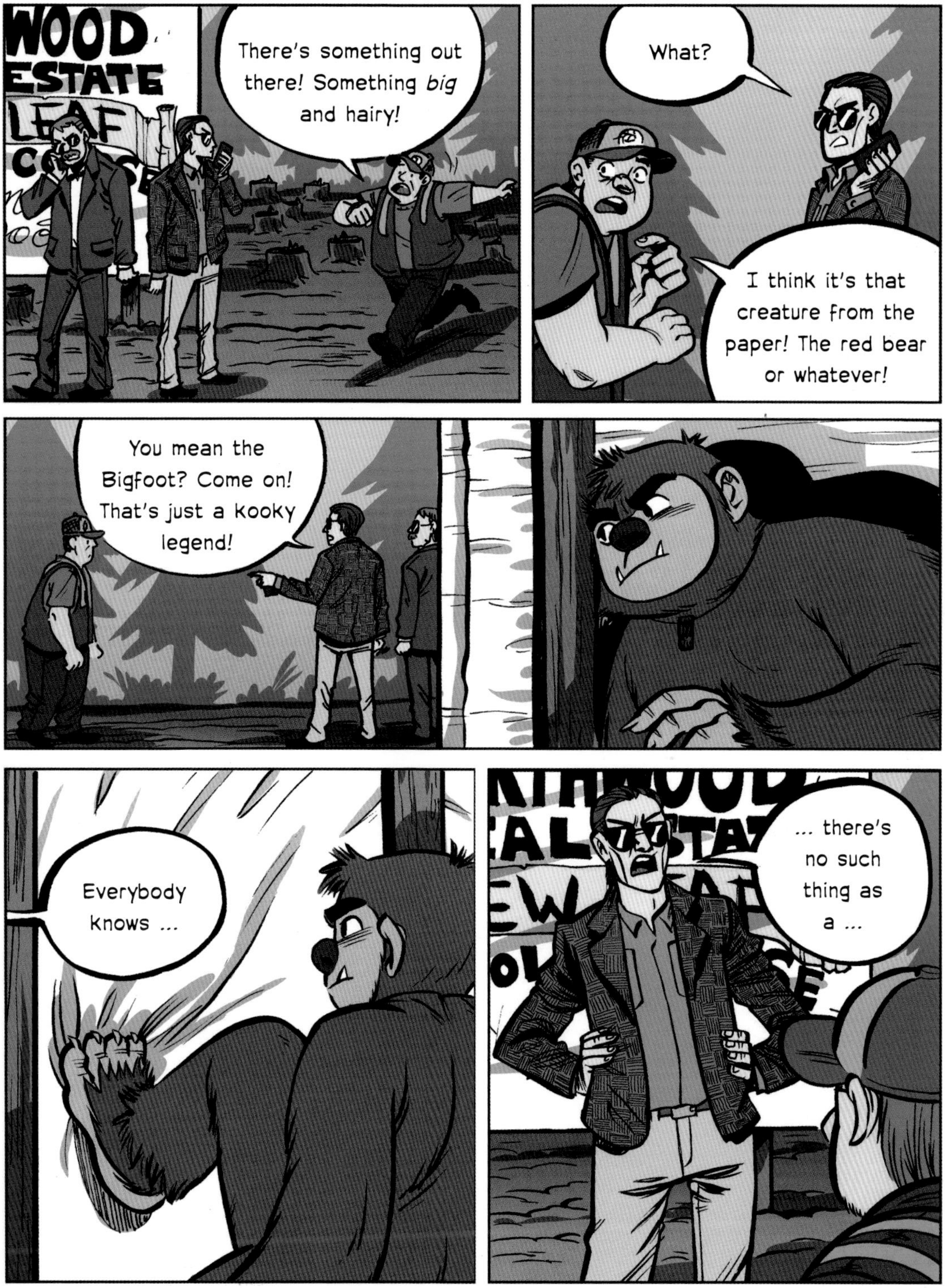
WOOD
ESTATE
LEAF
There's something out there! Something *big* and hairy!
What?
I think it's that creature from the paper! The red bear or whatever!
You mean the Bigfoot? Come on! That's just a kooky legend!
Everybody knows ...
... there's no such thing as a ...

... Bigfoot?

WHAAAAAAAA!

NORTHW
REALE
NEW LEA
GOLF COUR
Coming Soon!

See! I told you!
They saw it, too!

Saw what?

All of you
stay put!

Meant to kick down the sign! Now I'm stuck!

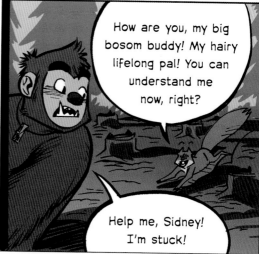

How are you, my big bosom buddy! My hairy lifelong pal! You can understand me now, right?

Help me, Sidney! I'm stuck!

Eek! Someone's coming this way, too!

This is so *not* legendary! Pull, Sidney! Pull!

This isn't going to work!

Keep pulling!

Where are you going???

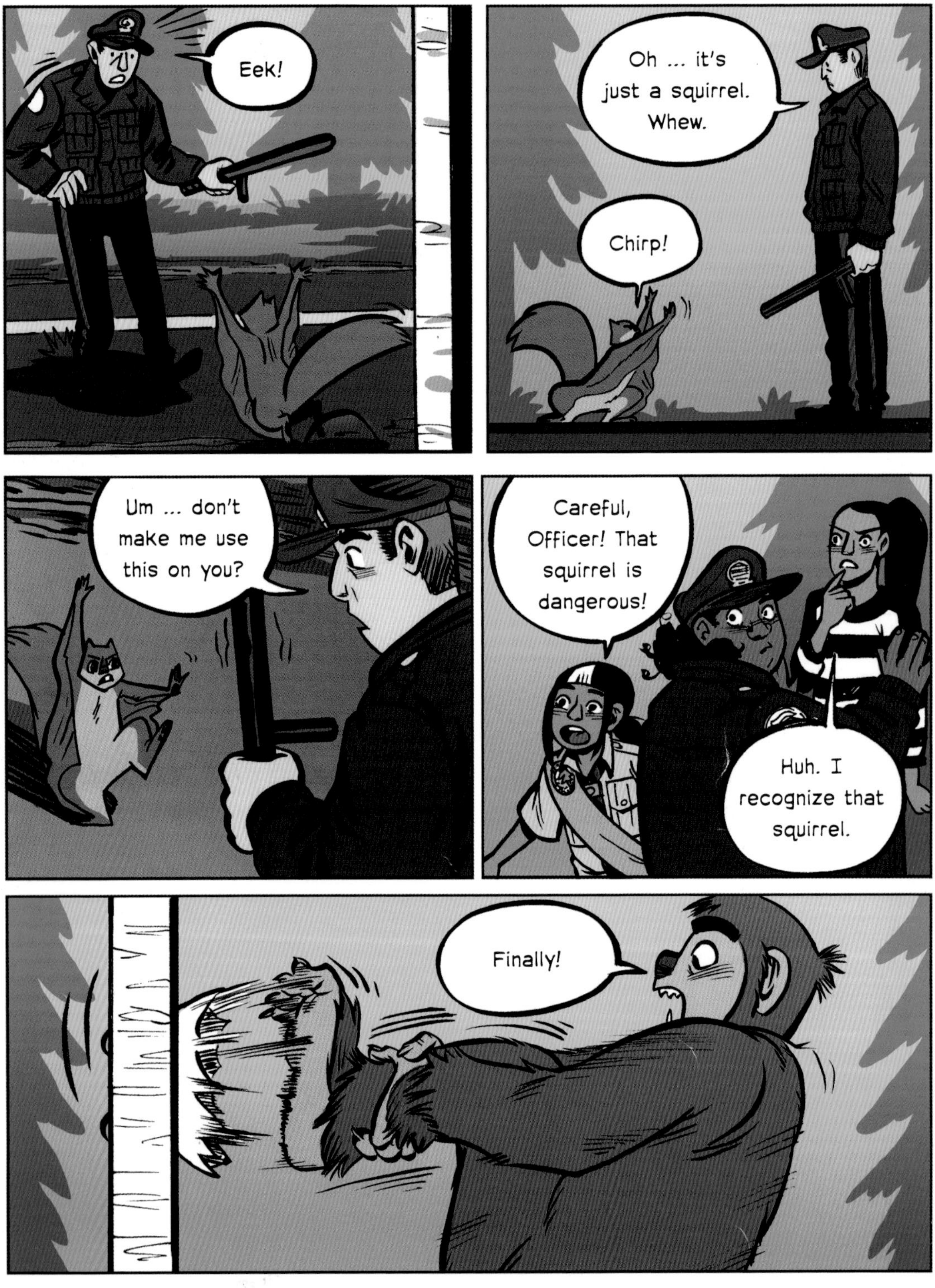
Eek!
Oh ... it's just a squirrel. Whew.
Chirp!
Um ... don't make me use this on you?
Careful, Officer! That squirrel is dangerous!
Huh. I recognize that squirrel.
Finally!

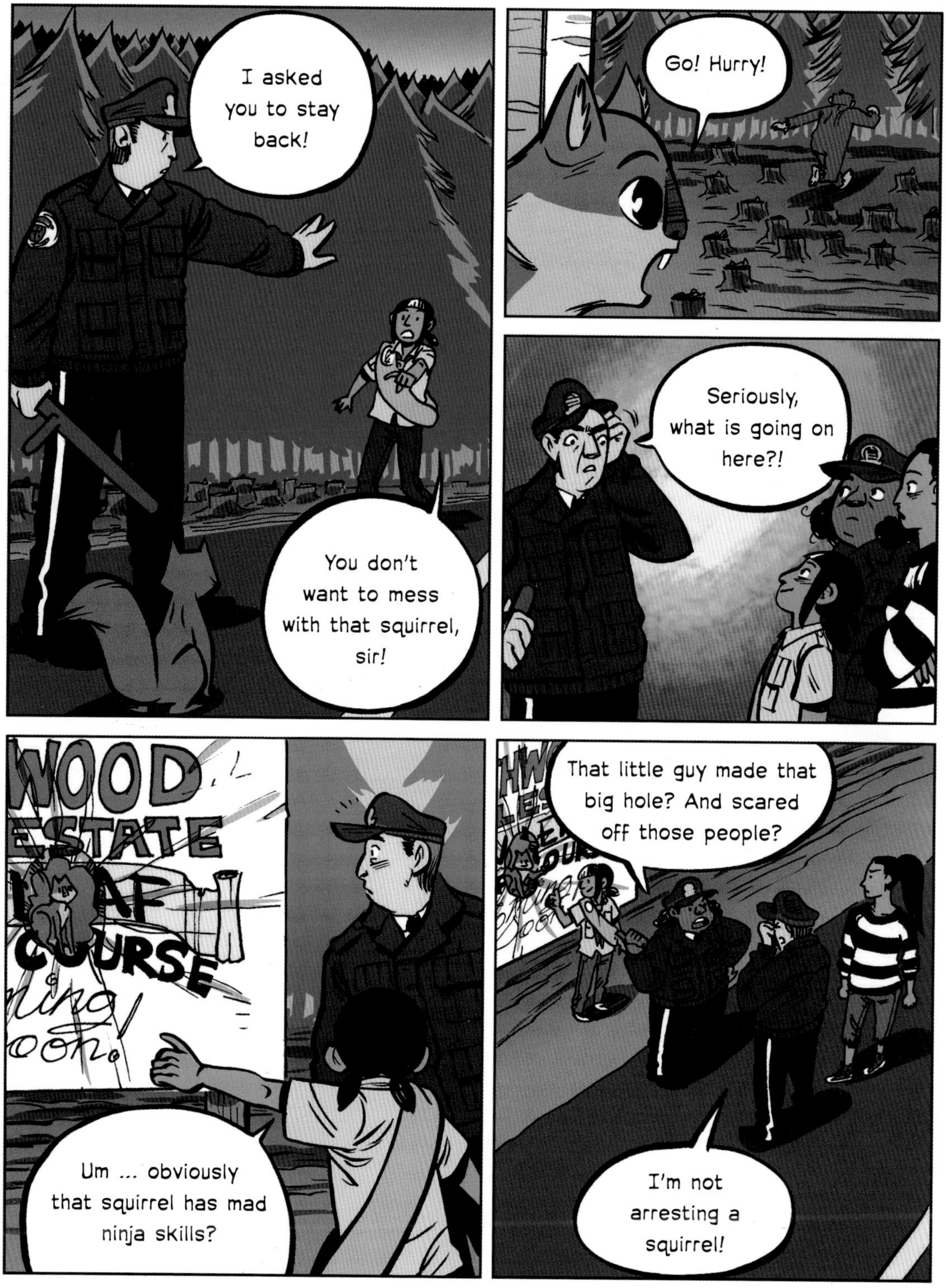
I asked you to stay back!
You don't want to mess with that squirrel, sir!
Go! Hurry!
Seriously, what is going on here?!
WOOD
ESTATE
COURSE
Um ... obviously that squirrel has mad ninja skills?
That little guy made that big hole? And scared off those people?
I'm not arresting a squirrel!

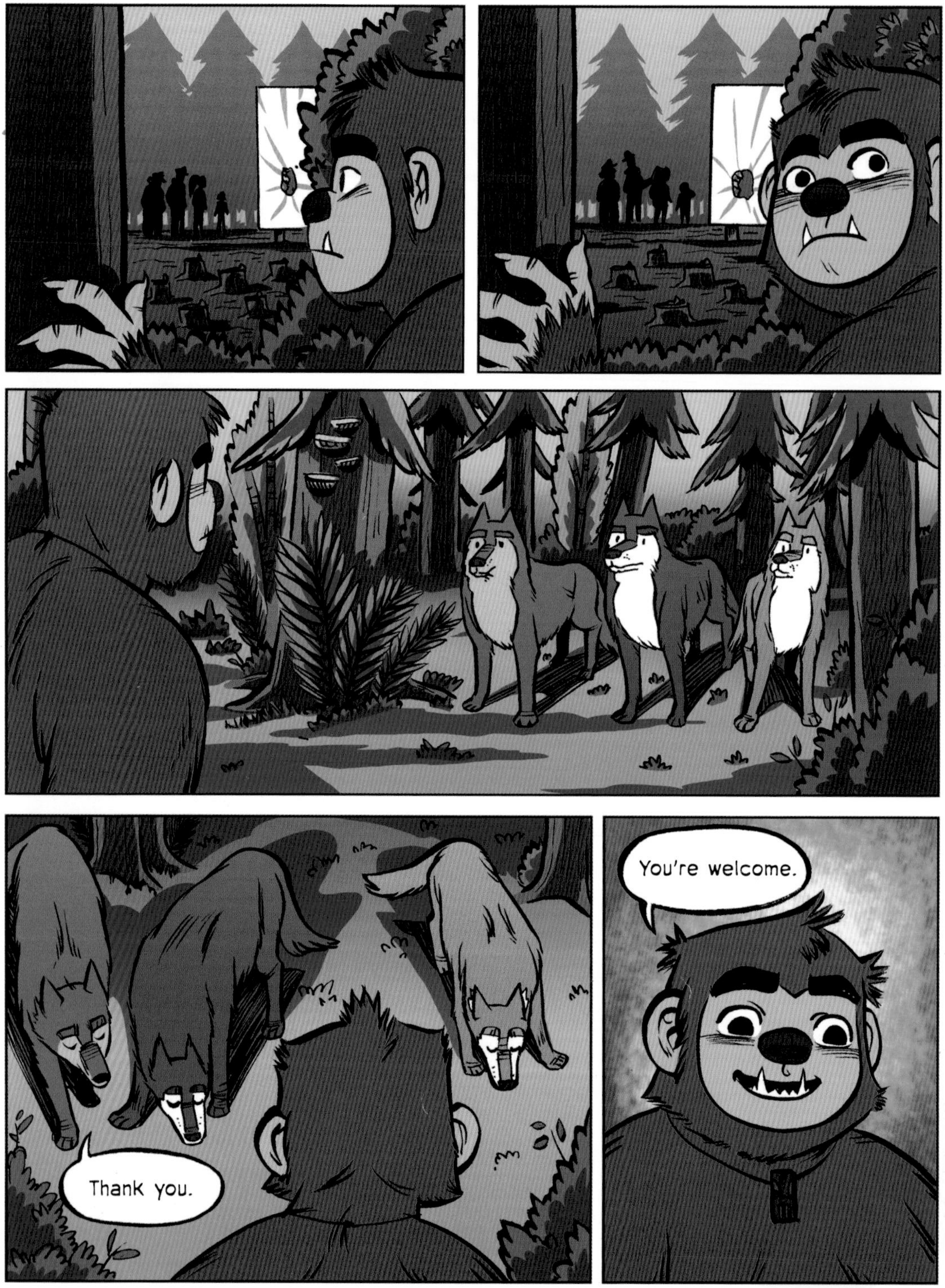
Thank you.
You're welcome.

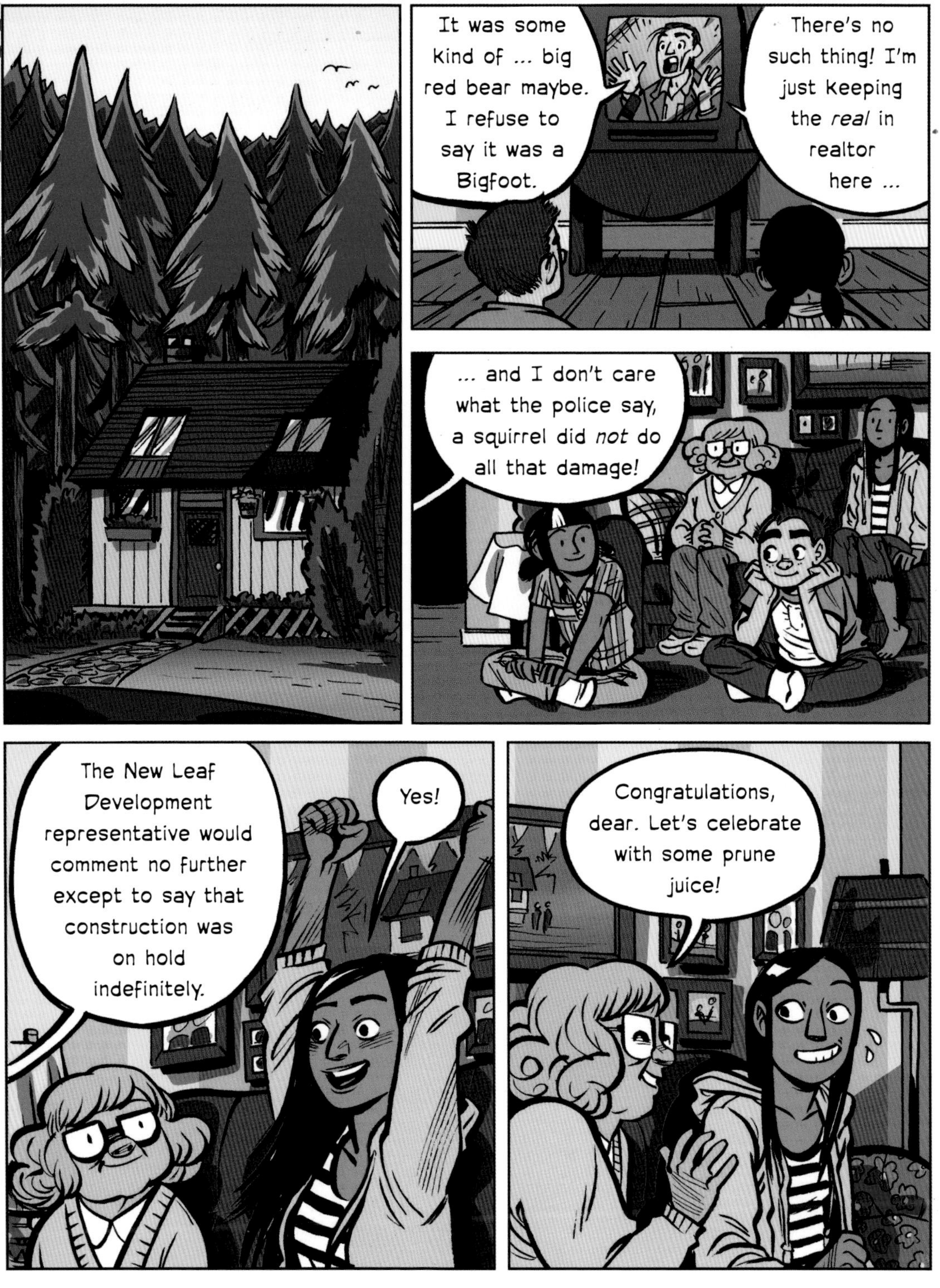
It was some kind of ... big red bear maybe. I refuse to say it was a Bigfoot.
There's no such thing! I'm just keeping the *real* in realtor here ...
... and I don't care what the police say, a squirrel did *not* do all that damage!
The New Leaf Development representative would comment no further except to say that construction was on hold indefinitely.
Yes!
Congratulations, dear. Let's celebrate with some prune juice!

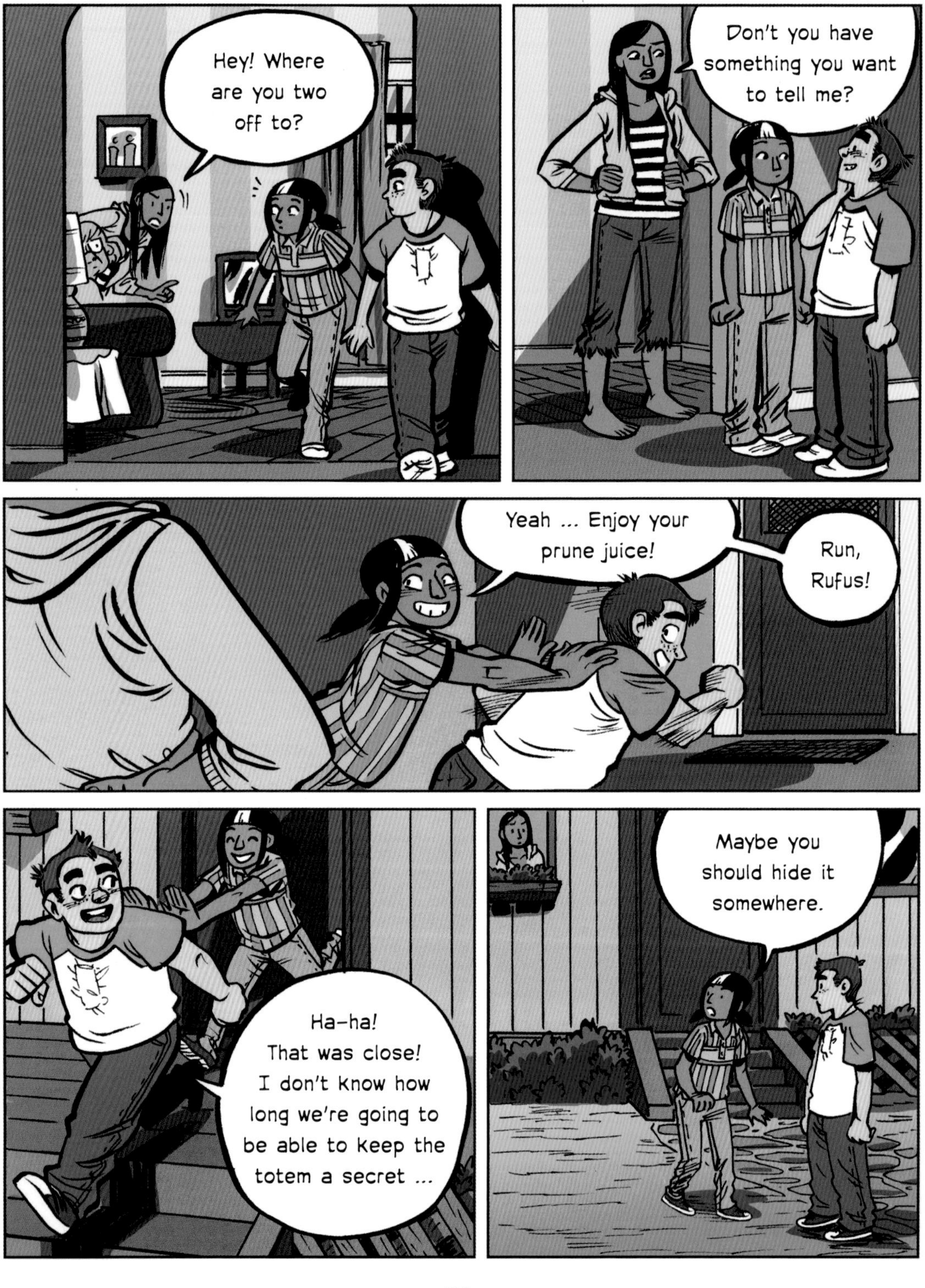
Hey! Where are you two off to?
Don't you have something you want to tell me?
Yeah ... Enjoy your prune juice!
Run, Rufus!
Ha-ha! That was close! I don't know how long we're going to be able to keep the totem a secret ...
Maybe you should hide it somewhere.

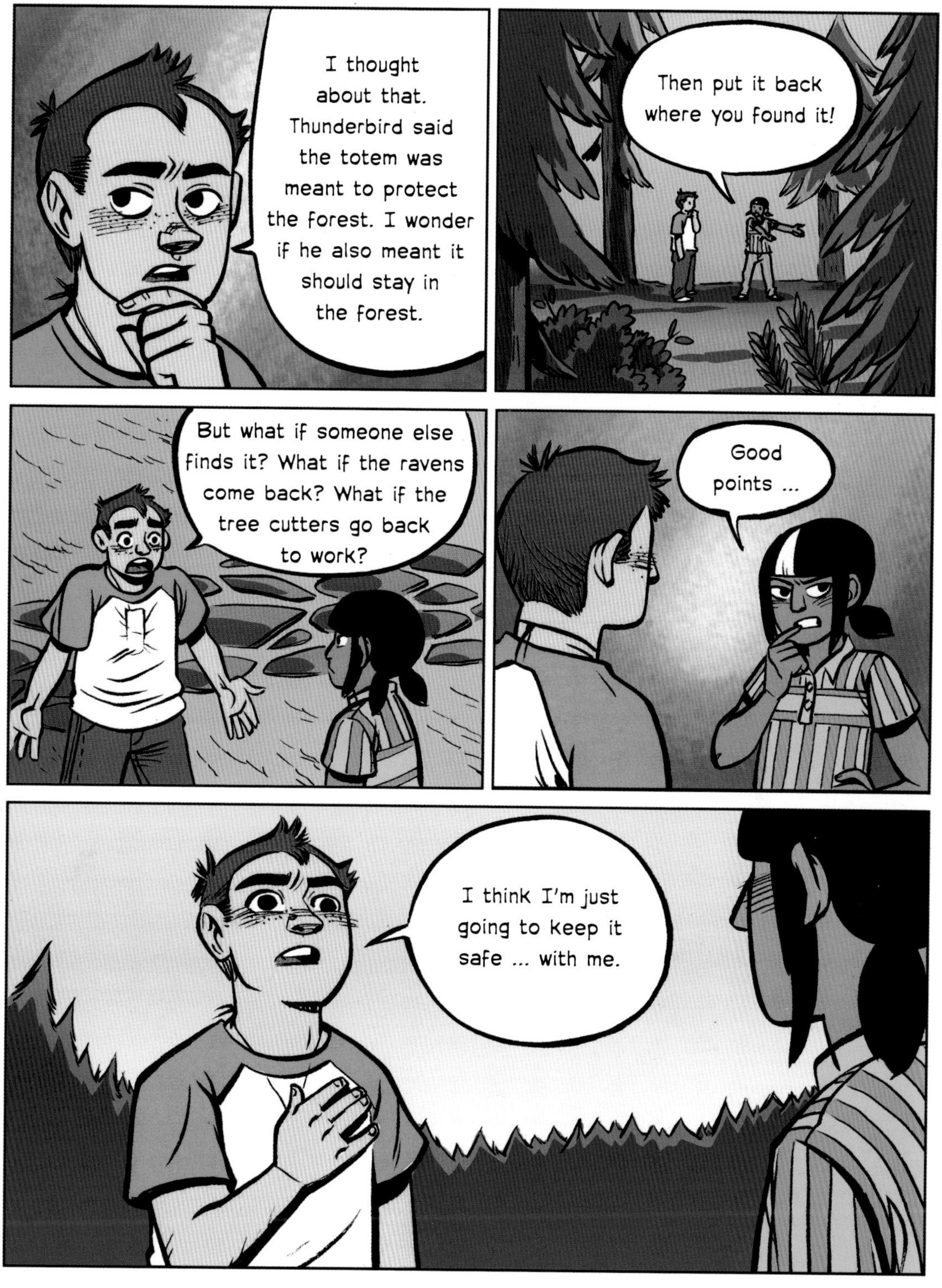
I thought about that. Thunderbird said the totem was meant to protect the forest. I wonder if he also meant it should stay in the forest.
Then put it back where you found it!
But what if someone else finds it? What if the ravens come back? What if the tree cutters go back to work?
Good points ...
I think I'm just going to keep it safe ... with me.

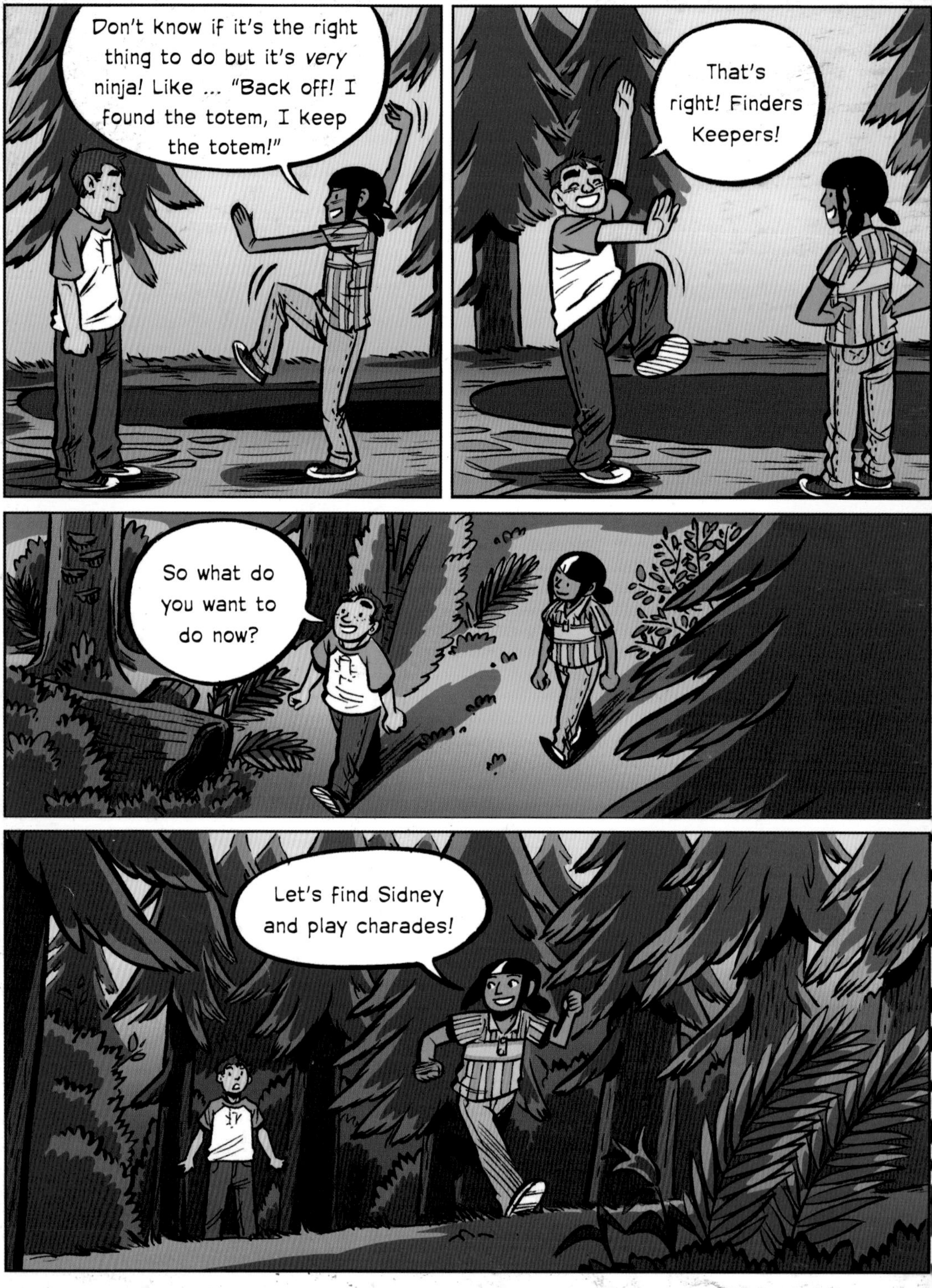
Don't know if it's the right thing to do but it's *very* ninja! Like ... "Back off! I found the totem, I keep the totem!"
That's right! Finders Keepers!
So what do you want to do now?
Let's find Sidney and play charades!

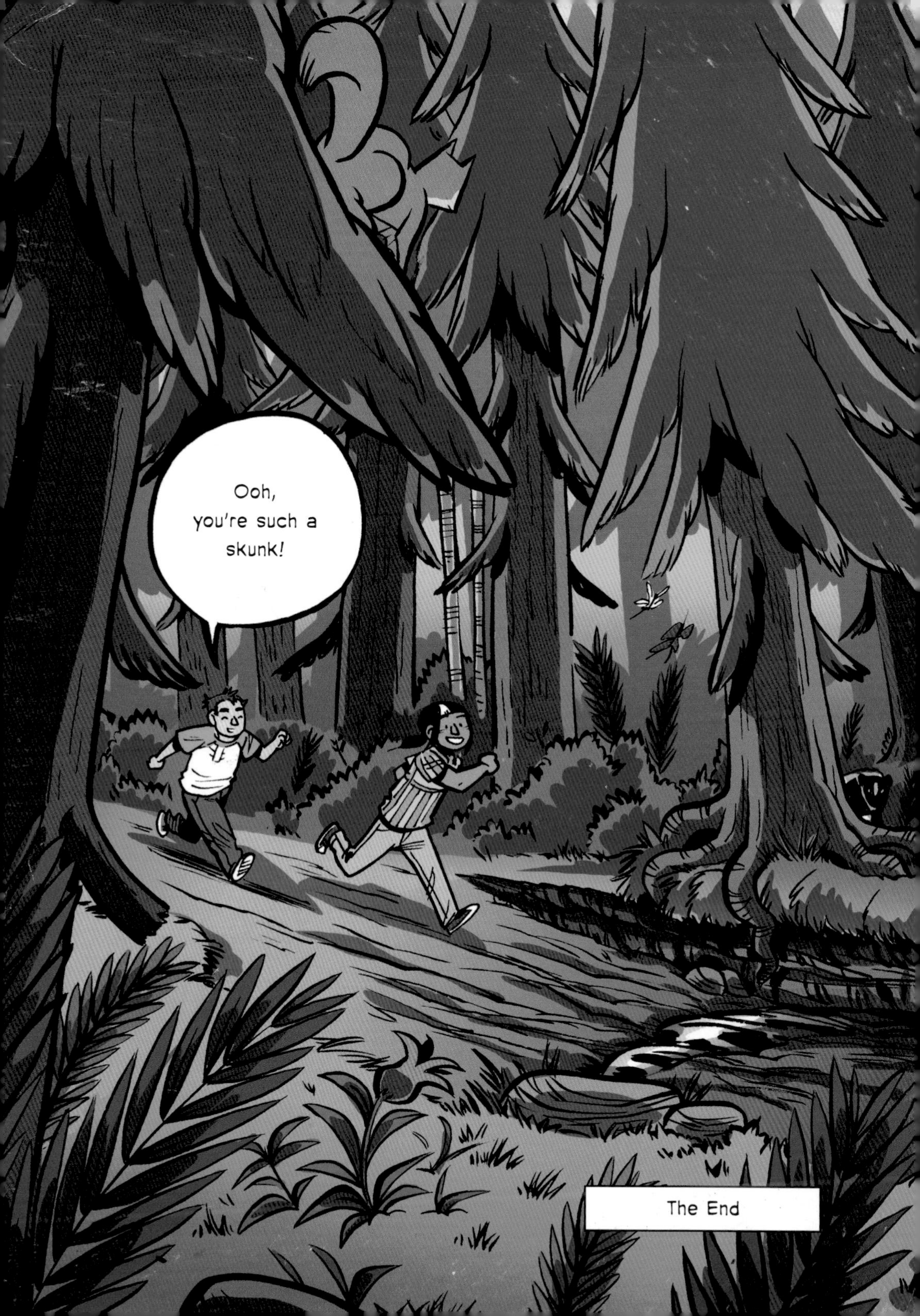
Ooh, you're such a skunk!
The End

DON'T MISS ANY OF THE BIGFOOT BOY BOOKS

1
BIGFOOT Boy
Into the WOODS
J. Torres and Faith Erin Hicks

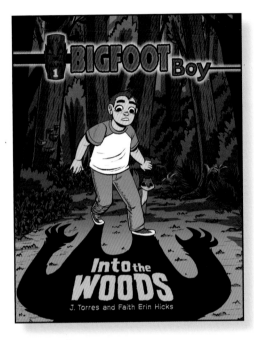

HC 978-1-55453-711-2
PB 978-1-55453-712-9

2
BIGFOOT Boy
The Unkindness of RAVENS
J. Torres and Faith Erin Hicks

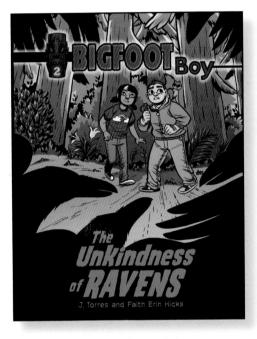

HC 978-1-55453-713-6
PB 978-1-55453-714-3

Praise for the Bigfoot Boy series

★ "Be prepared for young Sasquatch fans roaring for more."

—*Kirkus Reviews,* starred review

"The rich, expressive full-color artwork shines, adding humor and ably carrying the story."

—*School Library Journal*